WITHDRA

D0394734

ALSO BY CHUCK KLOSTERMAN

Fargo Rock City:
A Heavy Metal Odyssey in Rural Nörth Daköta

Sex, Drugs, and Cocoa Puffs:
A Low Culture Manifesto

Killing Yourself to Live:
85% of a True Story

Chuck Klosterman IV:
A Decade of Curious People and Dangerous Ideas

Downtown Owl:
A Novel

Eating the Dinosaur

THE
VISIBLE MAN

A NOVEL

CHUCK KLOSTERMAN

YOLO COUNTY LIBRARY
226 BUCKEYE STREET
WOODLAND CA 95695

SCRIBNER

New York London Toronto Sydney New Delhi

SCRIBNER

A Division of Simon & Schuster, Inc.
1230 Avenue of the Americas
New York, NY 10020

This book is a work of fiction. Names, characters, places, and incidents
either are products of the author's imagination or are used fictitiously. Any resemblance
to actual events or locales or persons, living or dead, is entirely coincidental.

Copyright © 2011 by Chuck Klosterman

All rights reserved, including the right to reproduce this book or portions thereof in
any form whatsoever. For information, address Scribner Subsidiary Rights Department,
1230 Avenue of the Americas, New York, NY 10020.

First Scribner hardcover edition October 2011

SCRIBNER and design are registered trademarks of The Gale Group, Inc.,
used under license by Simon & Schuster, Inc., the publisher of this work.

For information about special discounts for bulk purchases,
please contact Simon & Schuster Special Sales at 1-866-506-1949
or business@simonandschuster.com.

The Simon & Schuster Speakers Bureau can bring authors to your live event.
For more information or to book an event, contact the Simon & Schuster Speakers
Bureau at 1-866-248-3049 or visit our website at www.simonspeakers.com.

DESIGNED BY ERICH HOBBING

Manufactured in the United States of America

1 3 5 7 9 10 8 6 4 2

Library of Congress Control Number: 2010047309

ISBN 978-1-4391-8446-2
ISBN 978-1-4391-8448-6 (ebook)

For Melissa

THE
VISIBLE MAN

FROM THE OFFICE OF **VICTORIA VICK**

1711 Lavaca St.
Suite 2
Austin, TX 78701
vvick@vick.com

July 5, 2012

Crosby Bumpus
Simon & Schuster
1230 Ave. of the Americas
11th Floor
New York, NY 10020-1586

Mr. Bumpus:

Well, here it is. I never thought I'd type that sentence, but now I have!

This is such a bizarre sensation, Crosby. I have no idea how you're going to react to what's here, but I'm exhilarated, terrified, and mentally prepared for whatever is supposed to happen next. Let me reiterate (one last time) how flattered I am by your dogged interest in this project and how grateful I am for your limitless reserve of support, despite the apprehensions of your publishing house, your co-workers, your new boyfriend (!), and every other rational person in your life. If this really works out, it will be a testament to your vision and spirit.

I know we've had this discussion dozens of times over the telephone, but I need to say it once more, just to satisfy my own conscience: I am not a writer. I have no further ambitions in this regard, and this is the only manuscript I'll ever submit to a publisher. I also need to stress (because there seems to be some confusion over this, at least with your assistant and with the woman I spoke with from your publicity department) that I am not a psychiatrist, even though I'll undoubtedly be described as such if this manuscript is ever received by the world at large. I have not attended medical school and I'm not in a position to prescribe medication. It's important we're all clear on this point, because I don't want to mislead anyone. I received a masters degree in social work from the Univ. of Texas after earning an undergraduate degree in psychology from Davidson College in North Carolina. I do not have a Ph.D. I've been a licensed therapist and analyst for exactly twenty-one years, but my roster of clients is small (no more than twelve patients in any given week) and has never included anyone of public interest, sans the lone individual I will describe in the enclosed file. I'm sure my professional credentials will be savaged, but—if that has to happen—I want them to be savaged for the proper reasons.

Is this manuscript ready for publication? I think we both agree it is not (nor does my agent). I have no idea how the fact-checking process works in your industry, but I cannot fathom any system that would accept the majority of this text on face value. Like I said in our very first conversation: I can't verify the story I'm trying to tell. All I have are the tapes (which prove nothing) and one photograph of a seemingly empty chair. How will this not be a marketing disaster? I know you're strongly against recasting this work as fiction (and my agent has already informed me that such a switch would force a reworking of the contract's language and a substantial decrease in the amount of my advance), but I don't see any other option. Obviously, you understand the publishing game more than I do, and I trust your judgment completely. Perhaps we should revisit this conversation when you've finished reading my draft.

Five annotations regarding the structure of this manuscript:

(A.) After my second phone conversation with the Scribner lawyer in June, I've elected to use the pseudonym "Y___" in place of the patient's name or his actual initials. I now understand why using a fabricated name might create more problems than it solves. I initially used a different letter as a placeholder (first "V," then "K," then "M"), but my agent explained how those specific letters might cause their own unique dilemmas. I'm still open to your thoughts on this, assuming you have any.

(B.) During the very early phases of my relationship with Y____ (and particularly during the initial few weeks when we interacted exclusively by telephone), I took almost no notes whatsoever. Why would I? At the time, the case did not seem abnormal. The only things I wrote about Y____ were for my own rudimentary record-keeping, primarily so I could reference whatever we'd last discussed at the opening of our next session. These notes were brief e-mails I sent to myself, so please excuse the sentence fragments and incomplete thoughts (I've tried to fix misspellings and abbreviations, but I have not altered the language or syntax). Obviously, I had no way of knowing how unusual this situation would become. Hindsight being 20/20, I realize I should have asked him more pointed, expository questions about what was really happening here, but—keep in mind—it wasn't an interrogation. My intention was to *help* this person, so I allowed him to dictate the flow of conversation. So how should we handle this? My solution (at least for the time being) was to just print and attach those six self-addressed e-mails for your consideration. The e-mails are included in what's currently labeled as <u>Part I: The Telephone.</u> Should I try to turn that content into conventional prose, or should I exclude them completely? They're difficult to read and a little embarrassing, but I think some of the details are critical.

(C.) Once I became aware of my scenario's actuality, I started recording everything Y____ said during our sessions on audiotape (with his permission and at his urging). Much of this manuscript is a transcript of Y____'s unedited dialogue, augmented by my periodic queries and my (mostly unsuccessful) attempts at steering the conversation toward a reasonable resolution. It should go without saying that Y____ was among the most intelligent, most articulate patients of my career. His ability to speak in complete thoughts and full paragraphs was astounding, often to the point of pretension and almost to the level of discomfort; I will always, always wonder if Y____ had rehearsed and memorized large sections of what he said during our sessions. It's my suspicion that Y____ (consciously or unconsciously) long believed I would eventually publish the details of our work together and felt an overwhelming desire to be as entertaining and narrative as possible. He was never able to accept the concept of therapy for his own sake. Granted, that troubling view made the compilation of this manuscript extremely easy—much of the time, I simply had to type a transcript of whatever Y____ had said in its raw form. But this chasm between the clarity of Y____'s words and his stark inability to understand his own motives inevitably undermined whatever progress we seemed to make. From a purely therapeutic perspective, I can only classify my work with Y____ as a failure. I wonder if we need to make this clearer to the reader?

(D.)   The only other person who has read this manuscript is my husband, John (who, by the way, is doing much, much better and wanted me to thank you for sending us that wonderful book about Huey Long). He mentioned one potential problem: John believes Y____'s behavior and personality is too inconsistent, and that my portrayal of him generates (what he refers to, possibly incorrectly, as) "the pathetic fallacy." I suppose I see what he means, even though it didn't feel that way at the time. But if John sees this dissonance, other readers will see it, too. So how do I justify these contradictions? How do I overcome the fact that real people inevitably behave more erratically than fictional constructions? It's important to remember that—despite his rarefied intelligence and intermittent charm—Y____ was/is a deeply troubled individual without any sense of self, an almost total lack of empathy, and a paradoxical confusion over the most fundamental aspects of human behavior. I suppose it's no accident that he was seeing a therapist. Here again, I wonder if fictionalizing this story might be the best solution. Perhaps he would seem more believable if we made him more predictable?

(E.) Assuming this manuscript eventually becomes a purchasable book, there are a handful of private citizens who will see themselves in the text, sometimes in embarrassing contexts. I feel terrible about this, but there's just no way around it. I believe this work is important, and cultural importance often comes with casualties. It has to be done. I also believe the inclusion of those specific anecdotes will be critical to the commercial value of the book, and (as I explained in one of our early e-mails) that's something I don't necessarily want but very desperately need. It's humiliating to admit that, but you know my situation. So if this must be done, let's at least try to show these poor people the respect they merit. I deserve my humiliation, but they do not.

I think that's everything. Sorry this cover letter ended up being so long. Please call or e-mail when you receive this package, Crosby. I can't wait to work with you. Also, I'm curious—does your reception of this manuscript constitute its "acceptance," or does that not occur until you've finished reading and editing? I only ask because our contract states that 25 percent of my agreed advance will be delivered "on acceptance," and my agent can't (or won't) seem to give me a firm date as to when that will happen. I hate to keep bringing this up, because I know it's not really your department. But—like I said before—you know my situation.

Warmest regards,

V.V.

Victoria Vick

PART 1

THE
TELEPHONE

FROM: thevickster@gmail.com
SENT: Wednesday, March 05, 2008, 7:34 PM
TO: vvick@vick.com
SUBJECT: Y___ / Friday

Received phone message this a.m. from "Y___," local male,
inquiring about scheduling possible session as soon as possible.
Message did not elaborate on nature of problem; caller's voice
did not express urgency. Returned call in early p.m. Patient
initially seemed calm and asked typical questions about rates
and availability. Conversation changed when patient aggressively
requested that all sessions be conducted over the telephone
(and that this requirement was nonnegotiable). After explaining
to Y___ that this was not a problem, I casually asked why he
was unavailable for conventional face-to-face dialogue. Patient
immediately grew agitated and said (*something along the lines of*),
"That isn't your concern." When I mentioned that this information
might be central to our future interactions, caller became sarcastic,
then abruptly apologetic. Another brief discussion about rates
and insurance option followed (Y___ is uninsured). I told him he
would need to fill out a few basic forms, but he said, "No forms.
I don't fill out forms. I have money. The forms aren't needed."
This is unusual, but not unheard of. We discussed our mutual
distaste for paperwork. A telephone appointment has been
tentatively scheduled for 10:00 a.m. Friday. Call then concluded.
Difficult to ascertain if this behavior is a manifestation of shyness,
agoraphobia, or drug/alcohol dependency. Skeptical about whether
this patient will call again, but leaving the 10:00 a.m. hour open
nonetheless.

Sent from my BlackBerry Wireless Handheld

FROM: thevickster@gmail.com
SENT: Friday, March 07, 2008, 10:11 PM
TO: vvick@vick.com
SUBJECT: Y___ / Friday (1)

Opened work with Y___ this morning. Received call at 10:00 a.m. sharp. Patient seems bright but capricious; he oscillates between unnecessary levels of aggression and repetitive, contrite apologies. I initiated session with standard entry query [*editor's note: this is typically a straightforward question about why the patient has contacted the therapist*]. Y___ declined to answer. He suggested I would not be able to understand his reasoning at this time. I agreed to give him that emotional space temporarily. I then asked the following:

AGE: 33

OCCUPATION: declined answer (unemployed?)

CURRENT RESIDENCE: declined answer

FAMILY/MEDICAL HISTORY: declined answer but described self as "healthy"

Discussion throughout session was predictably circular. I was clear with Y___ that therapy would be ineffective if he refused to say why he wanted this process to occur, a suggestion he simultaneously agreed with and balked at. Y___ responded to virtually all questions by asking a similar question of me. He seemed preoccupied with making jokes about whether I physically resembled Lorraine Bracco, the actress who portrayed a psychiatrist on the defunct HBO series *The Sopranos*. When I responded to his humor in kind (by informing him that some form of this joke was made by virtually all my male patients), he seemed unusually offended and would not acknowledge my immediate apology. At the thirty-five-minute mark, I directed my questioning toward his day-to-day mental state, asking if he ever felt depressed. He immediately said, "Very much," but was unwilling to give any details as to why, always stating and restating the notion that his problems were more "exceptional" (his word) than whatever I might be "anticipating" (his word). When I told him this is a typical feeling among first-time therapy patients, he told an extremely long, unfunny joke about a clown. The premise of the joke is as follows: A little boy is humiliated at the circus. A clown makes sport of him, and the audience laughs. As a result, the boy spends his entire adult life trying to invent the funniest, cleverest comebacks for every kind of social embarrassment. The boy even travels to Tibet (?) to study the ancient art of banter. Years later, the boy (who is now a man) brings his own child to the circus, and—for whatever reason—the same clown is working and attempts to embarrass the man again by spraying him in the face with a bottle of seltzer water. The man has spent years preparing for this very moment. He dries his face with a towel, looks his adversary in the face, and says, "Fuck you, clown." (This, it seems, was the punch line?) Unclear how this joke is connected to his feelings of inadequacy. Session ended immediately after clown story. Y__ agreed to call again next Friday.

NOTES:

If Y__ is dealing with addiction, it seems unlikely that he was intoxicated during our session. His speech and thought patterns seemed unremarkable (although possible use of cocaine is not outside the realm of possibility, as his speech was sometimes rushed). More troubling is his paranoid obsession over the most minor details within his own life, almost to the point of caricature; he has wildly exaggerated the import of his own existence. Keeps using phrases like, "It's different for me. Everything is different for me." Y__ is emotionally overinvested in some undefined, unspoken idea (regarding his own sense of self), and this investment overwhelms all other components of his psyche. A grandiose or somatic disorder seems possible, although more info will be needed before making any strict diagnosis. This will take time. That said, my overall concern is mild. Patient does not appear to be in danger.

Sent from my BlackBerry Wireless Handheld

THE VISIBLE MAN

FROM: thevickster@gmail.com
SENT: Friday, March 14, 2008, 2:02 PM
TO: vvick@vick.com
SUBJECT: Y___ / Friday (2)

No progress with Y___. Initial conversation was pleasant (he mentioned how listening to songs by the ex-Beatle George Harrison had put him in "an effervescent mood"), but real dialogue collapsed soon after. Once again, I tried to direct our conversation toward his motive for seeking therapy. This quickly became a thirty-minute "intellectual cul de sac" (his words). He said he wanted to "see what other people see" but would not elaborate on what this meant. In response to my conventional follow-up ("What do you suspect other people see?"), he laughed and called my elocutionary technique "amateurish," claiming I should "try harder." At this point I informed him that he could seek help elsewhere if that was what he wanted. He then apologized, although not sincerely—he said he was sorry his words had insulted me but refused to apologize for what he actually said. Sensing this interaction was only exasperating our relationship, I returned to the topic of the Harrison album he had mentioned at the start of the session, mostly to get him talking in a nonconfrontational manner. He expressed preoccupation with one song, a track he identified as "Be Here Now." When asked what he liked about the song, Y___ suggested that the song's lyrics illustrated Harrison's guilt about becoming wealthy and the singer's "self-conscious hypocrisy" for choosing to advocate principles of Eastern spirituality while living as a conventional celebrity. He was smug about this analysis. "If he really believed what he sang," said Y___, "he would not have needed to write and record the song at all. It's totally fake. He wrote the song as a means of admitting he can't be the person he pretends." This alleged contradiction amused him. Being unfamiliar with the song, I did not comment. Session ended soon after, closing with another friendly (and most likely meaningless) exchange of pleasantries.

NOTES:

I have purchased "Be Here Now" via the computer application iTunes, initially confusing it with another track of the same name. Though I've listened to the song only twice, the textual interpretation by Y___ strikes me as unusually cynical. He seems to misread the song on purpose. At risk of placing too much emphasis on one tangential aspect of our second encounter, I now have fewer fears about addiction and more concerns about clinical depression and/or a specific break from reality—it seems very possible that Y___ is a highly functioning depressive. Have decided to take a more aggressive stance with Y___ next week.

Sent from my BlackBerry Wireless Handheld

THE VISIBLE MAN

FROM: thevickster@gmail.com
SENT: Friday, March 21, 2008, 10:44 AM
TO: vvick@vick.com
SUBJECT: Y___ / Friday (3)

Terrible session this morning. My fault entirely. Opened dialogue
by giving Y___ a false ultimatum: I claimed that if he was
unwilling to discuss why he was seeking therapy, I was unwilling
to continue working with him. My intention was to challenge
him, with the expectation that he would respect this challenge
and respond. At first, the exchange felt natural. He chuckled. He
asked what kinds of problems I normally dealt with, and I told
him the most universal problems among my other patients were
anxiety issues. He discounted this: "Anxiety is not a real problem.
It's only a modern problem." I tried to get him to explain why
he would believe that, and he started to explain his reasoning.
But then he stopped mid-sentence and asked, "What do you look
like?" I asked why that made a difference, particularly since he
had wanted to keep our interaction over the phone. Y___: "It
makes a difference to me." I accused him of trying to change the
subject. He said, "No, *this* is the subject [emphasis his]. Whatever
I want to talk about is always the subject." I told him my physical
appearance was irrelevant. He disagreed. I asked how it was
relevant. He said, "If you can't understand immediately, you will
never understand eventually. Why should I tell you something
you'll never understand? Why won't you answer my question? At
least I have the potential to understand the answer." His tone was
flat. I asked if this question was related to his previous reference to
the Bracco character (from *The Sopranos*). He said, "Of course not.
Get over it." I told him I looked like a normal person. I mentioned
I had red hair. Y___: "See, that first part is relevant. It is. If you
look like a normal person, that's interesting. But I don't care what
color your hair is. *That's* irrelevant. Your hair color is irrelevant.
You don't understand what's important and what isn't." I asked if

he thought he looked like a normal person. He said, "No, not at all. Not at all." I asked what he believed a normal person looked like. At this point, he ended the call without comment. Total time of conversation: less than ten minutes.

NOTES:

Very strong suspicion that Y__ is housebound due to obesity. Physical deformity also seems possible—is he a burn victim? Tremendous failure on my behalf. Completely overlooked this (fairly obvious) scenario, particularly when viewed in orchestra with his joke about the boy and the clown from session #1. I am a terrible therapist today. Really down about this. Today I am a failure. Need to be smarter next week. WILL be smarter next week. Will be smarter.

Sent from my BlackBerry Wireless Handheld

ADDENDUM[1]

[The evening following this episode, I received two voice mails from Y__ that were stored on the hard drive on my office computer (via the telephone service Vonage). I have transcribed the content of those messages here. It is my belief that Y__ was reading from a script. Midway through the second call, he appears to deviate from the script—however, I now suspect he consciously included this deviation to create the illusion of spontaneity. His delivery of these messages was intermittently measured and animated. Soft sitar music is audible in the background. Total length of first message: 48 seconds. Total length of second message: 222 seconds.]

---

1. Calls were received on Saturday at 2:55 a.m. and 3:03 a.m.; both messages transcribed on Saturday, March 22, at 8:55 a.m.

THE VISIBLE MAN

CALL 1

"Good evening, Vicky. This is Y___ speaking. I want . . . I want
to apologize for my juvenile behavior on the telephone today.
I understand what your intentions were and I don't know why
I reacted the way I . . . reacted. I don't want to jeopardize our
relationship. I've enjoyed our sessions thus far. I think they're
going extremely well. I've tried working with at least four other
therapists and none have gotten as far as we have. I like your
approach. Honestly. I like your approach. You aren't a control freak,
or even in any control at all. You don't mind taking a . . . less-than-
dominant, semidominant role. I like that. It's what I like about you
most. That's what I (*inaudible*). So I'm hoping we can just put this
whole episode behind us. I will call again next Friday, and we'll just
go on from there. Okay? If you're uninterested in continuing our
work, we can discuss at that juncture. I assume (*inaudible phrase*).
Thanks again. This was Y___."

CALL 2

"Vicky. Y___ again. So . . . I realize you had mentioned—again,
this was this morning, on the telephone—that you needed me
to explain why I was seeking therapy, and that you can't help
me unless I explain my reasons. I don't agree with that. I don't
think it's essential in any way. But because *you* believe this, I'm
willing to make a concession. If you can't continue under any
other circumstances, I will make this compromise. As I said, I
appreciate your approach. But I need you to accept that you'll
never truly understand my reasoning regardless of what I tell
you about myself. You will never completely understand what's
happened. Which might be difficult for you, as a professional.
It might toy with your confidence. It's just that . . . I spent my
mid-twenties on the most radical edge of science. I know that
sounds (*inaudible*), but it's the only means through which I can
explain my condition. In simplest terms, I worked with biological

17

(*inaudible*) light refraction, although that doesn't really matter to anyone and certainly should *not* matter to you. In fact, I would recommend that you don't even think about the technical aspects of my condition. What should matter—to you—is that my aptitude at science allowed me to do some negative, problematic things . . . actually, no. Let me rephrase that. I need to rephrase that. My aptitude at biological science allowed me to do things that *could be perceived* as problematic. The things I did, when viewed intellectually, are *not* problematic. I don't see them as bad. I don't think any intelligent person would. I view my actions as positive. But I know that "society," or whatever term we want to use, might disagree. I realize that the average person would consider my actions criminal, and maybe even that's optimistic. Now, that's their problem, as far as I'm concerned. Their wrongness is unrelated to who I am. But because we were all raised in the same society, and because I've unwillingly adopted a lot of the weaknesses inherent to other people, I can't help but feel the sensation of guilt that comes with my actions. Not guilt itself, because I know the things I did were good. But the *sensation* of guilt. That's what I felt. And that can be just as detrimental. And that is what I need to talk to you about. I want to find a way to manage this sensation. I also need someone to objectively view my actions and validate what I already know, which is that I've done nothing wrong. Like I said—I already understand all of this intellectually. I just need to know it emotionally. So that is where we will pick up. Good night, Victoria. Again, this was Y___."

THE VISIBLE MAN

FROM: thevickster@gmail.com
SENT: Friday, March 28, 2008, 2:00 PM
TO: vvick@vick.com
SUBJECT: Y___ / Friday (4)

Corner turned? Significant strides with Y___ this a.m.!

Opened session by thanking Y___ for his late-night phone
messages from the previous Friday, noting that these
calls—regardless of their content—suggest progress. Y___
expressed sheepish appreciation. I asked Y___ about the timing of
his calls, as they were received very late in the evening; I asked if
he had been having trouble sleeping. Y___ said he sometimes slept
during the afternoon, but that this was a preference (and not a
problem). "My work requires that I'm alert in the evening and early
morning hours," he said, and then playfully compared himself to
a variety of nocturnal animals. His metaphors were apt, but I also
noticed a degree of showmanship—he seemed to be referencing
exotic animals in a self-aggrandizing style, simply to show me that
he knew a lot about zoology. However, I did not press him on this
(at risk of reversing our newfound level of mild intimacy).

About ten or fifteen minutes into the session, I addressed the three
most compelling details from his second phone message:

*[Reader's note: Of all the exchanges I would eventually
have with Y___, this is the one I most wish I'd recorded.
Knowing what I know now, this was (almost certainly) the
most detail-rich exchange we ever had, at least in terms of
the scientific content. But—at the time—it just seemed like
we were clearing extraneous details out of our path. During
the most critical segment of the exchange, I'm ashamed
to admit I barely listened (and instead mentally prepared
for my next line of questioning). This being the case, Y___'s
quotes in the following section are not verbatim—were I a*

cub reporter for the **American-Statesman,** *I wouldn't use them in an A1 article. These were simply my present-tense attempts to paraphrase Y__'s jargon-heavy descriptions of how his situation began, which I have since slightly expanded. Though I suspect my memory is more accurate than not, I missed the minutiae that mattered most. It remains the greatest regret of my career.]*

1. "The most radical edge of science": This phrase struck me as unusual and pretentious. I asked why he chose those specific words. He proceeded to give an incomprehensible, extemporaneous speech on his field of study, something he referred to as "epidermal refraction theory." Y__ noted that this work was conducted through funding from the military, but that he was a civilian (originally employed by Chaminade University in Hawaii). He prefaced his description by saying, "There is no way you will ever understand this," and (again) claimed that the specifics of his research were not important. I pushed him to try. As it turns out, he was either correct or trying to confuse me on purpose. I have no idea what his research was trying to solve or create. The bottom line is as follows: Y__ was involved in something he referred to as the "cloaking initiative." At one point he asked if I had ever watched *Star Trek,* but I have not. He used the term "negative refractive index" several times. Whenever I asked him to simplify his description, he would say things like, "Imagine looking at the front of a woman's chest, but seeing only whatever was behind her back." He made reference to a "sheer suit." Though it's impossible to tell if what Y__ was saying was (a) even partially true or (b) some type of fantasy life, I'm now secure in the assumption that Y__ does have (at the very least) a legitimate background in science. Obviously, that background does not dismiss his pseudologia fantastica[2] (and may paradoxically serve

---

2. This is more commonly referred to as pathological lying.

to enhance it). I found myself generally unable to follow this stretch of dialogue. When I admitted this, he politely asked that I never ask him about this again, as it was a waste of both our time. I conditionally agreed. He needed to hear me say that.

2. "Problematic things": I mentioned that his phone call referred to some sort of criminal or antisocial behavior, but he immediately retracted his initial take. I asked what kind of specific behavior he was referring to. He said, "Surveillance. Invasion of privacy. Home invasion. Prowling. I did some prowling. Deception. A certain kind of intangible theft. Humanity theft." I asked what "humanity theft" meant. Y___ said, "I've consumed people's lives without their consent." I pushed him to explain this further. He said (*something along the lines of*), "I reached a point in my life where I became exclusively interested in the unseen reality of human behavior, and I did not think it was possible to study such behavior if the person knew they were being studied." He went on to say that the traditional means for understanding human psychology was by asking subjects questions about themselves, a process he finds futile. "The act of asking someone a question completely destroys the value of the answer," he said. He asked if I was familiar with the Heisenberg Uncertainty Principle.[3] When I told him I was, he said, "Well, then you already understand why psychology has failed." Though I wanted to pursue these points further, I realized time was expiring on our session and I needed to move to point 3.

3. "The sensation of guilt": This, I suspect, was the most important phrase Y___ said in his message (and the root of why Y___ is seeking help). I asked how *guilt* differed from *the sensation of*

---

3. In quantum mechanics, the Uncertainty Principle suggests that the act of measuring one magnitude of a particle, be it mass, velocity, or position, causes the other magnitudes to blur. In other words, the very process of examining something changes what that something is.

guilt, since guilt itself is a feeling (and every feeling is a type of sensation). Y____ vehemently disagreed. "A man is guilty when he subjectively thinks about what he has done and concludes that his actions were objectively wrong. A man feels the *sensation* of guilt when he objectively thinks about what he has done and concludes that his actions were subjectively wrong. My problem is that I conflate those two perspectives." I was shocked by both the eloquence and the forethought of these words; it was as if he had been waiting all month to make this statement. When I asked him to repeat those thoughts, he did so immediately (and with identical syntax, furthering my suspicion of rehearsal). I asked why he was so concerned with the notion of feeling sensations of guilt. Y____: "Partially because I do not deserve to feel guilt, but mostly because it gets in the way."

At this point I noted that we'd extended our allotted time by more than five minutes. Having now conducted four sessions, we discussed payment. Due to its abbreviated length (and because it was my fault, though I did not admit this), I waived the fee from session #3. Y____ expressed appreciation for my fairness. After giving him my mailing address, I told him the bill would be $450. He declined my offer of an e-mail receipt.

Sent from my BlackBerry Wireless Handheld

THE VISIBLE MAN

FROM: thevickster@gmail.com
SENT: Friday, April 4, 2008, 11:04 PM
TO: vvick@vick.com
SUBJECT: Y___ / Friday (NA)

Strange morning. No call from Y___ . Considering the progress of
our previous session, my hopes had been high for today's chat.
Mystified. *But*—I am choosing not to overreact. A missed call
could be the result of any number of things. Need to stay realistic
about this type of case. Don't want to have more situations like
[*redacted*] and [*redacted*].[4] Still: disappointed. Was beginning to
really relish my discourse with Y___ and remain curious about the
authenticity of his persona.

NOTES:

Did receive payment of $450 on Tuesday, sent standard mail as
(oddly) cash: twenty-two twenty-dollar bills (plus two fives). The
most cash I ever received through the USPS! Pretty dangerous, IMO.

Sent from my BlackBerry Wireless Handheld

ADDENDUM[5]

*[Received another two voice mails from Y___, this time explaining
his missed session. Unlike his previous message, he seemed to be
speaking off the cuff. Total time of first message: 299 seconds.
Total time of second message: 19 seconds.]*

---

4. These were two former patients. In both cases, I became overly involved
with their problems (the former regarding the death of an infant, the latter involv-
ing a rape that occurred during penal incarceration). In both cases, I had to
request that our treatment terminate prematurely.
5. Calls were received on Saturday, at 3:00 a.m. and 3:03 a.m.; both messages
transcribed on Saturday, April 5, at 9:58 a.m.

CALL 1

"Good evening, Vicky. This is Y___ speaking. First of all, I want
to apologize for failing to call you this morning. I did not forget
to call, if that's what you're thinking. I chose not to call. But
this is only because I thought about some of what you'd said in
our previous sessions—really, *really* thought about what you'd
said—and I decided that maybe you were more correct than I
initially believed. I was watching someone this morning—someone
on the TV, one of those variety shows—and it occurred to me that
people who don't talk about themselves are limiting their own
potential. They think they're guarding themselves from some
sort of abstract danger, but they're actually allowing other people
to decide who they are and what they're like. This happened to
George Harrison. He was the quiet Beatle. Right? But he was also
the Beatle people are most able to turn into whatever inaccurate
projection they need, and for whatever purposes they arbitrarily
decide. And I'm (*inaudible*) to make that (*inaudible*). Not that I'm
comparing myself to a Beatle, of course, but I think you (*inaudible*).
I probably am a little like a Beatle, within my own field. So here
is my proposal: The next time I call you, there's not going to be
any questions, or at least none from you. I need to talk to you
about what has happened to me, and I believe it's important for
you to get a full picture of my life. And, by extension, a portrait of
my problems. And if this goes well, and I have every expectation
that it will, I believe we could actually meet—face-to-face, as it
were—and start talking more directly about these issues. So this
is what we will do. Agreed? I will call next week, and you will
listen. I will talk and you will not. Now, this doesn't mean you
can't say 'hello' or ask follow-up queries to certain points you
won't understand. I'm not a fascist. However, I'd advise you not to
ask any more questions than absolutely necessary, even though
I realize that's your nature. Some of what I tell you will just be
impossible to understand, so trying to get your head around my
condition will not serve our progress. Second, I don't want to give

you some sort of false confidence that you can latently direct our conversation by asking a bunch of subtle, pointed queries. That's not what we're going to do. I know every smart person always believes that he or she can control a conversation without making a single declarative statement, and I know that—"

CALL 2

"Your machine cut me off. You should set it to record for a longer amount of time. But what I was saying, basically, is that I know what a smart person would do if placed in the position I'm putting you in. I realize how this must sound. Still, I'm hoping you will resist the temptation to interfere. You will have enough things to deal with when this process starts to accelerate. Don't overthink what's happening here, Vicky. I am not a swamp monster, Vicky. I'm not an invisible man. I'm not a vampire, and I'm not God. I'm just an incredibly interesting person. Good night, Vicky."

The First
Meaningful Phone Call

[After consultation with Dr. Jane Dolanagra, my own therapist and academic mentor, I concluded that the conditions Y___ proposed in his message were not as problematic as my gut reaction indicated. What was the risk? Why not allow Y___ to freely say whatever it is he wants me to know? Isn't the entire purpose of therapy to make the client comfortable? To put the client in whatever position makes them most willing to become emotionally vulnerable? To get them to talk on their terms, so that he or she can eventually have those same kinds of conversations inside their own head? That was my thinking at the time. Obviously, I'm less comfortable with that position now. But Dolanagra and I both postulated that—if Y___ was indeed as intelligent as I believed—he might naturally gravitate toward the same platform I would have pushed him toward.

Some context: After I opened our April 11 call by saying, "The floor is yours," Y___ lectured nonstop for forty-three minutes, at which point I informed him that less than two minutes remained in our session. This manuscript does not contain the entirety of that call (or the totality of any of our subsequent interactions), as those single-spaced transcripts stretch to well over 2,400 pages. What I have done (to the best of my abilities) is excerpt the most critical and illuminating passages from each individual exchange. Parties interested in reading the complete transcripts may do so by visiting the basement of the Univ. of Texas

Psychiatric Library, where the pages have been archived by local sociohistorian Daniel Arellano. They have also been transferred to microfiche and can be accessed through the attorney general's office in the William P. Clements Building, 300 West 15th Street, Austin, Texas.]

[Note to C. Bumpus: For purposes of simplicity and impact, I have elected to present Y___'s speech in a traditional prose style. Certain decisions—when to break paragraphs, when to include italics or employ unorthodox punctuation, when to encapsulate especially unwieldy stretches of dialogue—were dictated by my own peccadilloes. However, all of those decisions were solely driven by the desire to reflect Y___'s thoughts in a manner that best captured my experience. If this is a problem, we can address it later.]

APRIL 11 (Y___ calls office line, 10:00 a.m.):

Let's begin. You know, I don't mind talking like this. I'm sure you think I'm going to be one of those people who hires a therapist and then spends six weeks talking about how they hate talking about themselves, but I'm not that kind of guy. I'll never understand why people behave like that. Do they feel some kind of social pressure to prove they're not self-absorbed, even though the basis of this entire process is a critical examination of one's own self-absorption? In this day and age, no one would ever say, "Therapy is ridiculous." Right? Only a philistine would say that aloud, because we've all been conditioned to accept the value of this process. You'd have to be a jackass to think like that. Right? Yet when faced with the experience itself—whenever someone opens that interior door to the conscious and subconscious, fully aware they're paying money to talk about themselves in a completely one-way relationship—everyone feels an urge to say, "I don't really know what I'm doing here" or "I'm not very comfortable talking about myself" or "I don't even know what

I'm supposed to be figuring out." It's childish, really. At this point, who *doesn't* know what kind of conversation they're supposed to have with a therapist? You enter therapy in order to confront four-word sentences: Why am I here? Where am I going? What does it mean? It's not some kind of maze. I understand the expectation. I want to talk about my feelings. That's what I want. I'll never fight you on this. I don't have those prejudices.

[I attempt to interject in order to mention that there is no expectation. Y___ immediately cuts me off.]

Stop. Just stop, please. You're already blowing it. What did we agree to do? Isn't that kind of interjection the exact opposite of what we agreed? We agreed that this would not be a back-and-forth fabrication. This is not an episode of *In Treatment*. You're not Bob Newhart. I don't need your reassurances. I suppose some of the burnouts who pay your rent need a weekly litany of reassurances, but I don't. Did I not make that clear? Let me clarify again: If certain questions arise and you feel the need to ask them, either for clarity or because you're lost, go ahead and ask them. Our conversation will be impossible if you don't have that option, and I don't want to confuse you. But we agreed this was not going to be some kind of Nora Ephron chitchat that toggles back and forth while you sit there and nod on the other end of the telephone. That was not our agreement. We agreed on something else. If I misinterpreted our agreement, tell me now. Because that's the only kind of interaction I'm willing to have. I decide how this will go. I decide.

If this is acceptable, say nothing. If not, tell me now.

[Ten seconds of silence]

Okay then. Thank you, Vicky. I appreciate your cooperation, Vicky.

Where do I begin? I suppose I'll begin by saying that my goal in life, pretty much from infancy, has been to understand the truth about human nature. And—yes—I did say *infancy*. This is not hubris, and I don't care if it sounds pompous or unrealistic. It's the way that it was, and it's the way that I am. My earliest memories all involve staring at people and wondering who they actually were. Staring at my mom, for example, and wondering who she was and what she really felt, and how her mother-centric worldview compared to mine. I didn't know the definition of the word *worldview*, but I still had one. My mom was a different person around my brother and a different person around my dad and a different person on the telephone—why would I be the one exception who saw the real her? I would play by myself, alone in my bedroom, aligning my little green army men on the floor or throwing a Nerf ball against the window, doing childish things in a childish way. I wasn't abnormal. But I'd inevitably find myself thinking difficult thoughts. I'd think, "You know, this is really who I am. Right now, right here. *This is me*. And this is the *only* time I'm me." With my parents, around other kids, sitting in a pew at church, sitting in my desk at school—in all of those situations, I was someone else. I was a *version* of myself, but not the actual me. I understood this separation before I understood anything else. I understood this before I had the language to explain it to other people, or even to my own consciousness. The question was always there, whenever I went out in public: *Who are these people?* I knew this was central to everything. I knew I was looking at a world that wasn't there. I knew I was looking at a simulacrum of life, despite the fact that I had never been introduced to the word *simulacrum* and wouldn't be able to define it for more than a decade. This has been the only thing I've ever thought about, for as long as I can remember. Everything I did, everything I accomplished . . . it was all in the service of this one question. So this is where we start: We start with the recognition that the things I have done were done in order to understand the truth about people. If I've done bad things, or if

we agree that these things could be *viewed* as bad, or if someone
was hurt collaterally because my actions created a domino effect,
we always have to weigh those consequences against what was
learned. Or—in some cases—what I *hoped* would be learned,
even if that ultimately proved fruitless. I say this only because
I want you to feel comfortable judging me, Vicky. Most people
hate being judged, but I am not most people. You can judge me
all you want. However, I do insist that you judge me *accurately*,
and—in order to do that—you need to be aware that nothing
I've done was committed without cause. My motives have always
been one hundred percent good. Now, sometimes, an individual
can have totally pure motives and still do terrible things. I'm
not discounting that. But keep my words in mind. We'll both be
better off if you do. I will absolutely accept any judgments of my
character at face value, but only if those judgments are fair and
balanced.

Back to me: I was always singular. Most children want to believe
they're different, but I actually was. I say things other people
won't even think. The week I started second grade, they skipped
me ahead to third grade. When I was supposed to start eighth
grade, they advanced me into high school. I graduated at fifteen.
Most of the time, this is the worst thing you can do to a child.
It makes them insecure. It makes them fragile. I saw it happen
to other kids. But that never hampered me, or at least I never
noticed if it did. It was a nonfactor. I didn't mind skipping
grades. It made me feel abnormal, but in a good way. Plus, I was
unusually tall. I was almost six feet by the time I was twelve. I'm
sure that helped. Tall people are naturally confident. History has
proven this—Alexander the Great, Wilt Chamberlain, Gisele. The
tallest person in the room always runs the show, and I'm a show-
runner. When I was fourteen, I applied for a summer job with a
telemarketing company. When I showed up for the interview, the
little Willie Loman running the shop asked why he should hire
me. I said, "Well, for one thing, you could probably fire some of

the dead weight around here. I don't see anyone irreplaceable." I got that job. I crushed it.

But you know what? The thing that really made me different wasn't my height. It wasn't my confidence, or the fact that I could read fast or multiply three-digit numbers in my head. What made me different was that I didn't care about socializing with other kids. I never enjoyed the experience of having friends—they always seemed like a bunch of illiterate teenagers pretending to be other people, trying to impress each other, obsessing over bad music and sexually explicit movies, talking too loudly about where they bought their jeans. Outside of my classes and a few of my teachers, the only thing I enjoyed about high school was the gossip. I really, really loved gossiping about other students. I know that's a lowbrow confession, but it was always the best part. Gossip was the only thing I found interesting about my peer group. We would speculate on who was dating whom and we would talk about why so-and-so thought she was so awesome and about how so-and-so got an abortion, and it was all conjecture and analysis. There were certain kids we analyzed every single day. To us, they were celebrities. Of course, there were also a lot of jejune bozos we *never* gossiped about, but that demarcation had it's own little meaning, too—gossipy people define themselves by who they ignore as much as by who they care about. You establish that delineation organically. What can I say, Victoria? I'm a gossip. I don't deny it. I wanted to be like that, so I was. But what I really wanted was to *know*. I wanted my gossip to be verified or disproven. I mean, how was I supposed to relate to these people if I didn't even know what they were really like or who they really were? And I didn't know those things. I didn't. I knew how they acted, but that's not the same thing. I started to wonder: How could I learn the truths that weren't visible? What was I missing? What was *everyone* missing? I became obsessed by these questions, so I started following people. I would follow them home and hide in the bushes. People always make jokes about freaks hiding in the bushes, but that's literally what I did. I was the boy in the bushes.

One particular memory stands out. There was a kid I decided to observe—a long-haired boy with glasses. Thick glasses, long bangs. I don't remember why I picked him. I guess because he seemed easy to follow. He lived eight blocks from my house. At night, I would tell my folks I was going to the library at the community college uptown, but instead I would sneak into this boy's backyard. His room was on the second floor, so I spent the first few nights observing his parents in the living room. They didn't do anything except watch TV, but then again, his mother and father were always in the same room. They were never alone, so they couldn't be themselves. My principal target was the boy, so I eventually took a gamble. There was this massive, sprawling tree behind the house, which I climbed. I climbed this tree, sat on a branch Zacchaeus-style, and looked straight into his bedroom window while the kid played Nintendo. It was incredible! I totally remember that first night—it was the first night I was able to see a person who wasn't me. He was doing nothing, but he was doing it *for real*. No pretense. No self-awareness. I was seeing him as he really was. And I know this probably sounds like voyeurism, but that's not accurate. Voyeurism had nothing to do with it. I wasn't getting cheap pleasure from seeing something I wasn't supposed to see. I was learning. It was like school.

Now, this boy, this teenager—I don't even remember his first name, but his last name was Swanson—he mostly just played video games. Driving games, like *Pole Position*. That was his modus operandi, and it was unremarkable. But sometimes he did something else. Every so often, and without any forethought, he would pause the Nintendo, turn up his boom box, and physically act out whatever song he was listening to. He'd perform, but only for himself. And he didn't play air guitar, the way they always make it seem in movies and in rock videos; it was more like a Broadway musical. He would pantomime the lyrics of the song, lip-syncing all the words, jumping on the bed and spinning around the room like a woman. It was always the same songs off the same CD, always played at top volume. When his window was ajar, I could sit in my tree and faintly hear the music he would mimic: Rush. He listened to Rush. *2112*. An album that no one at our school cared about. An album I'm certain this boy never mentioned to any of his friends. I mean, I knew this person. I suppose I *was* his friend, from his perspective. I saw him every day, or at least I saw the version of himself he dragged into school. He sat behind me in geometry and across from me in French. We had P.E. together, two years in a row. I knew what he talked about and I knew the things he pretended to like. And I can assure you, the version of the kid I knew from school did not give a shit about Rush. Not at all. Not in any way. And yet . . . and this seems so obvious now . . . he clearly did. He *did* care about Rush. He *loved* Rush. It must have been more important to him than all of the things he pretended to adore in public, because that was the music he played when he was himself. *2112* was already uncool and outdated, but it was the one thing he loved, simply for what it was. So I was fascinated by this. I was fascinated by this one minor detail that wasn't remotely minor—his secret relationship with *2112*. His secret bedroom performances, devoid of anything performative. I always wanted to ask him about it. I wanted to just casually walk up and say, "Hey, Swanson. So, what do you think of Canadian power trios? Any opinion? Do they inspire your very being? Any plans to do an oral book report on *Anthem*?" But, of course, I never did. I couldn't. Too risky. Instead, I just watched him through his window. Over time, I lost interest and started following someone else. But Swanson was the first. He was the first person I knew.

This, I assume, is exactly the kind of information you want from me. You want me to go back through elementary school and middle school and high school and college, and you want me to talk about all the things that supposedly made me who I am. And maybe I'll do that, assuming these sessions go well and we need to keep digging for bones. Maybe I will and maybe I won't. But—right now—I want to accelerate. I want to talk about why I built the suit and why I developed the cream. You could argue, I suppose, that those things were not necessary. Certainly, there are easier means of surveillance. Wiretapping, for one. Hidden cameras, motion detectors. I had an intense interest in hidden cameras, and I used them on my roommates during college. Very often, hiding under a bed or inside ceiling panels can accomplish the same goals, at least in a limited capacity. But none of those things can truly reflect the sense of being inside a room. If you want to be in a room, you need to be *in the room*, you know? Even though that's an infinitely more difficult endeavor. Even though the suit and the cream are uncomfortable, and even though the physical toll it takes on my body is ludicrous. I'll never feel the same. I'll never be the same. But it had to be done.

[Note to C. Bumpus: In retrospect, I should have stopped Y___ at this juncture and asked him to provide greater details about "the suit and the cream." He might have complied. However, in my defense, I want to stress that I was still under the impression that "the suit and the cream" were part of Y___'s fantasy life and not tangible artifacts. I was also trying very hard to comply with Y___'s prearranged conditions, which demanded that I not interject during his monologues. At the time, gaining his emotional trust seemed more important than the credulity of his claims. If you're wondering what I was thinking internally when he started talking about the suit and the cream, my answer is simple: I thought, "This is interesting. I wonder where this is going?" I assumed Y___ was doing something many patients do when they begin to feel relaxed around a therapist—I assumed he was expressing an obvious metaphor about how he viewed himself. The idea of donning a special "suit" or costume is a common symbol for someone hiding his true self from the world. The concept of "the cream" initially struck me as sexual, which was a subject Y___ had never alluded to previously. I was genuinely excited by these revelations and wanted to hear more. Only later did I discover my silence had been a mistake. I waited one session too long.]

As I believe I already mentioned, research and development for the suit and the cream was financed by the second Bush administration, technically through standard grants but ultimately via the NSA.[6] This was when I was in Hawaii. It started as an extension of optical camouflage, which originally came from the University of Tokyo, but—at Chaminade—we were more occupied with metamaterials. Now, to this day, I still don't know if the original intention for the suit was warfare or reconnaissance. As you might expect, there was a lot of debate about this among the staff at the lab. There was always an issue over whether we could accept funding for this research if the suit and the cream were going to be used in actual combat, since that would essentially make them weapons. None of those eggheads wanted to be working on weaponry. They were overt moralists. It was a little different for me, partially because I was younger but mostly because this was not my first rodeo. I was young, but this experience was arguably my fifth or sixth intellectual undertaking: I had started in chemical engineering as an undergrad, but then I pursued graduate study in sociology and then—immediately following that—psychology. I dabbled in investigative journalism for two years. I was a capable musician. I was a pretty decent playwright. I attended a city planning workshop. I did some organic farming. I invested eighteen months of independent study in mathematics before seriously returning to hard science. I can't think of any academic subject that doesn't excite me, except

6. National Security Agency.

maybe art history. So even though I was the youngest person in
the Chaminade lab, my worldview was much more diverse. I'd
already considered different levels of thought. I would never
refer to myself as a "renaissance man," although I suppose that's
precisely what I am. But virtually everyone else at Chaminade had
never done anything outside of research, so all their individual
concerns were a tad myopic and—frankly—unsophisticated. The
big question for them, it always seemed, was the relationship
between the unexplained motives of the military and their own
personal involvement. Basically, they felt they could chase any
technology as long as they pursued it under the guise of doing
something good, or at least something neutral. In other words,
if they made a weapon *but did not know it was a weapon when they
made it*, there was no moral crisis. They refused to consider the
possibility of someone misusing whatever we created; that was
something they viewed as beyond their control. They were fixated
on accepting all directives at face value, even if that information
made no sense or seemed like an obvious lie. What they wanted,
I suppose, was the proverbial "clear conscience." But because the
government would never directly say why they wanted cloaking
paraphernalia, the whole project started to hemorrhage and
collapse. Many of my colleagues felt that—because no one would
directly tell us *why* we were trying to construct human cloaking
elements—they were forced to infer that whatever we ended up
making had no use at all. If no one *told them* what the cloaking
was for, they looked at everything as an exercise. In their minds,
having no espoused explanation meant the suit couldn't be used
for anything. I know that sounds crazy, but there was a certain
silly logic to it: If something did not have an outlined purpose,
then any use qualified as misuse, and that meant they'd knowingly
be working on a project that was destined to be used improperly.
Because, I mean—rationally—we all knew these theoretical suits
were going to be used for *something*. All the grant contracts made
it clear that this was not just a scientific inquiry, and there was
so much money being poured into development that there had

to be a definite product when we finished. The NSA wouldn't throw that much money at an exercise. But nobody could get over the fact that we had no directive. In other words, if the military had told us *anything* about why we were supposed to develop cloaking technology, that would have been enough for most of my co-workers. I'm certain everyone at Chaminade would have been totally comfortable if the NSA had just fabricated some bogus memo about our intended purpose. It could have said anything. Just something on paper that stated, "This is why we want these magic suits." They could have sent us an e-mail that said, "We want to use these suits to imbed soldiers in dangerous areas so that they can provide emergency relief to displaced citizens without visually notifying enemy personnel." That would have been more than enough. For all I know, that might have been their actual intention! But because the NSA refused to give us anything quantifiable, people started to slowly abandon the lab on so-called ethical grounds. The first ones who quit did so for valid reasons, but—after a while—most people quit because one of their favorite colleagues quit before them, or because this fake philosophical problem provided an excuse to move back to the mainland, or because they were the kind of sheep who always did what everyone else was already doing. And this, of course, totally worked to my advantage. When the project was eventually eliminated, I was the only person left in the lab, so I just stole everything we had and finished the work in my apartment. I'm not generally a thief, but this was a special circumstance. Once I escaped the distractions, it took only three more years. Nobody noticed. This had never been a secret project, because the project never had a clear-enough purpose to keep secret. I just boxed up everything from the lab and put it in my car. Nobody asked me one question about all the shit I carried out, and all our collective notes and equations were on a shared computer network. And to be honest, even when the lab was at full strength, I'd done most of the work myself, anyway. I was the only one who immediately understood how important this was. And I've never minded working alone. I actually prefer it.

[It was at this point that I interrupted Y___, despite our agreement. I tried to be straightforward, saying only, "I don't understand what this means or where this is going." At the time, I was being truthful. Read in retrospect, it seems all too obvious where this monologue was leading—but it only seems that way now because I know what happened later. I didn't believe I was getting real information. I was mostly wondering why these specific fabrications were the lies Y___ was choosing to tell.]

I didn't anticipate that you would get this, Vicky. And I hope that doesn't seem condescending, because that's not my intention. I don't think anyone could understand this. I'm only giving you some background so that we can get to my real concerns, none of which relate to science. Look: I had a desire, and I built something that made that desire real. And there was a consequence to that. I suppose it's not all that different than any artist who ever got what he wanted, only to discover it made things harder. My desire was to study how people lived when they were alone, and I developed a means to do that. It's as simple as that. I don't have any issues concerning the value or morality of the science. I just want you to know exactly what I did. Moreover, when we really get into this, I don't want to waste our time going over the details of cloaking every ten minutes. It's difficult to explain to a scientist and impossible to explain to a therapist. You'll need to accept a degree of cognitive dissonance. You made it very clear that these sessions were for *my* benefit, and that I could dictate what we talk about. So I'm telling you what I want to talk about. Now, is that going to be a problem?

[I assure Y___ that this is not a problem, and I assure him that this will not become a problem. But I mention that it's difficult for me to

understand what we're talking about if he's not even willing to frame what we're supposed to be discussing.]

What part of this strikes you as "unframed"? Don't take this the wrong way, but I really can't make this any simpler than I already have. I know it's complicated, but what I'm able to explain is limited by what you're unable to understand. How about this: Imagine that you live alone. I know that you don't, but imagine that you do. Imagine that you live a quiet, solitary life in a one-bedroom apartment on the outskirts of town. Now, imagine that someone else was inside that apartment. Imagine that a stranger had managed to get inside your residence, and that this stranger just sat there, silently, and observed you. This stranger would learn a great deal about who you really were, wouldn't he? He would know you with a depth that only you can normally experience, in a context devoid of artifice. He would see the raw ingredients for whatever recipe you use to create the public version of yourself. He would learn things he couldn't unlearn. And maybe that would be tough on him. Maybe he'd feel sinister. Maybe he'd feel angry at no one in particular. Maybe he'd think less of himself.

I feel differently about people, and I feel differently about myself. And I don't think I'll be able to reverse those feelings. So that, I suppose, is what I want to figure out. I want to learn how to manage who I am and what I can do. And I'm serious about this, so I'll call you next week. I'll call you.

Goodbye, Vicky. I think this went well.

END OF PHONE SESSION 1

NOTES: This is going to be more difficult than anticipated. Y___'s problems may be beyond my faculties. He is mired in a profound delusion that's now intertwined with his functional reality. It is not simply that Y___ cannot separate his real life from his imagined life; it appears that the real now takes direct cues from the unreal. I'm now skeptical of Y___'s scientific credentials, mostly due to his obsession with avoiding all scientific details before I even ask for them. My first goal will be helping Y___ accept and admit that he is not a scientist.

I do, however, believe he spent time in Hawaii.

A deeper problem is his preoccupation with other people (and what he seems to think that preoccupation means). His story about the teenager he watched through the window, for example, seems genuine—although it's unclear why the music of Rush plays such a significant role in the anecdote. What's even more confusing (and less plausible) is his emphasis on voyeurism motivated by academic curiosity. All signs point toward an extremely lonely person—a loneliness that has lasted so long it's morphed into psychosis. If his description of being skipped ahead in school (not once, but twice) is true, that experience must be explored. Y___ needs to be jarred out of his own head. He's a stubborn one. This will be a challenge.

The Second
Meaningful Phone Call

APRIL 18 (Y___ calls office line, 10:05 a.m.):

Vicky. Hello. How are you? I will assume you're perfect. Now, I
believe we ended last week with—

*[I stop Y___ from continuing. I tell him that I've spent a week
thinking about his situation and I have some practical questions that
must be addressed. Nakedly annoyed, he asks what these questions will
focus on. I say, "The suit and the cream. I need to understand the suit
and the cream." He asks what I need to know. When I tell him I want
to know everything, he sighs so melodramatically that it's audible on
the recording, almost as if this is a radio play.]*

We've already talked about this, Vicky. I'm not going to talk
about it again. We went through the entire process weeks ago.
Why didn't you ask me these questions when I was explaining
it the first time? This is not what I want to do. I don't intend to
send you envelopes of cash in order to teach you about molecular
science. Why would I want that? Will you please inform me
why I should send you money in order to help you pretend to
understand something that'll never make any sense to you?

*[I apologize. In retrospect, I apologized to Y___ too often in these
kinds of situations, but I had no idea he'd use that against me. I*

asked if he would give me the Cliffs Notes version of how the suit and cream worked. He said, "I'm not surprised you're a fan of Cliffs Notes." When I told him that this type of response was insulting and sophomoric, he apologized.]

I'm sorry if what I said hurt your feelings. I'm sorry if you inferred my joke differently than the way it was intended. That was not my intention.

[Recognizing a window of vulnerability, I again ask if he would provide a rough sketch of the suit and the cream. Again, he sighs cartoonishly.]

Okay, sure. I don't see how this will do any good, but fine. Here, in simplest terms, is what we were working on in Hawaii: Are you familiar with Philip K. Dick? Have you ever heard of a book called *A Scanner Darkly*? They made a movie about it, too. An animated movie, which I didn't see. Doesn't matter. Basically, it was a futuristic novel about drug enforcement, and the police officers in the book wear something called a Scramble Suit. In the book, a Scramble Suit is this superthin material that a policeman wears over his body like a membrane, and it's made from some kind of malleable quartz lens, and the idea is that the suit allows you to look like a million different people interchangeably. Essentially, it makes someone look like everyone and no one at the same time. This is totally fiction, of course. It's totally impossible. But evidently, that book was the seed for an idea, at least from the military's perspective. They wanted us to make a suit that would make someone impossible to see, or at least very, very *difficult* to see. No one at Chaminade was told this directly, but we all sort of understood that this novel had been the genesis. We talked about it among ourselves. I mean, the type of person who worked in this lab was the same type of person who read a lot of Philip K. Dick novels. And you'd be surprised how often the military operates like this. They get so many ideas from bullshit

like *Star Trek* and Arthur C. Clarke and *World War Z*. At one
point they were trying to genetically engineer a Wookiee in
Greenland. I'm not kidding. They wanted to build an army
of fucking Chewbaccas for hand-to-hand warfare in arctic
climates. They tried for ten years. I have photographs. One of
my colleagues allegedly had hair samples, but it just seemed like
regular yak hair to me.

But, regardless . . . it was like this: We were instructed to make
these cloaking suits, although—as I said before—none of us really
knew why. And obviously, you can't make a fabric that disappears
on its own. That's nonsense. But we came up with a concept that
immediately felt semiplausible: What we needed was a sheer
suit that *reflected* light, but was covered by a viscous fluid. This
fluid would capture the light and move it. The elements within
the fluid are something we refer to as metamaterials, because
the components are smaller than the wavelength of light. Are
you understanding the premise? Do you remember talking
about this before? We called this theoretical fluid "ozone fluid,"
because it was loosely modeled after the way the ozone layer
traps ultraviolet rays: Light would pass through the cream, but
it wasn't reflected out. This was where *A Scanner Darkly* actually
played a role. There are certain natural elements—quartz being
one of them—that naturally bounce light back toward its source,
almost like a mirror. And if you combine a specific sequence
of these elements, they each refract a universal light source at
varying wave distances. So that was what we infused into the
cream: The cream is filled with crystallized metamaterial that
reflects light capriciously. But the surface of that cream provides
resistance. It's like the suit has its own visual atmosphere. This,
obviously, was the key—the key was developing a cream that
allowed light to pass through its membrane, strike the surface
of this highly reflective suit, bounce, and then bounce *again*. But
it couldn't refract at a right angle. It had to refract at an angle
that was either obtuse or acute. Because what we were trying to

do was make this light *move*. We wanted to move it one hundred and eighty degrees from the point of origin. Our hypothesis—*my* hypothesis, really, because I did all the heavy lifting—was that there would inevitably be a pool of light at the opposite pole of whoever was wearing the suit, since the refraction would be happening from both sides simultaneously and at the same speed. That pool of light would overcome the cream's resistance and become our quote-unquote "third-party visual." This was the plan.

Is this making sense? Any sense at all?

Now, what does that mean in a three-dimensional world? It basically means that any third party looking at a man wearing the suit would see whatever was directly behind that man. If the man in the suit was standing in front of a brick wall, the third party would see the bricks. These bricks would only be a reflection, but they'd match the rest of the wall. It would be an imperfect match, but close enough to fool anyone who didn't know what they were looking for.

Does that satisfy you?

[I say, "Not really."]

Of course it doesn't. How could it? I'm already dumbing this down to a level where it barely makes sense to me. Seriously, Vicky—don't concern yourself with science. I don't know why it matters to you, anyway. Here's all you need to know: At Chaminade, we constructed something akin to a ninja suit. They almost looked like a child's pajamas. In my apartment, two years later, I finished the translucent cream. It took another ten months to concentrate that cream into a mist so that I could apply it as an aerosol. That was harder than I thought it would be. In many respects, that was the hardest part. The only way I could do it was by trial and error. I don't even want to *think* about that period of my life. It was incredibly tedious. But like I said—these details are not your concern.

Now, if I put on this ninja suit, and I shave my facial hair and I put on a pair of goggles, and I spray down the suit and my hands and my feet and my face with this concentrated cream, an optical illusion occurs. You won't be able to see me. Instead, you will see what's directly *behind* me, and you'll interface with that false image at the speed of light. And like I said before, because this process unnaturally bends the light source, my fabricated image will be a little off. It will be less sharp and less vivid. The difference is roughly similar to the disparity between high-definition and standard-definition television, if that helps your imagination. The match won't be perfect. But it will be close enough.

Now: Does *that* satisfy you?

[I say nothing.]

The decision you're going to have to make, Vicky, is how much this mental hurdle is going to impede your ability to work with me. I understand how strange it must sound. But here's the thing: It's not that strange, or at least not as strange as it feels at this specific moment. What the military wanted—and what I eventually finished—was simply a way to be unseen. They probably wanted to be unseen in order to murder Afghani dissidents, but my motives were different. I'm not a terrorist. I'm just a person. So can we get back to the problems that matter?

["Yes," I say. But then I casually said something that enraged Y____. I said, "It's just hard for me to accept that you're the Invisible Man."]

Jesus Christ. Did you really say that? Am I drunk right now? Are we six years old? Are you really a therapist? Where did you go to school? Did they make you read books there, or did you get one of those online degrees? I am not an invisible man, Vicky. It's not the fifties. I'm not black. People can't be *invisible*. Sorry to disappoint you. You can't see directly through something that's not, you know, made of fucking Plexiglas. I didn't drink a potion and disappear. I'm not fucking Gyges. There's no magic ring. I don't wear a cape. That's not how it works. I was never *invisible*. I was always there. Jesus fucking Christ. Don't you know how the human eye works? An invisible person would be totally blind. You realize that, right? A transparent retina wouldn't register color. This is a little offensive, to be honest. More than a little. I spend all that energy explaining the cloaking process to you—despite my apprehensions, knowing you're not a scientist—and still, this is what happens. You think I'm H. G. Wells. Actually, that's not true. I'm sure you have no idea who H. G. Wells even is. They probably don't cover that at the University of Phoenix. He's probably not pictured on their home page. Do you know who Chevy Chase is? He was the invisible man, once. Maybe you think I'm like Chevy Chase. Do you know who that is? Did you ever see *Fletch*, or was the plot too complicated? Or maybe you're more of a Kevin Bacon fan.

[I inform Y___ that his behavior is abusive. I inform him that I will end the session if he continues speaking to me in this style.]

Then maybe we should end this session.

[Long pause.]

Okay, fine. Fuck my intentions. I was wrong to say those things. I'm sorry if I hurt your feelings. I shouldn't have said that stuff about Chevy Chase. You're not like a six-year-old. I know you're not an idiot, and I know that you know that. It's just that . . . I mean, seriously? Invisible? You should know better. You *do* know better. Tangible objects can't be invisible, ever. But they don't need to be. That's the crux of the concept. One of the most meaningful things I've learned from this is that people barely see what's openly in front of them, much less things that are camouflaged. We all have a fixed perspective on how the world looks, and that perspective generates itself. We mentally change what we see to fit our unconscious perception of order. I'm sure you're familiar with the phrase "People see what they want to see," but that's not really accurate. A more accurate phrase would be "People see what they assume must be seeable." If there's no sense of movement and no unexpected sounds, we typically let our mind produce a backdrop that matches our memory. People will look at the world without seeing anything beyond their unconscious expectation.

I can vividly recall a few nights I spent in Dallas, imbedded inside the home of a man with a high-stress, physically taxing job. This was maybe two years ago. He was a man who would leave home very early in the morning and return two hours after sundown. He'd return dirty and mentally exhausted—his phone would ring and he'd totally ignore it. Never answered it once. Wouldn't even check the caller ID. He'd take a shower, put a frozen pizza in the oven, drink a tumbler of iced tea, and watch MSNBC on the television, ninety percent naked. He usually went to bed before eleven. From an observational standpoint, the man did not give me much to work with. But I'll always remember how detached he was from the room itself. It was like the room wasn't even there. He had four pictures on the walls of his living room . . . images of vaguely sexualized women. Not photographs, but graphic art. Did you ever listen to Duran Duran? These paintings were sort of like the cover of the Duran Duran album *Rio*: Cheesy, I suppose, but tasteful to someone with blue-collar sensibilities. I'm sure when he originally bought 'em, they were replacing posters of Megan Fox or Dirk Nowitzki. He probably thought they were symbols of adulthood. On the third day I was inside, I swapped the location of two of these *Rio*-esque portraits while he was away at work. I wasn't surprised when he didn't notice they'd been moved. I'm sure I could have switched them around every afternoon. I probably could have painted one myself. That night, I sat unnecessarily close to this tired, seminaked man. I crouched on the carpet, maybe eighteen inches to the left of his couch. His sofa was in the middle of his living space, right out in the open, sort of like an island. Geographically, I was completely exposed. Except for the suit, I wasn't even hiding. But his behavior never changed. He just stared straight at the TV screen with his big, brown, bottomless eyes. He had eyes like a horse. In every way possible, he was horselike. I wondered, "Would this horse-man even notice me if I were uncloaked?" Frankly, I doubt it. I really doubt it. What would he have seen? I don't think he had the potential to see *anything*, real or imagined. But he was not the only one.

END OF PHONE SESSION 2

NOTES: This is going to be a problem. I am at fault. By agreeing to Y___'s terms (re: sustaining a one-way dialogue that he controls), I've only served to enable his delusions. He now believes he has the right to create any self-mythology for his own benefit, almost as if I am not there. Moreover, his anger at my mild skepticism prompts me to conclude that he's more fragile than I initially realized. He has built a massive interior world for himself—a comic book where he's a brilliant scientist who's turned himself into an amoral superhero. Moreover, his detail-rich fantasies about hiding inside the homes of strangers suggest genuine psychosis and a real measure of danger. At present, I don't believe that Y___ has committed any acts that would constitute felonious activity. But it's not outside the realm of possibility. This has to stop. During our next phone discussion, my goal is to convince Y___ to meet me for a face-to-face session; after that, I will concentrate on directing him to a medical facility for psychological testing and possible medication. I am not equipped to deal with this level of disorder. Extremely despondent over this turn of events, but what else can be done? I can't help this man. I am not a doctor.

The Third
Meaningful Phone Call

APRIL 25 (Y___ calls office line, 10:01 a.m.):

Vicky. Hello. I hope you're not sitting in a puddle, soaked to the bone. *[Reader's Note. It had been raining heavily throughout the greater Austin area.]* I tend to have bonko dreams when the weather is like this. Surreal, non sequitur vision quests, even within the surreal, non sequitur context of vision-questing. Last night I dreamed that I was talking to my gay sister. I don't even have a sister, much less a gay one. But I did in this dream. We were discussing her adopted children, and I had all these insights about the kids and how to discipline them. I knew all these highly specific details about these imaginary children, adopted by a person who isn't real. Plus, I could reference all these historical facts about my nonexistent gay sister—games we had played in our youth, bad relationships she had in high school. All of this arcane, distant background. But then, suddenly, the dream was different. I was no longer talking to my gay sister. I was in Venice. I was walking around Venice, alone, looking at the gondolas in the canals. Of course, I've never even been to Venice, I've never even thought about it as a place I'd like to visit. So I guess I was looking at whatever I must imagine Venice looks like? I'm not sure I've even seen photographs, although I suppose everybody has at some point. How else would I know what a gondola even was? But regardless, while I was walking around this city I've never visited, I realized my gay sister was dead, even though she'd never actually existed. I started to worry about her imaginary kids again—who would raise them, who would pay for their tennis lessons, that sort of thing. I think there was a cat swimming in the canal, or maybe a thousand little cats and one big cat. It's really too bad that dreams don't mean anything. I wish I could learn something by sleeping. But, of course, I can't. Nobody can, ever. Dreams are fake. Freud was a cokehead, you know. No different than Scarface. Who else would believe that shit? Dream talk is crazy talk, delivered by the drowsy uncrazy. Except for maybe those dreams where you look into the bathroom mirror and your teeth start to fall out—it does seem strange that everyone has that same specific dream. What does *chewing* represent for our collective unconscious? Probably something to do with horses.

Okay, before we begin I'd like to take a little—

[I stop Y___ and ask if I can pose a few questions—not conversational directives, but a few specific queries that I need him to confirm or deny. I tell him that it's essential I verify certain facts before we discuss anything further. He agrees to my request. These are my questions and his responses:]

Q: You are a scientist. Would you say that statement is true? Are you a scientist?

A: Uh, yes.

Q: And you have a college degree, and you've worked in the capacity of a scientist?

A: What? Yes.

Q: And one of the places where you worked in this capacity was at Chaminade University in Hawaii, and your central

scientific project was the creation of a suit that—while not making you invisible—allowed you to appear invisible to other people.

A: Yes. Sure, sure. Yes. What are you getting at? Am I missing something?

Q: And you eventually used this suit for your own personal gain?

A: No. Not for my *personal* gain. That's an incorrect reading of what I've described.

Q: Did you use this suit to enter people's homes?

A: Yes. To observe them. This was a scientific endeavor. I've stated this countless times. I wasn't robbing them, if that's what you're suggesting. I'm not a thief. I wasn't peeping for thrills. I'm no peeper. Is that what you're suggesting? That I'm some kind of thieving peeper?

Q: I'm not suggesting that. But I do need to ask one more question. Can I assume, or would it be safe to say, that the reason you have contacted me is to talk about how the process of using this invisibility suit to spy on strangers has negatively impacted your day-to-day life?

A: Yes. Yes. Yes! Have I been talking to myself for the past two months? Why are you asking me to explain the only things I've already explained at length?

[At this point I made a request for Y___ to come in to my office in person. I tell him that I can no longer help him over the telephone.]

What? Why? Where is this coming from? What will that accomplish? I thought we agreed on this. There were certain terms I outlined as imperative. Relatively speaking, this seemed like a minor one. You've expressed no problem having these conversations in this style. It's never been an issue. I'm more comfortable on the telephone. It allows me to think more clearly. And . . . it's more convenient. I'm a busy person. Don't you realize I'm a busy fucking person? Why do I need to come to your office and sit there like some housewife with postpartum depression? I'm not going to do it.

[In response, I give Y___ a host of valid reasons why face-to-face meetings would be to our advantage: they're more intimate, nonverbal language has significance, trust cannot be galvanized over the phone, etc. These are all fake reasons, but I express them out of courtesy.]

That's horseshit. That's fiction. You would have mentioned those things immediately if they were true. You have an ulterior motive here. Your lies are transparent. What are you trying to get for yourself? Is it that you want to see the suit with your own horsey eyes? Or is it that you want to not see this "Invisible Man" you can't stop yourself from mentioning? Are you falling in love with me? Are you falling in love with some childish notion of an invisible man? The Invisible Man is not real, Vicky. It was a book. There is no such creature. You need to come to grips with that. I'm just a person. You've seen men like me before. Don't you have a husband? Try loving your husband.

[I ask him to remain calm. I tell him this is a professional decision, not a personal one.]

But a professional decision would be based on reason. It would be built on specifics, and those specifics would be clear to both of us. You're communicating through abstractions. Your arguments are horseshit—you're just throwing around buzzwords to sound like you're not making an arbitrary, personal choice. Which, I would argue, is exactly what you're doing. If you can't tell me the real reason you want to meet with me in person, I don't see how my doing so could be helpful.

[On this point, I concede that Y___ is correct. I apologize. I proceed to tell him my actual reasoning for wanting a face-to-face meeting: It's because I do not believe the things he is telling me, and I suspect he needs a different kind of help. I tell him that he is not a bad person and that I can sense his intellect, but that his intellect is the reason he came to me in the first place—he knows that he has significant mental health issues. As such, he also knows it's not too late to become the man he used to be. I tell him that I am probably not the person who can provide that help, but that I can connect him to someone who can. Again, I reinforce the likelihood that he already knows I'm right about this. Y___ listens without interrupting, and then he says this:]

This is interesting, Vic-Vick. I'm surprised to hear you state your feelings so directly. I'm not surprised you *thought* these things, but I am very surprised you said them. I'm actually impressed. I've kind of been waiting for this.

I've told you who I am and I've told you why I called you. And you don't believe me. You think, "This is some kind of new insanity." Or maybe you think it's just the old insanity, repackaged as bad television. This is what your mind is telling you to believe. You view yourself as a therapist, which—in a broad sense, from your perspective—makes you a certain type of scientist. A rationalist. You view yourself a rational being who assists other people in driving their flawed relationships toward rationality. That's essentially your job, isn't it? Your job is to talk to people who see their lives irrationally, and you try to coax them toward a rational balance. You can't *tell* them how to feel or how to think, even if that's what they want. You can only ask them leading questions that force them to talk to themselves. "If they could just hear what they themselves are saying," you think to yourself, "they'd see how their view of the world is skewed."

That the view they hold is unrealistic, or maybe unnaturally personal. In order to do what you do, this is how you need to think. So when I call you up on the telephone, and I tell you I've done these unbelievable things, and I explain how I am unlike every other person you've ever met, you can't accept what I say. Your whole self-identity tells you that my unbelievable stories are *literally* unbelievable, and that I'm just a normal person with a delusion. So you ask me to come to your office. You want to prove to yourself that I have a different problem than the one I've outlined over the past two months. Now, honestly, I think you know that everything I've told you is true. I don't think I've said one thing that you don't believe. But there's no way you can admit that. It would make your own relationship with rationality unmanageable. So maybe you want to avoid the collision. Maybe you think if you demand my physical presence, I will refuse to comply, thereby ending our relationship on your terms. Or maybe you think I will show up at your office door and admit that this has been an elaborate hoax, perpetrated by one of your colleagues, and you will be a little embarrassed and a little relieved. You're in a peculiar position right now: You can't believe what you believe. And you want to void that feeling, so you're changing the rules. This is by no means irrational. I understand completely. I do it all the time.

Let me tell you a story. I don't know if it will help you understand where we're at, but I'm going to try nonetheless. It happened in Cleveland. This was a few years ago. Three years ago, if I recall correctly. I spent four months in Cleveland, following a variety of random Clevelanders. This was difficult, because absolutely everyone in Cleveland drives. It's like L.A. It was hard to find a decent mark, because I'd have to find an unlocked car in the afternoon, wait in the vehicle for several hours, and then stow away in the backseat while they drove home. Then I'd have to figure out a way inside their house, and—very often—the homes would be in suburban areas, like Lakewood or Mayfield or

Cleveland Heights. The upside to this was that it's much easier to sneak into a freestanding home than into an apartment, because modern houses have a lot of vulnerable openings. The mechanics are pretty simple. But the downside to watching someone in a suburb is that you're often trapped in the middle of nowhere. If things went wrong, it would take forever to get back to the center of the city, which is where I was temporarily living. Sometimes I'd have to walk the whole way back, because there's really no public transportation in Cleveland and I didn't like the risk involved with stealing cars. But these details don't matter right now. What I want to talk about is a particular guy I watched for almost a week. His name was Bruce.

I first noticed Bruce at a bar. Bars are good places to begin following someone. If the person you start following is already a little drunk, you can take more risks. For example, it's easy to sneak into a really intoxicated person's vehicle: All you have to do is trip them while they're opening the driver's side door. You just step on their outside foot and push them down with your shoulder, all in one motion. It doesn't matter if they feel something pushing them—they inevitably assume it's their own fault. Drunks always blame themselves. If a drunk person can't see who knocked him down, he immediately assumes he's just more wasted than he thought. Sometimes they lie on the ground and laugh at themselves, because drunkards love being drunkards. It feels great to be drunk, right? That's when you slip into the passenger seat. Granted, you then have to ride home with a person who's too drunk to realize he was just assaulted. It's sketchy. But people are good at driving drunk, especially in Cleveland. That's another thing I learned—drunk-driving laws are way too stringent in this country. Or at least they are in Ohio.

I didn't even have to knock Bruce down, though. He required no work at all. I found him in an Irish pub, late in the afternoon.

57

It was autumn. The sun was low. He was having drinks with a few people he worked with—it was easy to figure out what was happening, because they all got to the bar at the same time and they were all dressed identically. There were five of them, all men, all in their late twenties. I watched them through a window and tried to figure out which one I wanted to trail. Two of them had wedding rings, so they were immediately out. Remember: I watch people when they're alone. That's my thing. Of the three who remained, I thought two looked like viable candidates; the third guy was too handsome and gregarious, so I assumed he was either in a preexisting relationship or sleeping with a whole bunch of random hookups. I wasn't interested in those scenarios. I wanted people who looked like they had no important friends. Bruce fit the equation. Bruce had that sad, distant stare of a man who missed college too much. So did the guy sitting next to him. Neither one talked much as the group drank three or four beers. None of the five got drunk. They all left together, at the same time. My initial plan focused on the other loner—the quiet guy who wasn't Bruce. He just seemed swarthier and weirder—he had a strange haircut and thicker eyeglasses. He looked like someone who might have played in a ska band when he was sixteen. Bruce's principal upside was that he had less character. Bruce was just an American guy. Nothing about him was obvious.

Now, because my original target was not authentically intoxicated, and because it was still dusk, my best option was to distract him when he opened his driver's side door. I was going to wait until he started to climb into the driver's seat, and then I was going to kick the back fender of his Nissan as hard as I could. My hope was that he'd get out of the car to check on the mysterious thud, and then I'd scoot around and jump in the vehicle while the door remained ajar. My life is filled with these kinds of momentary misdirections. They only work twenty-five percent of the time, but how else can I do it? It's all trial and error. This time, however, I got absurdly lucky: Before I even had a chance to put my plan into action, Bruce opened the door of his own car and just absentmindedly walked away from it. Left it wide open for at least fifteen or twenty seconds. He opened his car door, walked over to one of his drinking partners, and said, "So, are we going to make this trade or not?" The other guy said something along the lines of, "I don't know, man. Anquan Boldin always gets hurt. Let me look at the schedule and think it over." It was too easy. By the time Bruce turned his ignition key, I was already in the backseat. Bruce was oblivious. Oblivious Bruce. I would say it was like taking candy from a baby, but babies scream. This was easier.

We finally arrive at his house, which is way the fuck out in somewhere I'd never even heard of. Most single twenty-five-year-old men don't own four-bedroom houses that are seventy-five minutes from the office, but Bruce did. He was an odd one. Bruce parks in the garage and waddles inside. I follow about five minutes later. The screen door isn't locked. He's already at the computer, masturbating. That might seem perverse, but you'd be amazed how common this is: Men get home, change clothes, and masturbate. There's nothing remotely sexual about it. They just need to get it out of the way. It's like taking out the trash. I've probably watched three hundred different guys masturbate, and not one of them seemed to enjoy it. I'm sure they did, but you wouldn't know by looking at them. I don't even think that pornography plays a particularly important role. It simply saves them a little time. Men are so lazy. They're too lazy to imagine naked women.

Anyway . . . so now I'm inside his house. This is always the most thrilling moment, because it means everything worked. I always spend so much mental energy trying to get into this position that I never know what to do with myself once I'm actually inside. I always want to celebrate, to congratulate myself for being so goddamn clever. But I can't. I just have to find a comfortable spot in a corner and sit down. I have to control my breathing. I have to keep it shallow. I also need to prepare myself for the inevitability of utter boredom: Very often, single people don't do shit. They do nothing, all night long. They sit in a recliner and watch TV. I've probably watched more television than anyone you've ever met, and I don't even own one. Terrible shows, good shows. Golf tournaments in Cancun. C-SPAN. Hours of Oprah. *Law and Order*. Lonely people love *Law and Order*, for whatever reason. They prefer the straight narratives. They'll also rent the entire run of a TV series on Netflix, and they tend to rent whatever Netflix promotes as popular. I'm pretty sure I've seen every episode of *The Wire*, but never in the proper sequence. I have no fucking clue what's supposed to be going on there.

Bruce is a different kind of guy, though. Bruce doesn't watch TV—he owns an awesome one, but he never turns it on. Bruce is one of these people who lives on the Internet. He has a house full of leather furniture, but he spends the whole evening in his desk chair. He plays RISK over the Internet for hours—he'll have sixty or seventy games happening simultaneously, all against strangers he'll never meet in person. He steals music constantly—he'd rip a live Paul Simon album, listen to the first track for thirty seconds, and then never play it again. He follows a bunch of political blogs and seems to comment on every post, usually with bitter sarcasm but sometimes with an LOL. He looks at YouTube clips and types terse, lowercase critiques of any videos that underwhelm him. His updates his Facebook page about ten times a night and elects to "like" some photo of a dead porcupine lying next to an empty champagne bottle. He never reads books, but he put a lot of effort into a website called goodreads.com: He looks at other people's reviews on Amazon and writes his own reviews from whatever he gleans. Bruce has, relative to a lot of the other people I observed, a relatively rich life. He isn't dark or depressed, or at least he wasn't while I was there. Never sighed, never cried. But I noticed one omnipresent aspect about his online activity: It was constantly interrupted by Bruce's ongoing attempt to write an e-mail. One e-mail, to one person. He would open his e-mail account, type a few sentences, delete a few sentences, and then close it back down and do something else. At first, I thought he was writing a bunch of different e-mails to a bunch of different recipients, but it turned out that he was only working on one. It was a single e-mail to one woman, maybe a hundred words long. The woman's name was Sarah. He would work on this e-mail like it was a sculpture. He'd type, "Long time no talk," and then he'd delete that and write, "Been a long time since we talked." Then he'd delete that and type, "It's been awhile, no?" Completely innocuous stuff, but he'd type different variations of these words and pace around his living room, saying these phrases aloud, testing them out. He kept trying to craft a joke about how his job was more boring than her job, but he was obviously paralyzed by the prospect of offending her. During the first night I was there, he probably built and rebuilt that e-mail five hundred times—yet he never worked on it for more than five consecutive minutes. He'd add something or delete something, and then he'd go back to the Internet to waste another quarter of an hour. He'd always return to the e-mail, fixate over its contents for another five minutes, and repeat the process all over. He finally sent the message at about two a.m., and when he did, it was the most bland, nonmeaningful letter you can imagine. I read it over his shoulder. Nothing romantic, nothing humorous, nothing clever. Zero insight. I watch him punch the "send" button. Bruce sits motionless and breathes through his mouth. It's like he's watching a person die in a hospital bed: He wants to do something, but there's nothing to do. So he ends up doing the only thing anyone can do once they've sent a message they can't stop thinking about: He goes back and rereads his own sent e-mail for another forty-five minutes, parsing and reparsing every line like it's the book of Revelation. It was excruciating. I felt terrible for him. It was eating him alive. He was eating himself alive. I was so relieved when he went to bed.

The next morning he wakes up early. He drinks a 7:05 Dr. Pepper for breakfast and checks his e-mail. He has dozens of messages, but nothing he cares about. Most are left unread. He leaves for work. I stay behind. I immediately turn on his computer, assuming a man who lives alone will not have his e-mail account protected by a password. But Bruce is the kind of man who does. I suppose the kind of guy who buys a four-bedroom home in order to spend his nights in a desk chair is the same kind of guy who protects his e-mail from roommates who don't exist. I look through his desk drawers and find nothing personal. He has a photo album in his bedroom, but almost all the photos look like they were taken during the same fraternity party. I look for anything that might indicate who Sarah is, but there's nothing. No trace. Outside of his hard drive, there's nothing in this house to indicate that Bruce is alive.

The day drags. Bruce arrives home at roughly the same time as yesterday. He walks in the door and checks his e-mail. He goes upstairs to change clothes, strolls back down, and rapidly masturbates. Today is yesterday. He boils a few hot dogs and eats them at his desk, wrapping them in white bread and smearing the meat with chili sauce. He starts playing RISK. He leaves some comments on the political blogs. The only difference is that, tonight, he's no longer composing a hundred-word e-mail a hundred different ways; tonight, all he does is check his in-box. He checks it constantly. It's robotic, mechanical. Bruce knows a lot of keyboard shortcuts—he can check and close his e-mail in less than two seconds, and he does so incessantly. He gets messages every hour, but not the one he wants. He downloads Billy Squier's *Don't Say No*, listens to half of "In the Dark," and then he checks his in-box. He attacks Alaska from Kamchatka, and then he checks his in-box. He reads a blog post about China's environmental policy, follows a Wikipedia link to a list of prominent Chinese entertainers, puts a documentary about Yao Ming into his Netflix queue, and then he checks his in-box.

He shows no emotion while compulsively rereading the message
he wrote the night before. I sit on the floor right next to him,
unseen; we both reread his letter to Sarah. Neither of us sees
anything worth rethinking. Around two thirty a.m., he gives up
and goes to bed. When he checks his e-mail the next morning,
there's still no reply. He drinks his morning Dr. Pepper and
leaves for work. I was in that house for five days, and Sarah never
responded. It was probably the only thing he thought about,
despite the fact that he was technically thinking about twenty-five
other problems.

Now, what do you think this means, Vic-Vick? Why do you think
I told you this story?

I told you this story because I'm curious about what element you
view as meaningful. What part of Bruce's life do you consider to
be most important? In my view, Bruce was living three lives. He
had his exterior life, which was composed of day-to-day work and
shallow friendships: This was his job, the people he had beers
with, all the normal daily filler. This exterior life was boring and
unsatisfying—I suppose I can't prove that he didn't like his day
job, but that's the impression I got. Now, he also had a second
life, on the Internet—a life that was simultaneously unreal and
fulfilling. It was a life he controlled completely, and it was the
means for his escape from the boredom of being a normal person
with normal responsibilities. But he also had a *third* life—this
hyperinterior life, within his own mind, where he incessantly
imagined an intimate, online relationship with Sarah. A life where
his first life and his second life were intertwined. Every time he
wrote and rewrote that e-mail, he was activating that relationship
inside his imagination and fighting the natural, irrational urge
to become fixated on a person he didn't really know. I mean,
Bruce was a sane man: He knew his connection to Sarah was
not real unless she responded to his e-mail, and he knew he'd
be living like a crazy person if he just sat at a desk with his arms

crossed, staring at his static in-box. So Bruce used the Internet to normalize his abnormal existence. As long as Bruce was engaged with his computer, it was not unusual to check and recheck his in-box, or to write and rewrite a single e-mail. That's what people do when they're sitting at a computer: They multitask and they daydream and they think about everything at once. One can easily fold obsessive self-absorption into the process of online communicating. In other words, the Internet was doing two things for Bruce—it allowed him to separate from the exterior life he hated, but also allowed him to stay engaged with an interior life he wanted. It was, ultimately, the single most important aspect of who he was: It removed his present-tense unhappiness while facilitating the possibility for future joy. It made the dark part of his mind smaller, but it made the optimistic part limitless. It added what he needed to affix and subtracted what he hoped to destroy. And maybe this was bad for Bruce's humanity, but I think it was probably good. I think it took a mostly sad man and made him mostly happy. The degree of authenticity doesn't matter.

Right?

Here's the bottom line, Vicky: You are an Internet. What the Internet did for Bruce, you do for me. You are the bridge through which I mind the gap between my exterior and interior life. Now, judging from what you've told me, you don't believe my exterior life is real. You think my exterior life *is* my interior life, and that I'm making up a delusion to compensate for some other problem. Personally, I don't care that this is what you believe. You don't need to believe what I tell you. My self-esteem doesn't hinge on whether you think I'm a reliable patient. I don't care what you think of me and I never have. I never will. *But right now, I need this experience.* I need to have you in my life, because you act as the control. I want to upload these images into someone who isn't me. And if the only way to make this happen is to meet with you in person, face-to-face . . . well, then I will do it. I will come to your office, because I want to keep talking and I don't want to start over with someone else.

Give me your address.

END OF PHONE SESSION 3

NOTES: On balance, I'm classifying today's conversation with Y___ as a success (albeit a strange one). He *is* coming into my office next week, or at least that's what he claims. That was my goal, and my goal was achieved. But this does not feel like a win. My confidence is shaken. I should not admit this (even to myself), but it's the truth. I feel uneasy with Y___'s casual aggression. Was Y___ describing himself when he told the story of Bruce? That's my gut feeling, but such a diagnosis seems imperfect. Did he make the whole thing up? His details oscillate between unnaturally specific and uselessly general. Was I wrong to accuse him of lying? It seemed like the honest move, but perhaps I've lost his trust. In general, I'm losing my grip on this process. Y___ is either fabricating his story out of whole cloth or completely believes these falsehoods to be true—I *must* keep both of those possibilities at the front of my mind at all times, and I need to keep them intellectually equal. He's articulate, but I can't let his articulation bully me. Perhaps I need to accept that I'm scared of this patient. I still look forward to talking with Y___ every week, but part of me is frightened. I don't think I'm very good at my job. Does Y___ know this? I fear that he does. I should have made different choices with my life. This is not something I'm good at.[7]

---

7. At the time I wrote this sentence, I was having minor problems at home and projecting that frustration onto other aspects of my life. It is not an accurate reflection of my professional self-image and should not be taken as such. I did not think it would ever be read by other people.

PART 2

THE SECOND INTRODUCTION

I was physically introduced to Y___ in the most standard of ways: There was a knock at my office door, and I told the knocker to enter. The entrance swung open and a man stepped into the room. I knew who he was before he told me. There were no surprises.

He was a man. A strange-looking man, but nothing more.

He was tall and he was thin. Cadaverous. Perhaps six feet five or six feet six, but no more than 175 pounds. His head was a skull on a stick; it was shaved to the skin, but I could see a subtle shadow where his hair would sprout. The hairline was receding. He wore an oversized black T-shirt, khaki pants, and garish white tennis shoes. His arms were wiry and unnaturally long. His nose was large, as were his Adam's apple and his ears. His teeth were jagged and yellow. "Ichabod Crane," I thought to myself. "He looks like an actor auditioning for the role of Ichabod Crane." It was a sweltering day in May, but he was barely sweating. I can recall this because I asked him where he had parked his car (at the time, I was in the midst of a minor parking dispute with a neighboring office building and lived in constant fear that my patients might get towed). He mentioned that he had arrived on foot. I could not imagine how a man in a black T-shirt could walk any distance in the 90-degree Texas heat without perspiring, but Y___ was immune. When he shook my hand, it was cool and dry, like a brick from the cellar.

I turned on the tape recorder.

When I treat patients in my office, I never sit behind my desk. The desk creates a barrier, and barriers are the enemy. Instead, I sit in a white Eames chair. My patients have the option of sitting in an identical black Eames chair or on the couch. No one ever takes the couch, particularly during their first session (too overt). Y___ looked at both options and requested that he sit in my chair. I said, "No, that's not how things work here." I don't know why I used those specific words. Y___ asked, "Does it matter where I sit? Can't I sit in the white chair?"

"If it doesn't matter," I responded, "then why not sit in the black chair, like everyone else who comes here?"

"Because I have a preference," said Y___. "I prefer white objects. If I express a preference for white objects, why not allow me to sit in the white chair?"

"Perhaps I have my own preference," I said.

"Do you have a preference?"

"Yes. I prefer the white chair. The white chair is my preference."

"Then by all means, take the white chair," said Y___. "I would never interfere with your preference."

We both sat. I smiled. He smiled back, but only for a moment.

"So here I am," he said. "You wanted to see me, and now you have. This is your office, and I am here. I'm in your office."

"You are," I said. "Thank you for coming in. It's really nice to see you."

"Yes, yes. Of course. Of course it's nice. Let's talk about how nice it is. This is a wonderful office—you have plants, carpeting, a relatively quiet air conditioner. It's contemporary in a classic way, or perhaps vice versa. Can we get to work now? Or do we still need to have a pretend conversation about how much your rent is?"

"We can absolutely get to work," I said. "That's a good attitude. I've really been enjoying our work thus far. The progress has been, you know—*progressive*. But let me ask you something, before we get going: You mentioned that you liked white objects. That's an interesting thing to like."

"No it isn't."

"Well, what if I think it's interesting?"

"What if I think it's not? There's no meaning here, Vicky. My affinity for the color white doesn't say anything about me. Look,

we're not going to do this. You need to accept that. I already understand the process. We both understand the process. I don't need
to slowly grow comfortable with the conceit, and you don't need to
understand why I like white objects. Let's get to the provocation.
Let's start with what matters: You think I'm telling a fictional story.
Your stomach tells you that I'm telling the truth, but your mind
insists your stomach is crazy. I've been thinking about this all week.
When we last spoke on the phone, I realized I misspoke. I said that
I didn't care if you believed me. That's not accurate. That was my
mistake. What I meant to say is that I don't care if you think I'm
an honest person. I don't care if you think I'm a good person or a
bad person. But I do need you to believe the specific things I've
told you. If you don't believe I've done the things I've done, it will
derail our conversation. You will hear everything I say as an extension of a delusion, and the content will get ignored. I will say things
like, 'I once saw Event A happen to Subject Zed,' and you will wonder, 'What is his inner motive for telling that particular story about
this particular fabrication? What does this story *represent*?' But that
won't be what's happening. Anything I elect to tell you won't be
theoretical or metaphorical. It will be something real that happened
in my life. So I need you to believe that what I've said—and what I
will continue to say—is not untrue."

Y____ stood up from the chair, jarringly, throwing himself upward
by pushing down on the armrests. It was like watching a giraffe
awaken from a tranquilizer. "May I walk about," he asked. He
began to pace around the room, erratically, looking down at the floor
while gesturing with his hands. This behavior is what I'd come to
classify as "the Y____ Character." Whenever Y____ became "the
Y____ Character," his dialogue would feel rehearsed. It was like
watching a one-man show. Though I'd already experienced several
of these moments over the phone, this was the first time I witnessed
it with my eyes. Over time, I've come to accept that the Y____ Character was (probably) the real Y____. It was everything else that was
(probably) the show.

"So how can we do this?" Y____ continued. He loved semi-rhetorical questions. "How can I make you believe me? What could I do, short of being cloaked in front of you, to make you accept my words at face value?"

"That's an intriguing question," I said. "Maybe it's an impossible thing for me to accept. So if I never accept this, how will it make you feel?"

"Vicky, we're not doing this," he said. "We're not doing some kind of exercise where I make a declarative statement and you ask me how I feel about that declaration. We're not going to talk about my *development* or my *primal memories*. Maybe we will eventually, but not today. Right now, today, I need you to tell me how I can make you believe I'm not like other people. That I can do things other people cannot."

He stopped pacing and looked at me, frozen, waiting, saying nothing. The moment I began to respond, he commenced his pace.

"If there were some witnesses to this partial invisibility," I said, "and those witnesses came in here and verified what you had said, honestly and scientifically, I might believe you."

"There are no witnesses to my life," Y___ said. "That's one of the keys to being unseen: If there are witnesses, something went wrong. So what else?" His pacing continued.

"Video evidence," I said. "A videotape of you doing something that only an invisible person could do."

"That would prove nothing," said Y___. This was a game to him. "I could fake that with any computer. And even if my video was perfect—even if it was so seamless and unimpeachable that it couldn't be faked by a moviemaker—you'd still assume it was somehow unreal. You would merely think it was the best fake you've ever seen. You'd believe I was David Fincher before you'd accept who I actually am. Try again."

"Any reported evidence that this could be done. A *Wall Street Journal* article that describes your research. A textbook about the process."

"There is no such article or textbook," said Y___. "I would be the only person who could write it."

"Maybe you should do that."

"Not my thing. Not anymore. I hate writing."

Y___ returned to the black chair. He was smirking. I asked if he wanted coffee. He said he didn't want coffee or need coffee. He seemed calm, smug. Not very adult. More like a high school senior in the final days of May.

"Well, what about *this*," he finally said. "What if you just considered everything I've told you and weighed that information against the degree to which I seem credible?"

"That's what I've been doing," I told him. "From the first day you called me on the telephone, I've been calculating that very equation. I've taken what you've said at face value, and I've considered the source. I've tried to be as open-minded and nonjudgmental as possible. I've taken all your statements seriously and professionally, and I've come to a conclusion. Do you want to know what that conclusion is?"

"Yes."

"Are you sure? Do you promise to be as open-minded and fair with me as I have been with you? Because that's essential."

"Yes, yes. Yes."

"Then my diagnosis is this," I said, as evenly as possible. "You are an educated, affluent, highly functioning person who has experienced a break from the life you used to live. You have become obsessed with an imaginary life, and you use your natural intellect as a crutch to make that imaginary life real. This allows you to ignore the pain that still exists from whatever caused that break to happen."

I waited for a reaction, but he said nothing. His expression did not change.

"Now, that probably sounds very bad to you, and perhaps even insulting," I continued. "I can't tell if you already know I'm right, or if you're about to walk out my door and never speak to me again. Obviously, I have no control over what you do or how you react. But this is a solvable problem. Your very presence in my office proves you understand that. You want to get better, and you know that a better life is possible. So here is what I want to do: I want both of us to get in my car and drive to Seton Medical Center. They don't have to admit you and you won't need to stay overnight. However, they will conduct a short interview and a few tests in order to decide what the next step should be. From that point on, it's totally your decision. There are people there who are better suited to deal with this situation than me. If you want to continue using me as your primary therapist, that would be fantastic. I enjoy working with you, and I care about what happens to you. But you need to talk to a medical doctor, and I am not a medical doctor."

Y___ waited until I finished. He wordlessly thought about what I had said (and seemed to treat my words seriously). But then he stood up and resumed pacing, instantly rematerializing as the Y___ Character. It was as if I had said nothing at all.

"What about this," he began. "What if I told you something I couldn't possibly know? What if I knew something that could only be known by someone who was able to make themselves unseen?"

"I'm not sure what that would be, and I'm not sure what that would prove."

"You read a Malcolm Gladwell book last year," Y___ said.

"What?"

"You read a Malcolm Gladwell book. Last winter. Try and tell me that you didn't read a Malcolm Gladwell book last winter."

"What does that have to do with anything?"

"That happened. Right? It happened. So how do I know this?"

"What Malcolm Gladwell book did I read?"

"I can't remember. One of them. The first one, or maybe the other one. The third one? All the covers look the same to me."

"So, the fact that I read a book by one of the most popular writers in America, an author who sells several million books every year—this proves you have the ability to be invisible?"

"Well, I would have liked to use a more specific example. But you don't seem to read many books."

"So, what . . . are you implying that you've been watching me? Is that what you're claiming? Because that's a crime. Be careful what you say right now, Y____. Don't make up a story that will create a new problem for us."

"Well, that's why I only mentioned the Gladwell book," Y____ said. "I don't want to scare you. If I told you something too specific—if I told you the color of your living room carpet, for example—you'd probably freak out. I'm not going to freak you out."

"What is the color of my living room carpet, Y____?"

He said nothing. Maybe he smiled, but I can't be certain.

"There's a reason you're not telling me the color of my living room carpet," I explained. "And the reason is not that you don't want to scare me. The reason is that you don't know what the color of my carpet is. Now, maybe you *think* you know, or maybe you *know* you don't know. I can't tell. Right now, that's our problem. And this is why we need to go to Seton Medical. *This*—this scenario, right here. This thing we are dealing with, right now. This incongruity. *This* is the problem. Not your guilt over spying on people, not the stress from being an 'almost invisible' man. Nothing that involves the outside world. Our problem is the chasm between who you are and who you want to be. Everyone deals with this problem, Y____. Everyone. You are not alone. Half the work I do with my other patients is about the difference between who someone is and who they wish they were. The only difference here is the degree. You have a fixable problem. Your condition just happens to be a little more severe than what I typically encounter. But I am on your side here. Do you see that? I want to help you."

For the next thirty seconds, I thought I'd broken through. Y____ stopped walking and stood at the center of my office. He looked sad. He looked defeated. There was a moment when I anticipated (hoped?) that Y____ was going to cry. But then he changed entirely. His concern melted into stoicism, and then evaporated into low-level joy. He smiled and ran a hand across his bald skull; it was like a different person had jumped inside his bones.

"Okay, Vic-Vick: You win," he said. I thought this meant we were going to Seton Medical Center. It did not. "Next week. I will see you next week. Things will be different a week from now. But just try and remember what we talked about, okay? Remember what I said today. Really think about the things I said. Digest my words. They will make sense later. How about this: If you still feel this way seven days from now, I will go to the hospital. That is my promise. But only if you've *really* considered the things I've told you. Okay?"

I did not believe him, but I shook my head up and down. What else could I do?

"Goodbye, Vicky. Your skepticism is adorable. Don't ever lose that, no matter what happens."

And with that, Y—— walked out of my office. For the rest of the day, I seethed at my desk. He had dodged me again, and he talked to me like a child. He was so uniquely troubled. I should have known what was coming, but of course I did not.

May Ninth

(The Revelation)

What can I tell you?

Nothing you will believe.

Nothing I would believe. But this happened. And this is when everything changed (and never changed back).

There was a knock at my door. I knew it was Y___. I had been daydreaming about this meeting all week. I had so many condescending, incisive things to say to him, although I can scarcely remember any of those things now. They all seem irrelevant in light of what transpired when Y___ opened my door and was not there.

"Who is it," I asked, seeing an empty doorway. I said "hello," and then I said "hello" again. I said it a third time. I stood up with the intention of walking across the room, assuming someone (a confused child?) had opened my door by accident and fled upon the cognition of his mistake. I simply wanted to close my door. But the door closed itself, and then the door spoke.

"Come here, Vicky."

It was the signature moment of my life.

I tried to step backward and forward simultaneously, and I fell to the ground, knocking most of the contents of my desk onto the carpet as I tried to catch myself. I got up as quickly as I could and tried to scream, but the only sound that came out of my mouth was garbled, muted nonsense. It was a terrifying ten seconds. You'd think I would have assumed I was losing my mind, but I instantly knew this moment was real. It was not a dream or a hoax.

"Please don't hurt me," I said. I'm not sure why this was my first thought, but it was.

"I won't hurt you, Vicky," said the void. "Calm down. Sit down, if you need to. I'm not going to hurt you. I am not . . . going . . . to hurt you. Remain calm."

I did not sit. I tried to balance against my desk like a Christmas party lush. I was staring at my door, trembling. I could vaguely taste vomit on my tongue. Suddenly, Y___ spoke again—but I could tell from his voice that he'd come closer. He was maybe three feet away. My desk was the only barrier.

"There was a reason I didn't want to do this," he said. "This is the reason."

"What the fuck are you doing to me," I said. "Why are you doing this? I'm sorry I didn't believe you, but don't do this to me. I'm so sorry. You can take whatever you want. I don't care. I'm sorry. Why is this happening?" I had no idea what I was pleading for or what I was pleading against.

"Just think about all the things I've told you," Y___ said, "and accept that those things are true. That's all that I want."

I stood and did nothing. I think a lot of time may have passed, but I can't be sure.

"I will give you time to absorb this," said Y___. His voice was recognizable, but the tone was dissimilar to that of the person I'd met the week before. It was lower and leathery. More AM than FM. "Put out your hand. Give me your hand."

I lifted my right arm and extended it outward and upward, almost as if I were trying to pick an apple off the lowest branch of a tree. I could see my hand shaking, but I couldn't make it stop. Suddenly, I felt something: I felt the fingertips of another hand. Reflexively, I pulled my hand back. But then I extended it a second time. I started to relax. I touched Y___'s fingers, and then I touched his palm. I felt a glove, but a glove so sheer I could still detect the texture of the skin underneath. When I pulled my hand back, my fingertips were lightly coated with a silvery, greenish film that reminded me of the glitter a child would use to make a Valentine. I rubbed my fingers together and the film seemed to vaporize, even though I could still sense the grittiness. I collapsed into my desk chair and reflexively put a hand over my mouth. My fingers smelled like antibiotics, so I rubbed them on my pant leg. I wanted to say something, but my head was both empty and full.

"Now . . . this *is* what you wanted," Y___ said. "It is. Remember that. You demanded that I show myself in this way. It was my only recourse. And—to a degree—I respect that request. It's what your job requires, and it's what your personality dictates. Those who believe without seeing are blessed, but they tend to be bad conversationalists."

"Well, Christ—why didn't you just show me the suit?" I asked. "Why didn't you just bring the suit into my office? Why did you walk in here like *this,* knowing what that would do to me?"

"If I had shown you a suit on a hanger," he asked, "would that have been enough? Or would we still be having the same argument?"

For a long time, I sat and said nothing. Eventually, I spoke like a child: "I'm sorry I did not believe you." I thought he would respond by saying, "I forgive you." Instead, he said, "I'm sitting down now."

I looked at the black chair. Then I looked at the white chair. It seemed like Y___'s voice had come from the white chair, so I moved over to the black one, feeling it with my hand before sitting down. I sat and looked across at the empty white lounger, unsuccessfully pretending that this was not exploding my perception of reality. "This," I said, "is incredible. It's incredible. It's incredible."

"Can you see me?" he asked.

"No! I can't see you! I can't see you!"

"Let your eyes adjust," he said. "Get over the dissonance between what you expect to see and what's actually there. Are you sure you can't see me? Not even a little bit?"

At first, I had no idea what he meant. But as the minutes passed, I understood. It was exactly as he had described: The silhouette of his body *was* vaguely visible (although I would have never recognized this on my own). It was as if the outline of his body was ever so slightly out of focus; it was like someone had completely painted the world over him, but the fuzzy imprint of his being was still faintly present.

It was so amazing.

I am tempted to type that sentence over and over again. *It was so amazing. It was so amazing. It was so amazing.* But there's no purpose to that, and what would it prove? Either you believe me or you don't. I don't have the command of language to describe what it's like to see something that isn't there. If you can't imagine this experience on your own, I can't help you. Try to look at a white chair and see (almost) nothing. That's what it was like. It was (almost) exactly like that.

I did not audiotape our meeting. Obviously, I should have. But (a) I had knocked my tape recorder off my desk when I fell, and (b) I was not thinking straight. To his credit, I must concede that Y___ was remarkably patient during our encounter. He answered all of my questions, most of which were technical (whenever I get anxious, I worry about technicalities). Here are the key specifics I scribbled from memory after he departed:

1. The cloaking suit was tight and uncomfortable, but Y___ had grown used to it.

2. He didn't know if the "cloaking cream" he sprayed over himself was toxic or benign, but that didn't concern him. "Part of the risk," he said. "A small part. If I get cancer, I get cancer. We're all going to end up with cancer, anyway."

3. Before he encamped in a subject's home, he was able to store four additional cylindrical canisters of aerosol cream in a pouch sewn into the stomach of the suit. By reapplying the cream every thirty-six to forty-eight hours (done when the subject was away), he could stay inside any given residence for up to a week. If a subject proved especially compelling, Y___ might return to the residence for multiple stints.

4. In order to remain alert during these long observation periods, Y___ would consume copious amounts of oral stimulants, most notably low doses of Merck cocaine and methamphetamine in tablet form (this, he noted with some discomfiture, was the reason his teeth were so gnarled). Because stimulants are a diuretic (and since he often could not use the bathroom for long stretches of time), he'd regularly force himself into a state of dehydration. "There were signals I'd use as guideposts," he said. "When my piss was the color of Pepsi, I knew it was time to drink some water." He would eat when he was alone during the day, though constant amphetamine use had all but eliminated his appetite. "I can get by on five hundred calories a day," he said. "Usually less. I'll probably live to be two hundred years old. I mean, there's nothing worse for us than food, right? Food is what kills us."

5. When cloaked, Y___ wore tiny mirrored goggles with a soft gray tint. They were similar to swimming goggles. These lenses were the only part of his body uncovered by the cream. Y___ claimed that the easiest way to see through his illusion was to locate his eyes, but I found this totally impossible.

6. Through yoga, he had learned how to control muscle discomfort and to regulate his breathing. This was more imperative than people might anticipate. "I'd be the world's most in-your-face yoga instructor," he insisted. "I can lock into any physical position I want for five hours, six hours, eight hours. I've done this dozens of times. I can turn my bones off."

7. Y___ noted that—while he's difficult to see when stationary—he's flat-out impossible to see when in motion. "On the street, and especially in a crowd or in an airport, my individual movements disappear into the chaos of everything that's moving around me. The fuzziness evaporates, because everything surrounding

me seems equally unfocused. The human eye isn't fast enough to adjust. It's easy for me to walk straight onto commercial airplanes or into office buildings. The faster I walk, the less people see."

8. When I asked how he sustained himself financially, Y___ said, "My situation is unique. I don't really need money. Outside of my rent and my cell phone, life is free." He said he would sometimes steal high-end items (mostly jewelry) from major retailers and return them for cash the following day. Sometimes he would shoplift from pawnshops and immediately resell the items at competing pawnshops on the same block. Sometimes he'd just take two hundred dollars from unattended cash registers. He'd sometimes lift money out of people's homes, but only when absolutely necessary or when he felt the victim was asking for it. "I've stolen from the rich, and from the not so very rich, and from the almost poor. But never from the pure of heart, the chronically depressed, or the very, very, very poor."

9. His omnipresent concerns were rain (which diluted the cloaking cream), dogs, and birds. "Hounds hate me," he said. "Cats don't care if I live or die, but hounds catch my scent and go off the reservation. Birds are even worse. Have you ever had a pigeon fly straight into your face? I'm like a picture window to those goddamn shit machines."

By the end of our hour, it seemed like everything about our relationship had reversed itself. During the final ten minutes, we were downright jovial (almost flirtatious). It was like being high for the very first time. Y___ was flattered by my attention. I kept apologizing over and over. He finally said, "I forgive you, Vicky. I forgive you. But you have to make me a promise: From here on out, I decide what we talk about. No more of this 'How did you feel when your father said something dismissive about your haircut when you were eleven?' I already know the answers to those questions. *I know how I feel.* And no more discussions about how this suit works or how I invented the cream. Okay? No more debates about science. It bores me to talk about things I already understand. I want to talk about what I have seen, and I want to do it my way. So can we agree to this?"

"Yes." I said. "Yes. Anything you want. I will never question you again. I will do anything you ask."

At one point, I felt an urge to photograph this person who wasn't there. I asked if this was okay. Y____ laughed and said, "Why not?" He was in a great mood. I used the camera on my cell phone. This photographic image, as anyone can see (*fig. 1*), is distorted and grainy and useless. It looks like a chair. But when I see this photo, I can see Y____. I know what I'm supposed to be seeing.

Suddenly, I glanced at my wall clock. It was 11:45 a.m. We both commented on how rapidly our time had disappeared. We said goodbye, and Y____ left. He wasn't there, and then he wasn't there. I had another appointment at noon, but when the patient arrived I told her I was sick. I canceled the rest of my day's appointments and drove home. I spent the rest of the day drinking vodka in bed, completely awake. I did not tell my husband (or anyone else) about this experience for several weeks. I did not know how.

PART 3

Y___ ASSUMES CONTROL

The game, as they say, had changed.

None of my other patients were interesting, even though I knew they were important; I would sit and nod and listen to their problems, but I was always imagining their problems being described by Y____ (and how much that transference would change the meaning). I surrendered to him completely. I lost interest in my hobbies. I lost interest in television and in whatever new movies I was supposed to see; those things had never been that crucial to me to begin with, but now I couldn't even force myself to follow the plots or remember the names of characters. My college friend Cheryl sent me an e-mail politely expressing concern that she and I were "not connecting" and drifting apart; I didn't respond to the message and found myself alarmed by how little I could remember about the last phone conversation we'd shared. I began investing my free time into practical activities that required no thought (scouring the bathroom, trimming the hedges) so that my mind could drift without consequence. Nothing was as stimulating as thinking about Y____'s condition. To this day, whenever I slip into boredom, I find myself fantasizing and reimagining the stories he told me. From a therapeutic standpoint, it was an unhealthy situation. I don't deny that. But—in my meek defense—I need to reiterate how unusual this scenario had become (and not just because it involved invisibility). Professionally, it's the kind of problem that can't be solved by reading a book.

Here's what I mean: A few years before meeting Y____, I'd worked with an adult female patient still coping with the abusive relationship she'd had with her father. The father had sexually abused her during her teenager years and she remained paralyzed by recurring dreams of these encounters, inevitably describing her father's appearance in these dreams as vampiric. She saw her father as a sinister, seductive figure who became a monster at night, and she often imagined him draining the life out of her body. She loved and hated him against her will. On more than one occasion, she directly referred to him as "That fucking vampire." We talked about these memories for many weeks, and in every possible context. However, at no time did I ever suspect the patient's father *was literally Dracula.* Why would I suspect that? Why would anyone? The central philosophy behind treating the delusional is to understand why that specific delusion has been selected. You never entertain the possibility of the delusion not being a construction. So when that happened with Y——when I was forced to accept that the impossible situation he had described was not symbolic—I allowed the dynamic of our relationship to invert itself. From this point forward, I rarely questioned anything Y—— said, nor did I stop him from lecturing about whatever topic he desired. In short, I stopped being his therapist; I essentially became a vessel for his thoughts. My peers will criticize me for this, and I deserve the criticism. But I'm the only person who will ever fully understand how this felt, and I know that I did my best.

As the weeks blurred together, my sessions with Y—— became strangely consistent. He would arrive at my office uncloaked, sit in the white chair, and tell me what we were going to talk about. This usually entailed Y—— opening with the words "Today we're going to discuss my time with ——," and a story would advance from there. He'd periodically pace about the office, talking with his hands as much as his mouth. I would listen, take notes, and occasionally pose questions (which he'd sometimes answer but often ignore). Sometimes we'd talk about the same subject for consecutive weeks; sometimes he would spend long stretches dissecting a particular person, abruptly change topics for ten minutes, and then return to the original person he'd started with (without explaining the digression). For simplicity, I have packaged our most remarkable encounters into their own separate rubrics. We were (allegedly) talking about these various people so that Y—— could better understand his guilt over his invasions of privacy—and sometimes we really did touch on that specific issue. But as I reread the transcripts today, I suspect his larger motives were stranger and more egocentric. Y—— felt guilt, but not in the way guilt is supposed to be felt.

As before, I have reconstructed and truncated Y——'s transcripts into traditional prose (with my sporadic interjections in boxed italics). They are in chronological order, except where noted.

I cannot vouch for the veracity of the narrative details, because I was not there.

The Valerie Sessions

[The Valerie Sessions were a three-session dialogue that initiated the week following May 9. Though Y___ never specified where these events occurred, I got the vague impression that "Valerie" resided somewhere in Northern California. The log time of every excerpt is annotated at the conclusion of each passage.]

1 This person, this Valerie person, made things easy for me: She left her door unlocked. Not all day, of course, but whenever she went running. I assume she didn't want to be encumbered by house keys. Runners despise their house keys. And this was a understandable decision, because she lived where crime wasn't. I have no doubt she could have left her door unlocked twenty-four hours a day without incident. It was an excellent neighborhood. I was wandering outside the apartment complex when I saw a woman in her late twenties exit the building. She was wearing bike shorts, a sports bra, and a headband. This was Valerie. There was no way she had any pockets in that getup, so I made my move. I simply entered the front of the building and started ringing doorbells. If no one answered the bell, I tried the knob. It didn't take long. She lived on the second floor, in an efficiency apartment—essentially a studio with a kitchen. Not really decorated, a little messy. A bed, a love seat, a treadmill. Loop carpet. Books, but no bookcase. Way too many shoes. Everything smelled human. Earthy. Musky. I rifled through the mail, checked her medicine cabinet for antidepressants, and then sat in a corner and started to wait.

Val returned about an hour after she'd left, bathed in sweat. She closed the door and took off her sports bra in the same motion. Now, I'm sure—as a woman, and maybe just as a person—you find this description creepy. You think it's sick that I would sit in some unknown female's apartment and watch her get undressed. But this kind of visual experience was never sexual for me. Never. I looked at Valerie the way her gynecologist looks at her. Was she attractive? Maybe. I don't think I'm in a position to say definitively. Seeing naked people is just part of my job. I take no pleasure in it.

So, as I was saying . . . Valerie strips off her clothes and takes a shower. I wait for her in the living room. It's darker now—almost eight o'clock. Valerie comes out of her bathroom in a robe and underwear. Her hair is fucking bizarre. It's wet and vertical—it looks like a koala is crouching on her scalp. She checks her voice mail messages. She looks through her snail mail and separates the bills from everything else. She checks her work e-mail on her phone. And then—and this surprised me—she opens her closet and pulls out the biggest Pyrex bong I've ever seen. It was three feet high. She lights the carb port, takes a massive hit, and exhales a thundercloud of smoke. The whole apartment gets blue and thick. She walks through the fog and into the kitchen.

This is where the war was waged.

What I would come to discover about Valerie was that she was at war with herself. It was a ground war—a hundred-year war of attrition. She was at war with the size of her body, her desire to smoke pot, and an obsession with eating all the food in the world. She was compulsive about all three, and all three were connected. Thirty seconds after getting high, she was eating spoonfuls of Jif peanut butter, straight from the jar. Her eyes were crazed as she did this, somewhere between ecstasy and fear. I've never seen a person enjoy peanut butter so much. After ten minutes of chowing, she smoked more pot. Then she ordered a Domino's pizza. For the next twenty-nine minutes, she sat on her love seat, listening to the Beatles with her eyes closed; when the pizza arrived, she ate five of the eight slices like a she-wolf. She threw the last three slices away and emptied the garbage. This alone seemed like a full night's gluttony, but—once again—she returned to the bong. Again, the room turned blue. She listened to a little more of *Abbey Road,* swaying with herself to "Sun King." It was charming. But then she surprised me again: She ordered a second pizza. A different kind of pizza from a different pizza place. When it arrived, she did the same thing—she ate a little more than half the pie and threw the rest away.

By now, it's almost midnight. Valerie smokes more pot, changes the CD to *A Hard Day's Night,* and softly sings along with "You Can't Do That." She gorges on more peanut butter, this time swabbing it on Ritz crackers. Again, I assume the night is over. But suddenly she's lying on the floor, topless. Now she's doing sit-ups! She does one hundred sit-ups, rests for five minutes, then knocks off one hundred more. She attacks the bong a fourth time, refogging the apartment like a machine. Eventually, she crawls into her twin bed and falls asleep. She doesn't even turn off her table lamp. I spend the night watching her sleep in the light. For six hours, we're equally motionless but unequally bored.

Valerie awakes without an alarm. If she's feeling haggard, it doesn't show. Immediately, she's doing sit-ups. She's isolating her abs. She does a few push-ups, but she doesn't do them well. No upper-arm strength. She stretches her hammies and stretches her quads. She puts on her running shoes and pulls on her headband, and—once again—she's jogging out the door. I'm a little surprised, because yesterday she ran at dusk. It's only been twelve hours since her previous run. Her morning jog lasts forty-five minutes. When she returns, she showers and prepares for work. No breakfast required. She puts the bong back in the closet, spends ten minutes looking for her car keys, and finally leaves for wherever she needs to be.

I sleep on her floor for most of the afternoon. When I awake, I look for any innocuous food scraps in the kitchen. This is generally how I feed myself when I'm inside a stranger's home: I eat whatever food seems least likely to be missed. I'm not judgmental. I'll eat anything, and I don't need much. I can last days on uncooked pasta and raw sugar. But Valerie doesn't have either of those items. She doesn't have *anything*, except for peanut butter, olive oil, ketchup, and a (now empty) box of crackers.

It occurs to me that Valerie is afraid to keep food in the house.

Valerie gets home early—somewhere in the neighborhood of 5:20 or 5:30. I can't get a read on what she does for a living, beyond that it requires her to wear pencil skirts. By 5:45, the headband is back on her brain and she's jogging out the door. Tonight she runs for ninety minutes; when she gets back, I momentarily worry she might collapse. She literally staggers into the apartment, panting like a sheepdog. She needs a moment to compose herself. But Valerie rallies. She takes off her clothes and stands in front of the bathroom mirror, looking at her stomach in profile. When she steps out of the shower, she stares at her stomach again. To me, she looks neither fat nor thin, but I can't imagine what she sees. Judging from the expression on her face, she's either mildly concerned or mildly depressed.

Valerie get dressed and starts cleaning her apartment, although cleaning is not really the right word—she just sort of organizes the disorder into four separate piles. Around eight, her doorbell rings. It's another woman, roughly Valerie's age but significantly heavier. This is Jane. She has a lot of wavy hair, a lot of teeth, and one of those omnipresent, face-dominating perma-grins that makes her look like a lesser Muppet. Diabolically upbeat. She's carrying two buckets of Kentucky Fried Chicken. The two women hug hello, but I can tell they've seen each other recently; the hug is brief and their conversation is neutral and nonexpository. Valerie asks things like, "What's Jim doing tonight?" and Jane responds with, "Oh, you know Jim." They have a brief discussion about when they should start smoking marijuana, and the verdict is "immediately." They're comfortable with each other. They enjoy the process of agreeing. They sit on the floor and light each other's weed. They talk slower, but their personalities don't change. They start eating the chicken. This must be the thing they do together.

At 9:20 they turn on the television. They've digitally recorded that popular program about the good-looking airline passengers who accidentally travel through time. Every so often, they pause the action to bicker about the plot: Valerie seems angry at the episode because she doesn't know what's happening. Jane seems pleased by the episode because she doesn't know what's happening.

"Why are they all doing that?" says Valerie. "Why doesn't anyone ask why they're doing the things that they're doing?"

"They're doing it because that one guy told them it was the only way."

"But isn't that guy the same person who wanted to kill them?"

"No, that was the first guy. The guy who can't die."

"But why would they follow the other guy? The smoke."

"I don't think they're following the smoke."

"In this reality, or in all the realities?"

"Yes."

This goes on for a long time. When the show concludes, they keep disagreeing about what did or didn't occur. "I think that already happened." "We don't know that yet." "She's actually his half-sister, right?" "No, that was the woman from the airport bar." "He was killed a long time ago." "He might not be dead anymore." It's the worst conversation I've ever heard two people have about something that wasn't true. They finish the first bucket of chicken and decide to eat the legs and wings from bucket number two for dessert. Valerie hits "play" on her CD player; *A Hard Day's Night* is still in the carousel. Jane says, "Have you ever heard that song about the Beatles? It's not by the Beatles." Valerie looks at Jane like she's from Atlantis. Valerie says, "What?" Jane says, "Wait," and runs outside to her car. She returns with a cassette. "I can't play tapes," says Valerie. "I don't have a tape player. I don't play tapes." Jane says, "You should get a tape player." Valerie says, "But I don't have any tapes." Jane says, "But now you have *this* tape." Their relationship is founded on the repeated deconstruction of meaningless contradictions.

Jane gets ready to go home. She asks if she should leave the remainder of the chicken with Valerie. "Sure," lies Valerie. "I'll have it for lunch tomorrow." Jane walks out the door. Valerie smokes more pot and gets on the treadmill. She runs for three simulated miles, drinks a huge glass of water, and eats the rest of the chicken. It's the skin she loves most—she tears it off the flesh and drags it through the gravy. Every mouthful is succulent, decadent fat. It electrifies her spirit as it clogs her ventricles. When the chicken is gone, she returns to the peanut butter, finishing the remainder of the jar. She jams her whole hand into the jar and licks her fingers clean. There's no food remaining in the house. It's been erased by her mouth. Upon this realization, she inhales more weed, does forty abdominal crunches, takes another shower, and falls asleep to John Lennon's *Plastic Ono Band.*

Valerie was the fittest, hungriest, cleanest person I'd ever encountered. (**5.16.08, 10:08 a.m. to 10:33 a.m.**)

2 Now, let me ask you a question, Vic-Vick: What's the most transparently interesting thing about this Valerie person? To me, it's that she's a liar. Even to her closest friends, Valerie is lying about how she lives. She doesn't want Jane to know that she could never save half a bucket of chicken until tomorrow. She doesn't want Jane to know that she instantly knew she'd eat it all immediately, and that such an action was beyond her control. Instead, she chooses to exercise with the intensity of a decathlete, simply to sustain the physical appearance of normalcy. It's a hidden cycle: The stress of this fraud makes her want to escape from reality, which prompts her to smoke marijuana, which makes her eat compulsively, which forces her to exercise obsessively and without reward, which makes her original dishonesty so shameful. But I am the only one who knows this. Only I see her secrets. So I find myself thinking: Is this lie the totality of who she is? Is there any part of her personality that isn't dictated by this cycle? Is her secret the only thing that matters about her?

While she was at work, this was what I worried about. (**5.16.08, 10:47 a.m. to 10:48 a.m.**)

3 On the third day of my occupation, Valerie came home with two boxes of doughnuts, two cans of Chef Boyardee ravioli, and a bunch of bananas. I knew where that shit was going, and I knew it would be gone by midnight. She went out for her evening run and returned to do a few dozen burpies, or whatever they're calling burpies now, in the middle of the living room. Burpies are what convicts do. Burpies are designed for people in prison cells. She takes her second shower of the day and settles in for another night of smoking and gorging and listening to dead hippies sing about the Maharishi . . . her life is so calcified. It drives me crazy. How can she not realize how terrible her life is? And yet—she seems happy. I see no explicit depression within her existence. Does she not understand that this is no way to live? I *want* her to be depressed. I want her to want to be different. But she just doesn't get it.

[I interject to ask Y___ if he sees his own contradiction; I ask if he sees how his espoused intention to "objectively observe" these subjects seems to be false, and that his emotional relationship to Valerie is greater than his interest in her actual life.]

That's not true. That's wrong. Just because I care doesn't mean I can't be objective. That's what's wrong with the world, Vicky: We've given up on the possibility of overcoming our biases. Did I like Valerie? Yes. Sure. Yes I did. But I never *surrendered* to her. That's the part you can't comprehend.

Going in, I knew that watching people during their private moments was going to be emotionally confusing. I mean, I watched Valerie go to the bathroom many, many times. When she was alone, she never even closed the door. I've watched her defecate, and that's a pretty humiliating experience, even when no one's watching. And seeing someone humiliated is always going to make you like that person a little more. If an author wants to make a fictional character sympathetic, the easiest way to make that happen is to place them in a humiliating scenario. Humiliation preys on our deepest fears of what it means to be alive. So *of course* I was going to like Valerie. I liked everyone I watched. That was just something I had to mentally fight through. Newspaper reporters do this all the time, or at least they're supposed to. It's not impossible. The larger problem, at least for me, is the inherent inequality within this kind of relationship. Valerie believed she was alone, so—for her—our time together was neutral. There's no emotional charge to being alone. She felt nothing, because she had nothing to feel. Meanwhile, I continually spent my time, one on one, with unguarded strangers who act completely open and completely vulnerable. For me, these episodes became extremely intimate. But it's a one-sided intimacy, and that's something you can't prepare for.

Easy example: Our fourth night together. It rained that day, all afternoon and all night. Valerie couldn't run outside, so she used her treadmill. It was unnerving to watch how hard she ran—she was going nowhere, but she was getting there fast. She sprinted. And she sprinted *loud*—she took these heavy steps that went *boom boom boom boom boom boom boom,* like an automatic weapon with the trigger jammed, banging away for almost two hours. Val has an OCD tic about the treadmill: There are three LCDs on the machine, and she won't quit unless they all fall on perfectly round numbers. Like, she would hit her goal of four miles on the "distance" gauge, but she wouldn't stop because the "minutes" gauge might read 36:33. She'd decide to keep running until the minutes gauge was exactly 40:00. But the moment that LCD read 40:00, the "calories" gauge would be at 678, so she'd need to push it to exactly 700. But then the distance LCD would be at 5.58, so she'd need to make it exactly 6.00. This never balanced out, of course. It was hopeless, and it was exhaustive to watch. After she finally gave up and showered, she got high and boiled a massive bowl of spaghetti, which she ate with butter and black pepper and string cheese. She ate a bunch of Twix bars, too. But something else happened that night. It was the kind of something that makes me feel bad about myself. And I still don't know why I feel that way, which is why I'm talking to you.

Sometime around ten p.m., woozy and stuffed, Valerie started looking through her closet. At first, I had no idea what prompted this seemingly random, seemingly spontaneous decision. But she got down on all fours and really went at it. This was a dogged, focused search—the kind of search that can only be conducted by the very worried or the deeply stoned. After twenty minutes, she pulls out a clock radio. "Ah ha," she says to no one. I have no idea what her intentions are, because Valerie already has her own internal alarm clock. Besides, this is a massive, ugly clock. Unwieldy. Almost like a boom box, but not quite. Very much from the eighties, when plastics were bigger. No one would accept such a monstrosity today. But she plugs it in, and it blinks "12:00." She doesn't fix the time. And—suddenly—I know why she needed to locate this device. It's because it has a cassette player. She is going to play that cassette Jane gave her two days ago.

Now, the song on this tape, the song that Jane wanted her to play—I don't know how to describe it, really. It's barely a song. It's just drums and a singer and an accordion, or some instrument that resembles an accordion. The singer sounds broken, but not in the way we typically use that term. He literally sounds like a mentally handicapped child. And this song—well, it's almost like the singer is trying to be sarcastic, because it's just a straightforward explanation of who the Beatles were and what they did. One of the lines in the song is "They really were very good. They deserved all their success." Whenever the guy says the word *Beatles*, he sings it with a bad Cockney accent. None of it rhymes. It seems like a song written extemporaneously. Any listener's natural impulse would be to hate it, or to laugh at it. But Valerie kept playing and rewinding this same song. She probably played that song twenty times in a row, and she could not stop smiling. It was the happiest I ever saw her—even happier than when she was eating Jif. And this is because that song is fucking *profound*. It's like this quasi-homeless guy had tapped into the most primitive explanation as to why Valerie liked the Beatles, or, I suppose, why anyone likes the Beatles. There's a few lines where the singer mentions how the Beatles' career is like a fairy tale, and that the trajectory of their fame and their impact on the world would seem completely implausible if it were presented in a fictional context. That was the part that made Valerie smile the most—the not-so-obvious idea that the Beatles were not imaginary. It's so not-so-obvious that only an insane person could conceive it.

Now, for Valerie, that night was just about the song itself. There was no subtext. There was only text. She was just a spaced-out person, sitting in a love seat and listening to low-quality audio from a crappy clock radio. There was no exchange of feeling, beyond how she felt about the song. Her feelings were her own, and they were shared with no one. But the experience was different for me. I felt extremely close to Valerie that night, even though she had no idea I was in the room. I could hear the rain against the window, intertwined with the fragility of the music. I could see her amorphous affection for the Beatles being demystified—and then amplified—by this one weird song, and to see someone love one thing is to see someone love all things. She was alone, but we were together. The intimacy was overwhelming. Every time she rewound the tape, I felt like we were burrowing deeper and deeper into a hole. Was it the most romantic night of my life? No. That would be an overstatement. But it felt *important*. And Valerie didn't care at all. She couldn't. It wasn't like unrequited love. It wasn't even like having a crush on a person who doesn't know you exist. It was more like being seduced by an amnesiac. It was like she was forgetting who I was, while I was still there. It was terrible. I mean, I was really seeing this person. I was truly seeing who she was. Someday, Valerie will fall in love. She will get married. But her husband will never see her the way I did. No one will ever be as close to her as I was that night, because no one else can ever be with her when she's alone. Only I can do that.

So what is your real question, Victoria? Did I *like* Valerie? As I said before: Yes. But I probably didn't care about her. I've barely even thought about her since the last time I saw her. If I wasn't talking about her to you, I probably wouldn't be talking about her at all. Maybe I'm lying to myself, but I doubt it. I eventually found that song she played online, and it's by a local named Dennis Johnson (*sic*).[8] A pretty hopeless case, from what I can tell. That song doesn't even sound good to me anymore. I never want to hear it again. But now I'm left with the memory of having heard it that night. It feels like we shared something. But we didn't. I know the truth. I understand the truth. We didn't share anything. Valerie was in the room, but what happened to me didn't happen to her. And I know that I need to understand this. (**5.23.08, 10:32 a.m. to 10:42 a.m.**)

4 You're looking at me like I'm lying. You're looking at me like you think I'm saying the opposite of what I really mean. Either that, or you're looking at me like I'm some kind of terrible person. Like I'm some kind of brilliant troll.

[I tell Y____ that I am not looking at him in any particular way.]

Well, good for you. Great. Whatever. You can certainly say that, and maybe you're being honest. I can see how you're looking at me, and I'm never wrong about these things . . . but, you know, I understand your reactions. You're wondering why I could be so uncaring toward Valerie, and why I almost seem proud of my emotional detachment. I seem inhuman to you. Your eyes tell me everything. Your eyes are like a search engine.

I get the impression that talking about Valerie has actually made you more confused about what I do and why I do it. You probably think I'm just a sick person who likes to spy on strangers, and that I've created this elaborate, faux-sociological framework to justify my behavior. You can tell me if that's what you think.

[I tell Y____ that I don't know what I think.]

Yes, you do. You're thinking without even trying. You can't stop yourself from thinking. But here's what you *ought* to be thinking:

8. Daniel Johnston.

"What was gained from this observation? What do we now know about human nature that we didn't know before?" That's what you should be thinking. Those are the questions you should be asking yourself.

[I say, "I would love to know the answer to those questions."]

Don't pressure me. I'll answer your questions, but only when I'm ready. You won't really understand, anyway. The information will be useless to you.

[I say, "It seems like you want me to ask you questions, just so you can decline to answer them."]

That's not true. You lack self-confidence. We're almost out of time, anyway. The session is basically over. Wait a week. Next week. I'll talk about this next week. And I don't appreciate your tone, Victoria. It makes me think you're against me. (**5.23.08, 10:44 a.m. to 10:46 a.m.**)

5 I started to feel responsible for Valerie. She might have been comfortable with her life, but I wasn't. I didn't like where her life was going. She didn't realize how enslaved she was. Here was a single woman with no obligations, but with a life devoid of freedom. She didn't even understand what freedom meant. There are convicted murderers with more freedom than Valerie. I truly believe that.

Did she like exercise? No. She exercised only so that she could smoke pot and gorge herself on pizza. Did she like being high? Probably when she started, but not anymore. Now it was just a ritual that accelerated her hunger. Did she enjoy food? No. If she loved food, she would not be shoveling canned ravioli down her throat. Did she enjoy the *process* of eating—the chewing, the swallowing, the filling of the stomach? No way. All that did was remind her that she needed to exercise again. I'm not even sure if she really liked the Beatles. I think she *thought* she did, but how would she know? She clearly sucked at knowing things about herself. I think it's more likely that she believed the Beatles were simply what a person like her was supposed to listen to. Valerie had no agency. I don't care if she didn't realize that. I realized it for her.

This, my Vic-Vick, is the type of realization that can happen only through surveillance: If anyone else had been in the room, Valerie would have "become" happy. She wouldn't have *been* happy, but she would have acted happy and assumed that her actions were somehow related to feelings. Jane came by again—the following Tuesday, just as before—and they watched their little TV show that didn't make any sense and argued about a sequence of numbers and laughed and got excited and chewed on fried chicken skin. I'm sure they thought they were fulfilled, but they were wrong. That was not fulfillment. It was just another way to avoid the cognition of their imprisonment, and their banal interaction made that easier. They could feed off each other's fabricated joy. But when Valerie was alone, I saw the desperation she could not comprehend. She was running herself into the grave, just so that she could space out and pig out and not care about things that mattered. It was pathetic. She deserved better. I saw potential in Valerie that she refused to see in herself, but she was too busy being Valerie to see anything that wasn't already there.

So—now—I had to make a decision. I had to decide if watching Valerie was more important than helping Valerie. Did I have a responsibility to this person? Jesus would say, "Yes." Nietzsche would say, "Don't ask a question when you already know the answer." But let's not get political. I had to decide for myself. And what I elected to do would be—at least in theory—beneficial to both involved parties. I decided that I would help Valerie *in order to observe Valerie*. That was my plan. I thought that moving this person from a bad life to a good life would make her core qualities more clear, because those would be the only qualities that'd remain unchanged. I still see the logic in this. I do.

The way to help Valerie seemed obvious. What I needed to do was alter the sequence of her unhappiness cycle: I had to stop her from exercising, stop her from smoking pot, or stop her from eating. If I stopped one, the other two would cease to exist. In order to stop her from exercising, I assumed I would need to physically injure her. That struck me as wrong, even if my motives were good. What if I accidentally paralyzed her? What if her health insurance was shit? The risk was too high. Stopping her from smoking marijuana was flat-out impossible—her whole life revolved around that experience. If I threw away her marijuana, she'd just call Jane or buy more. But there *was* a way to stop her from eating, and that's what I pursued.

As I mentioned before, I always carry stimulants whenever I'm on an observation. This is done out of necessity: I need to stay mentally alert, and I need to stay awake for long periods of time. I can't sleep at my own discretion. As a consequence, I'm never hungry. I can barely remember what being hungry feels like. What I needed to do was make Valerie feel the same way I did. So when Valerie went to work, I turned her weed into an appetite suppressant.

It seemed like the best solution.

Val kept her pot in a music box, inside the freezer. And she had a ton of it—she was clearly the kind of nervous addict who always bought four or five months' worth whenever she saw her dealer. It looked like a soft, green brick. Now, like I said before, I had a whole buffet of stimulants at my disposal: Adderall, oral meth tablets, Ritalin, Dexedrine, medical coke, modafinil. I'm my own pharmacy. I always keep a little of everything on my person, because I don't like to use the same stimulant for too many days in a row. I can't risk addiction. So here's what I did: When Valerie left for work, I made a speed cocktail. I combined everything I had in a plastic bag, and I found a rolling pin under her sink—I'm not sure why a person with no food would possess a rolling pin, but Valerie had a nice one. It was perfect. I crushed all this coke and speed and meth into a powder. It was a sandwich bag of zombie dust. There ended up being a lot in there, way more than I expected—there was enough granular stimulation to make a Clydesdale climb a Christmas tree. And I poured *all of it* into her dope. I used my fingers and a fork to really drive it inside the buds. I had to make sure every future hit housed a modicum of speed. Obviously, this process caused the brick to disintegrate. It no longer looked like a brick. I started to worry that she'd notice how different it looked, because stoners tend to be meticulous about their weed. It's usually the only thing they really pay attention to. But then I had a moment of divine inspiration: I remembered that one of the only household items Valerie happened to own was olive oil! It was like organic gorilla glue—one tablespoon was more than enough to rebuild the brick. To this day, I'm kind of shocked how lucky I got with Valerie. When I needed a rolling pin, she inexplicably had a rolling pin; when I needed olive oil, it was pretty much the only item she had in the kitchen. It was almost like she unknowingly wanted me to save her life.

I put the dope back in the music box and I put the music box back in the freezer. Val gets home at her usual hour; she strips off her clothes, looks at her profile in the bathroom mirror, and prepares for her second run of the day. She's a robot. As she stretches, I can faintly hear her joints cracking, but her face expresses nothing. Mary Decker never had this level of resolve. She runs like a deer. She returns like a carrier pigeon. She showers like a porn star, and then she smokes like a tire fire. But this new smoke smells different; that's obvious to both of us. It doesn't smell like weed. It smells like a Nerf ball melting in the microwave. But Valerie assumes it's just the sediments in the bong water. She sniffs the chamber of her bong and makes a face. I can't get inside her mind, but I know what she's thinking: *I'm just really high right now.* That's the only rational conclusion she can draw. *I'm so high, this pot smells like poison.* It's an illogical assumption, but more logical than the truth.

I'm not sure if you know this or not, but smoking cocaine and marijuana simultaneously makes a person idiotically high. The feeling is unique. You get up as rapidly as you go down, and there's this unique third twist behind your eyes—it's kind of like how people describe the movement of earthquakes. I can tell Valerie notices this immediately. Her reaction is transparent. She knows something is different—her pupils are pinned and kinetic, and her pulse is running downhill. Plus, *she thinks she should be hungry.* I can tell just by looking at her. It's obvious. She knows this is the point where food always becomes a nonnegotiable desire. But the feeling is just not there. She looks at all the groceries she grabbed on the way home—some turkey meatballs, bread, cheese, ice cream—but none of it appeals to her and she doesn't know why. She sticks it in the fridge and starts to organize her apartment. She smokes more speed weed and cleans the bathroom. She smokes again and aligns her CDs in alphabetical order. She collects her dirty clothes and starts to do laundry, separating everything by color and fabric. Pretty soon it's ten o'clock and she still hasn't eaten. The shackles of hunger are broken. She's free. She can do whatever she wants. She opens her unopened mail and writes checks for all the individual bills. She balances her checkbook, smiling to herself as she does so. She smokes again and goes back into the bathroom—she's already cleaned it once, but now she *really* cleans it. She scrapes the toilet. She waxes the floor. She scrubs the walls of the shower with Ajax. She looks at herself in the mirror and poses like a model. She practices her casually-trying-not-to-care expression for future photo ops. She looks at puppies and kittens on the Internet. She's like three people at once. "I've done such a great service," I think to myself.

Valerie finally goes to bed without supper at 4:30 a.m. She wakes up at nine, looking awful, immediately late for work. When she gets home that night, things seem unchanged: She takes her normal run—maybe a little shorter than usual, but not by much—and then she showers and resumes her regimen of destruction. This time the smoke smells *really* bad, but the strangeness bothers her less. I can see her spirits lift. She brought home another grocery bag of food, undoubtedly presuming that last night had been an anomaly and that she'd be extra-hungry tonight. But she's not. She looks at her bacon and her white bread and she thinks, "I don't need this." I'm helping her. I know I'm helping her.

But I guess I did one thing wrong.

I guess I put too many drugs into her drugs.

I must have. It didn't seem like too much, but maybe I used my own tolerance as a yardstick, or maybe I should have added every-

thing except the meth. Maybe she just had a weak system. I don't
know what happened. I know it was an amateur mistake, but I'd
never tried anything like this before. Pharmaceuticals are tricky.
Doctors make mistakes all the time. That's why they need all that
insurance. Plus, this was partially her own fault. She smoked like
mad that night. Like, way more than the other nights. I started to
wonder if perhaps she'd traditionally used the sensation of hunger as
a barometer for when to stop. Because now she was smoking *compulsively,* every ten or fifteen minutes. Instant basehead. And suddenly
she's acting all crazy: pacing around, arguing with herself, calling
people on the telephone and hanging up when they answer, running
to the bathroom every half hour with explosive diarrhea. She listens
to "Revolution 9," which *nobody* does. She locks the front door and
pulls down the window blinds—totally cliché behavior. I suppose I
was concerned, but not *over*concerned—I mean, lots of people act
paranoid when they take stimulants. Everyone knows this. Uppers
are always worse than downers. But Valerie was off the reservation.
I don't know if she liked how it felt, or if this combination of narcot-
ics somehow confused her, or if she was just the type of person who
didn't realize how much she enjoyed drugs. But she was definitely
smoking too much, and there was no way I could stop her. At this
point, I was merely an observer. I was just sitting in the corner, silent
and unseen, waiting for her to crash and sleep. I was waiting for her
to recognize that her life was different now . . . better . . . less suffo-
cating. But she didn't seem to get that. She just got higher.

Around nine thirty, she takes another gargantuan hit and changes
into her regular workout clothes, then changes into a similar but different outfit, and then combines the two outfits into a third. She
jumps on the treadmill. That was the first red flag. Now I'm getting
worried. She starts running, sweating, grunting. And tonight she is
really obsessed with the LCD monitors, crazily obsessed, in a manner that totally dwarfs her previous behavior. Instead of wanting
all the gauges to line up perfectly, she *needs* that to happen; she
needs them all to share the same numbers, and she keeps adjust-
ing her pace and the incline to make it so. It never works. It's like

watching a person accidentally attaching themselves to an electric chair. I'm mesmerized. This is real science. I'm finally seeing the fundamental qualities of an isolated human in trouble. Pretty soon, I realize she's been sprinting for over two hours. She gets off the treadmill, inhales a massive quantity of speed smoke, coughs manically, chokes down four aspirin for (what I assume) was her pounding headache, and returns to the treadmill. Now, as you probably know, stimulants dramatically thin the blood. Aspirin is just about the worst thing to combine with cocaine. But Valerie doesn't even know there's cocaine in her system. Her nose starts to bleed, and maybe her ears. It takes her too long to notice, but she eventually does. She steps off the treadmill, tries to wipe her nostrils on the shoulder of her T-shirt, and immediately falls to the carpet. I see her hold two fingers on her neck, just below her cheek; she's checking her own pulse, and I can tell that she's worried. She hasn't looked right for the past ninety minutes, but now she looks like an animal at the pound. Her left leg starts to spasm, so she grabs her calf with her hands. It doesn't stop trembling. She starts crying, but she can't force out any tears—she's too dehydrated. She starts panting, and I think she says, "Help." I guess I'm not *sure* she said "help," but I thought that's what it sounded like. It was a one-syllable word that starts with an *H*.

So now I had to make a decision.

I am not a bad person. I'm not going to let any person—and certainly not someone I like, such as Valerie—die in front of me. No way. That's obscene. And I will concede that—in many important ways—I was responsible for this turn of events. If Val were to die, and if someone were to say I was responsible for her death . . . I'd have a hard time arguing against that. But I didn't think Valerie was dying. I really, really did not. I thought she was having a terrible reaction to a bunch of drugs she probably should not have been metabolizing, but I was 98 percent sure she'd live. Yeah, I know what happened to John Belushi and Len Bias and Ike Turner. I know, I know. I read all the same books as everybody else. It can happen. But people don't die the second time they try cocaine. It *can* happen, but it never does. Part of me thought I should just stay cool and ride the situation out. But this was a major blunder, and I knew it. My confidence was totally shot. I would have never forgiven myself if Valerie died. It would have contradicted the purposes of my research. I made the decision to intervene.

This, certainly, creates its own kind of special problem: How does one intervene in an emergency situation if one isn't really there? I mean, I was in the room, but I wasn't *in the room*. You know what I mean? So I knew this intervention would be shocking to Valerie, and her mental state was already fragile. My biggest fear was that I might give her a heart attack that might not have happened on its own. But life is a gamble. I finally just stood up, walked over to her cell phone, and called 9–1–1. I told the dispatcher the address, I gave him a rough idea of what was happening, and I left the building. I don't know what ultimately transpired, but I do know that Valerie is fine today. She lived. I was right.

[At this point, Y____ just stopped talking, as if the story was over. I waited for him to continue, but he quit pacing and sat down in the white chair. He just sat there, silently. Finally, I asked the obvious question: "How did Valerie react to what you did?"]

Oh, not well. I'm sure she thought she was hallucinating, or maybe dying. When I started dialing the phone, she initially said something like, "What's happening?" I said, "Remain calm." She screamed a few times. She said stuff like, "Who the fuck is there? What's going on? Oh my God oh my God oh my God!" Again, I said, "Remain calm. Everything will be okay." She started shaking. It was a little like the first time you saw me when I was cloaked, except way worse. She lost her shit completely. But this would be a lot for any person to handle, particularly if that person was superhigh and possibly dying and had just finished a cardio workout.

As I talked to the 9-1-1 operator, Val just sort of lay there and writhed around on the carpet. "What's happening? What's happening?" That was her refrain. When I was finished with the call, I walked over to where she was lying. I was sort of looming over her body, but I tried to be as casual as possible. It's funny—even when I know a person can't see me, I worry about semiotics. "Things will be okay," I told her. "The paramedics are coming. You've inhaled a lot of stimulants. When they arrive, give them what's left of your marijuana and tell them it was laced with other drugs."

"What are you saying," she said. "Who are you? What's happening to me? I want this to stop. Stop! Stop! I'm so sorry. I'm sorry. I want this to stop."

"Remain calm," I told her. "You don't have the ability to understand what's happening to you right now, so don't even try. Let it go. Breathe deep. Stay on the floor and wait for the paramedics."

"I'm dying," she said.

"You're not dying," I told her. "You're a decent person. I was trying to help you, but I made a mistake."

"Who are you? Where are you? Who is talking to me? Who is talking to me? Who is talking to me?"

"No one is talking to you," I said. "This isn't happening. Just make sure you give the paramedics the drugs in your fridge. I know you won't want to do that, but you must. They need to know what's inside you. It's not what you think."

And, with that, I left. And—like I said before—I don't even know if Valerie was ever in real danger. She lived. I do know that. A few weeks after that last night together, I went back and made sure she'd recovered. I didn't reenter her apartment, because I was kind of scared to go back in there. It seemed like the wrong thing to do. But I did follow her on a jog. She seemed fine. I'm sure she spent at least one night in the psych ward, and I assume she was placed into an outpatient rehab program for an amphetamine addiction she never actually had. I regret that. It's one of my regrets. She didn't deserve that hassle. On balance, I suppose my plan failed. Even now, I'd classify my time with Valerie as "bittersweet." But that's the consequence of getting involved with other people. If my job was easy, I wouldn't need to see you. I did the best I could. **(5.30.08, 10:11 a.m. to 10:50 a.m.)**

An Attempt at Reason

When Y___ finally concluded the Valerie Sessions in late May, I was relieved. This is not because I found his stories uninteresting—quite the contrary. I was still in awe of almost everything Y___ said; I still preferred to see him as superhuman. The cognition of his invisibility usurped my critical distance. He would arrive at my office and lecture me like a child, and I accepted those lectures unconditionally. But after he'd leave and I'd start to think about what he'd told me—when I relistened to the audiotapes and forced myself to seriously consider the information he was presenting—I grew troubled.

"This is not a moral judgment," I told him at the beginning of our June 6 session, "and I'm not trying to dictate what you discuss here. Certainly, I have problems with how you treated Valerie. But that can be addressed later. The one thing I do need from you, however, is a better sense of what you were hoping to learn from this observation. Because I must be honest with you: What you're describing doesn't seem like science to me."

I was nervous as I said this. I was tentative. My intellectual infatuation with Y___ was interfering with my judgment; I felt privy to the interior thoughts of an authentic genius and I didn't want to jeopardize our relationship. I'm certain Y___ suspected this. His response was hypersensitive, almost as if my question had wounded him. "What do you want to know?" he asked. "How can I help you understand this?"

What I told him was what anyone would have told him: I said that he didn't seem to be learning anything important about the people he was watching. It seemed like unadulterated voyeurism and a misuse of power. I noted that secretly drugging a person was immoral (not to mention criminal). But regardless of how things ended, I wanted him to explain why he ever thought the best use of invisibility was to watch a randomly selected woman smoke marijuana inside her apartment. I wasn't even that concerned with his involvement in Valerie's life; I was more occupied with his original intentions. My suspicion was that he didn't really have "intentions" at all. So I told him this.

He looked at me for a long time. He smiled, but it was the kind of condescending smile that said, *You don't really get this, do you?* At least that's how it felt. Maybe it's just how I remember it. The one thing I do know is that I believed what he said next, at least at the time.

"What is the purpose of science?" Y___ began. (How did I accept such pompous rhetoric? I'll never forgive myself.) "What's the purpose of building a telescope, or going to the moon, or assembling a laser that can slice through a diamond? Is it to make our lives better? Partially. That's the obvious, unimportant, superficial justification for technology. We study dielectric heating and nonionized radiation in order to create an oven that cooks popcorn in two minutes. We understand internal combustion so that we can travel sixty miles in sixty minutes. We research T-cells so that homosexual heroin addicts don't die in their late twenties. In general, brilliant people study complex things in order to make life simpler for the average and the less-than-average and the infirm. Talk to an eighth-grade science teacher, and that's what he'll try to tell you. Science, for most people, is something we use. But there's a fallacy in that. There's a problem. That logic suggests science is *improving* the world, and that's not happening. This is what gamblers call a push. Science is always a push.

"Everything science gives us immediately becomes normative. To an eighty-year-old man, a computer is this amazing device that creates instantaneous access to limitless information. He can't get his head around it. But to a twenty-year-old man, the computer is a limited machine that costs too much and always needs to be faster. Because humans live finite lives, all technological advances immediately feel banal to whatever generation inherits their benefits. Any advance can be appreciated only by the handful of people who happen to exist within the same time period of that specific technology's introduction. You follow my meaning? Those are the only people who notice the difference. To a seven-year-old, a computer doesn't even qualify as technology. It's like a crowbar. Everything magical is temporary. So the idea that science makes our life 'better' is kind of an ephemeral illusion. Take vulcanization, for example. That's a manifestation of science that seems to improve everything about modernity. Right? Of course it is. We couldn't drive without it, or at least not the way we drive now. But if vulcanization *wasn't* possible, would we miss it? No. Of course not. We wouldn't miss it at all. We'd find a way around it, or we'd effortlessly live without it. We wouldn't even have the capacity to miss it. Vulcanization seems to make life better only because we already know it exists. We wouldn't *miss* rubber tires if they had never been invented, in the same way we don't *miss* cows that taste like lobster or shoes made out of glass or sexual time machines or anything else that science can't create. Over time, the net benefit of technology is always going to be zero. Children born into Amish communities don't miss TV until they discover such contraptions exist, right? There's just no real evidence that proves people in the fifteenth century were less happy than people are now, just as there's no reason to think people in the twenty-fifth century will have happier, better lives than you or me. This is a strange notion to accept, but it's true. And once I accepted that truth, it forced me to reevaluate everything I did as an intellectual.

"The more I thought about this—and I thought about this *a lot,* for many, many years—the more it seemed like the only essential purpose of science was to define consciousness. To define reality. I know I overuse that word, but it's the only word for what I'm interested in: *reality.* Over time, I realized it was the same instinctive reason I'd dabbled in sociology and journalism and mathematics and music and every other discipline that hopes to make order out of chaos. It consumed me. For a long time, it was the only thing I ever thought about. It just seemed like an impossible conundrum. Everything I did moved me farther away from my intended goal. The *process* of everything I tried—experiments, surveys, interviews, whatever—inevitably created its own false reality. The process was always the problem. Obviously, I'm not the first person who's ever come to this conclusion; we talked about this before, very early on, long before you knew who I was or what I can do. By now, it probably sounds like common sense. But when I started at Chaminade, and when I realized what we were doing and what the end results could be, I saw a new potentiality for the very first time. I saw a way to repurpose science. I could use it to get me closer to reality. So that would become both my starting point and my ending point.

"Remember when I told you about that Swanson boy? The boy from my school? The boy who liked Rush? To me, watching him through his window was a rare glimpse of reality. Watching a single person, away from other persons, was the only way. There was no process to interfere with the experience. So that's what I've turned into my life's work: I've built a suit that allows me to see the unseen life, because unseen lives are the only ones that matter. Now, what you seem to be asking is 'What am I hoping to see?' My answer is this—I have no expectations. In fact, *I can't* have expectations, because the creation of expectation is its own independent process. Let me say that again, for clarity: *The creation of expectation is its own independent process.* If I expect anything at all, it will change my perception. So if your issue with my observation of Valerie is that nothing 'interesting' happened while I was there . . . well, I have no rebuttal for that. Clearly, you're not designed to do what I do. You'd be a bad scientist. You will never be able to see reality. You're just a person."

As I type these words today, Y___'s reasoning strikes me as dubious. But that's not what I thought at the time. Every time Y___ insulted my intelligence, I paradoxically trusted him more. Instead of disagreeing with his logic, I accepted it; instead of demanding further explanation, I told him he had a good point and changed the topic. For example, I asked how he could justify drugging Valerie if he did not want any "process" to impact his reality. Wasn't force-feeding a woman methamphetamine a process?

"Look," he said. "I'm here in your office. Right? I'm talking to you about what I did. Don't you think I realize dosing Valerie with cocaine and meth was a mistake? I realize that it was. I do. Obviously, I shouldn't have done that, or at least not so aggressively. Valerie was not ready for her life to change: She wanted to be unhappy, and you can't help a woman who refuses to help herself. I'm not saying that incident was entirely her fault, but it was *partially* her fault. We're all partially responsible. So what are you trying to figure out here? Are you hoping to understand what I'm trying to learn? If so, you won't succeed. This isn't social work. This is complex. There's no precedent for my behavior. I'm the first and last person who's ever attempted this. You won't be able to solve me. Quit trying to be someone you're not. Are you judging my actions? If so, stop judging them. That's not why I came here. I came to you so I could manage the guilt I don't deserve to have. I'm trying to understand why I feel bad about things that—intellectually—I know were good. Why does every conversation we have devolve into a treatise about the things *you* don't understand? When do we talk about the things *I* don't understand?"

I apologized.

Stupidly, I apologized. I didn't want to lose him.

I told Y___ he was right. I said that therapists sometimes make mistakes (just like everyone else), and that (of course) he had the right to dictate what we discussed in our sessions. I told him that my inability to comprehend his scientific methodology did not entitle me to question his means. I gave him a few sycophantic compliments and told Y___ he was so unlike all my other patients that I was still learning how to help him. I wanted him to like me as a person and to respect me professionally, which—in retrospect—is probably the most humiliating thing I've ever done. I deserve what happened.

1711 Lavaca St.
Suite 2
Austin, TX 78701
vvick@vick.com

July 5, 2012

Notes RE: Invisibility (Message to Crosby Bumpus)

Hey, Crosby, me again—I was originally going to mention what follows in my cover letter, and then I considered including it as an appendix. However, John thinks I should just cut-and-paste it here, as its own separate chapter, right in the middle of everything else. But is that a potential mistake? I'm afraid it might hurt "the narrative flow" (as you are wont to say). However, John insists this info *is* the narrative, because so much hinges on these details. Do you have thoughts on this? We've briefly discussed it in passing over the phone, but I need some concrete direction. My gut reaction is that John's usually right about this sort of thing.

It goes without saying that the most interesting thing about Y——far beyond anything he saw or did or claimed to have done—was simply his ability to disappear. When serious people study this case, that will be the detail they fixate upon. However, all my attempts to truly understand this phenomenon did not succeed, and for one glaring reason: Y—— almost never spoke about it.

It was, I suppose, the 800-pound gorilla in the room. However, our 800-pound gorilla evidently wore the same suit Y—— had designed for himself. There were only three occasions when Y___ explicitly discussed his capabilities at length, two of which were unrecorded. After our third discussion on the topic, he made it abundantly clear that he wasn't going to elaborate on that aspect of his being, even though (a) I was incredibly curious about it, and (b) it was the crux of who he was and what he did.

So why didn't Y___ talk about this? I've asked myself that question many, many times. If we are to believe his own explanation, it was mostly because he was paying for these sessions (and therefore reserved the right to dictate what we discussed). He repeatedly told me I wasn't qualified to understand the science of his cloaking and that he had no desire to waste time "teaching." The fact that he'd revealed his invisibility to me firsthand on May 9 also played a role—he believed there was nothing left for me to question, and that I should simply accept this supernatural ability and move on. And I suppose that's what I did. As so often happens in therapist-patient relationships (and to paraphrase the same hokey words Y___ so often used), our dialogue became "its own kind of reality"—we were living inside a vacuum where whatever Y___ said was accepted as infallible. At some point, I stopped thinking about how unusual this was; it just became a weekly part of my life.

Still, I always kept a separate record of any instance where Y___ casually alluded to the sensation and practicality of being an unseen person. These statements often came up as asides, generally when he was trying to change the subject or explain how he found himself in a certain position. All of these statements can be reaccessed within the unedited transcript at the UT psych library. Please note that the following quotes are not thematically connected and were drawn intermittently over the span of our entire relationship—they are not sequential. If you have any ideas about how they can be incorporated, send me an e-mail or give me a call. Thanks— V.V.

- **On being unable to see one's own body:** "It took a long time to be comfortable with that. I mean, imagine trying to turn on a table lamp in a completely dark bedroom. It's difficult, and we reflexively assume it's difficult because we can't see the lamp. But it's also difficult because we can't see our own hand—we can't gauge the relationship between the object and ourselves. We can *feel* our hand, and we *know* where the lamp is. But we reach for the switch and we miss. This happened all the time when I first started playing around with the suit. I had to imagine hands and feet I couldn't see. Getting up and down stairs was a trial. Even now, I'd never attempt to run down a flight of stairs. That's a death wish."

- **On the suit itself:** "It gets a little disgusting because I loathe to wash it. It operates so much better when there are multiple layers of mist on the surface—those trace remnants of cream harden into something that's almost like a polish, and nothing refracts light like polish. Every time I clean the suit, I'm basically starting over. But, of course, I sweat like a boar in that thing. I'm essentially wearing a second skin that doesn't breathe. To cover the smell, I try to spray down the inside of the suit with scentless Lysol. It really eats at my skin. My thighs will never be the same."

- **On the notion of using his ability for the common good, potentially in the vein of a stereotypical superhero:** "That's funny. The thought never occurred to me."

- **On mishaps:** "It wasn't uncommon to have a minor crisis. You can't control how people live. I had a hilarious, terrible situation near Houston. I was observing a nervous middle-aged man—he couldn't sit still. He never stayed in place. His movements were hard to anticipate. He had ants in the pants. I was hunched in the corner of his living room, and he started walking directly over to my corner so that he could jiggle the cable plugged into his stereo speaker, because the bass kept cutting in and out. At least that's what I thought his intentions were. When I saw him coming toward me, I stood up and moved a little to my right to clear the area. But at the last possible moment, he changed his mind and turned ninety degrees to his left. He walked right into me. We collided,

head on, skull to skull. It sounded like two coconuts. *Bonk!*
Our heads went *bonk*. We were both knocked to the floor.
He jumped up and started swinging his arms, punching the
air, saying all these outrageous things to whoever or whatever
he imagined was there. I stayed on the floor, which seemed
safer. But then the guy goes into his bedroom and comes
back with a fucking gun. This was a huge gun—I think it was
a .357 or a .44 Magnum. A Dirty Harry gun, for all intents
and purposes. And now ol' Ants in the Pants is filling the
chamber with bullets in the middle of his living room. He's
looking all skittish, breathing through his mouth, sweating
under the armpits. There's nothing like watching a nervous
man load a gun. Of course, he doesn't *see* anything, and by
now I've crawled into the kitchen. So now I'm watching ol'
Ants in the Pants from the other room, peeping my head
around the doorway. He's waving the gun around, trying to
figure out what the hell just happened. He *knows* someone
was in his living room. He knows his skull hit a skull. He
knows it. But he's also not going to randomly shoot up his
own house. His eyes dart from corner to corner to corner.
For some reason, he gets the idea that whoever broke into
his home must be hiding in the basement. I have no idea
why this possibility occurred to him, but I suppose he was
grasping at straws. He opens the door to his basement, gun in
hand, and slowly creeps down the stairs. I hear them creaking
as he walks. When he got to the bottom of the staircase, I just
sprinted out the front door. There was no way I was playing
around with that motherfucker. Owning a gun doesn't make
the average person safer, but it makes the average person safer
from me."

- **On fear:** "The one thing that constantly terrifies me is crossing
the street. I mean, if anybody ever hit me, I'd just have to lie
on the pavement and die. Every other car would drive right
over my body. I'd probably have to hope that somebody drove
over my head and put me out of my misery. The worst was

when I was in west Florida: Crossing the street there is flat-out impossible. No crosswalks, lots of old people driving blind, and no other pedestrians. I was more relaxed in Detroit!"

- **On troubleshooting:** "I completely miscalculated how cloaking would impact my shadow. We all did. We were all working under the assumption that shadows would be no issue whatsoever, because—in theory—the light I relocate should negate the absence of light we recognize as shadow. But it didn't work that way. The suit absorbs a tiny percentage of light, so it doesn't refract the full one hundred percent of what remains. This wasn't something I realized until I started wearing it on a regular basis: People can't see me, but the sun can. I still cast a dim, undefined silhouette. It's almost like projecting a shadow through a funhouse mirror. There are ways around this, though. If I'm traveling outside, I do my walking at night or at noon, or on days that are overcast. When I'm inside a room, I always stay cognizant of any windows that face directly east or directly west, and I try to avoid walking in front of south-facing windows during the afternoon. It's really more of a hassle than a problem. And like I said before—you'd be surprised by what people see, yet refuse to notice. I think about that a lot. Like, have you ever heard of a Mexican tribe called the Huicholes?[9] The so-called Running People of Mexico? There's a great book about these freaks. They're this hermetic society known for two things. The first, as you might expect, is running—the Huicholes are the craziest athletes in North America. Members of this tribe regularly run forty, fifty, a hundred miles at a time, barefoot, over unspeakable terrain, subsisting only on corn beer and mouse meat, purely for pleasure. No one knows how they do it. But—interestingly—the other thing they're known for is invisibility. They live in caves around the Sierra Madres, and

---

9. It has been pointed out to me (by a colleague) that Y____ was incorrect here. The tribe he meant to reference was actually the Tarahumara.

these people can virtually disappear into the rock. The first time a nineteenth-century explorer came across the Huicholes, he walked straight through one of their villages and didn't see anything. They were right there in front of him, and he didn't see one person. So if it's possible for an explorer to overlook an entire tribe he's actively searching for, imagine how difficult it is for an untrained person to see one stranger they don't expect to be there."

- **On who could wear the cloaking suit:** "Are you asking me if you can wear the suit? Because you can't. No one can wear it but me. I'm sorry if this disappoints you, but that's just how it has to be. You can't wear my suit. You can't." *(Note to Crosby: At no point did I ever express a desire to wear this garment. I'm still not sure why Y___ inferred that this was something I was angling for.)*

- **On side effects and addiction:** "Because there was no way to test this stuff, I have no idea if continually covering myself with an aerosol mist is basically going to guarantee I'll eventually get sick. I'm sure it's a bad idea to live like this, but I don't know to what degree. At first it burned my nostrils, but that stopped after a while. Of course, I was also taking a lot of stimulants at the time . . . the idea of becoming addicted has never been an issue. I understand my body. I got used to the stimulants gradually. Now they're just a tool, no different than a pen or a camera. The only people who talk about the dangers of drugs are the people who can't handle them. How does that old Richard Pryor line go? 'I know guys who've used cocaine every single day for ten years and never got addicted.' "

- **On the nature of this ability:** "What I do is not metaphysical. It does not transcend science in any way. It only feels metaphysical because no one else can do it. I'm sure the first person to build a fire with a flint seemed to be dabbling in the metaphysical, too. What I do is much closer to illusion. I relate to people like David Blaine: We both do something visually confounding that demands physical endurance. The only difference is that I'm doing something essential. Magicians only want to get laid."

- **On what he wanted:** "You call me invisible because you can't comprehend this any other way. I suppose that's fine. It's the wrong application of that term, but I understand why you keep using it. For you, any person who can't be seen is invisible. But there are invisible people in plain sight, Victoria. Most of the world is invisible. I wanted to see the visible man. That's what's happening here. That's really all it is."

The Unclear Story
of the Half-Mexican Ladies Man

[This content emerged from a rambling one-hour session on June 13. I'm including portions of the conversation not because it seems revelatory to me, but because it seemed so important to Y____. There was an element of nostalgic desperation to his storytelling. I've elected not to log the specific times these statements were made, although I have kept the passages in chronological order. Conscientious readers may have already noticed how Y____ oscillates between past and present tense; this may have been accidental, but I suspect it was not. As such, I've kept it faithful to the original audio. I got the sense this encounter had happened in the very recent past—perhaps as recently as the previous week. But when I asked when it happened, he said nothing, nor would he explain why he declined to answer.]

1 Elderly people present unique problems. It's harder to get inside their homes, because they're more cautious. They don't leave doors or windows unlocked. They don't trust people. The world gets scarier. Now, granted, once you're inside, old people are incredibly easy to observe. They don't hear footfalls and they're less aware of their surroundings. But the real problem is that they never fucking leave. They'll stay inside the house for two, three, four days straight. It's like working a double shift with no overtime.

2 I once had an old woman die while I was watching her. Died on Thanksgiving morning. She just never got out of bed. I decided to stick around until someone found the body, because I wanted to see the reaction of whoever discovered the corpse. I wondered how quickly the visitor would recognize that they were in an apartment with a dead body—would they sense this instantly? Would they check for a pulse? Would they cry? I was especially curious to see if the person who found the body would *talk* to the corpse, which we've all been conditioned to do by TV. On television, people are always talking to the dead. "Live, dammit. Come on, live!" "No, grandma, please don't leave us!" That sort of thing. But after two days, I started to suspect no one was going to show up, and the bedroom started to feel awkward and stale. We would all have a less romantic view of death if we regularly had to smell it. It seemed wrong to be there, and kind of gross. I left on Saturday. I left the front door wide open. Seemed like the right thing to do.

3 There was one old man I really liked, though. He lives right here in town. Liked him. Liked him a ton. A half-Mexican. I genuinely liked him. He lives not far from here, out beyond the Mount Calvary Cemetery. A barrel-chested half-Mexican. I broke into his house in the morning, when he was out watering the lawn. I remember watching him drink from the hose after I slipped through his sliding door. He must have been at least eighty years old, although that's a hard thing to tell with half-Mexicans. He wore flip-flops and suspenders and he walked with a slouch. He had a gray mustache. These details don't matter, but I remember them. He was in great shape for someone who probably shouldn't have been alive.

4 It was a nice house. It fit the universally accepted definition of "nice." There were pictures on all the walls of people who must be his kids. He must have had multiple wives, because there were at least three different women in the various photos and some of the kids look totally unlike the others. Some of the kids looked like borderline albinos! He had several framed pictures of himself, but they were all in the bathroom. No idea if this was irony or vanity. The picture over his toilet must have been taken when he was nineteen or twenty. As a younger man, he was handsome. I remember thinking, "I bet this guy used to run the show." He was standing in front of a Chevy with a cigarette and a Lone Star, posing in the way people from that era always pose in photographs: No smile, hand on hip, one eyebrow raised. Now, obviously, all old people seem cool whenever we see black-and-white images of their younger selves. It's human nature to inject every old picture with positive abstractions. We can't help ourselves. We all do it. We want those things to be true, because we all hope future generations will have the same thoughts when they come across forgotten photographs of us. But this codger had genuine charisma. I'm sure of it. His cigarette looked delicious.

5 I never deduced this man's name. I'm sure I could have if I'd tried, but I never tried. Didn't seem important. When he came in from the lawn, he took off his damp flannel shirt and sat at the kitchen table in a wifebeater, reading the newspaper. He read every word of every story. It's been my experience that solitary people are generally more engaged with the mass media. They have no alternative.

6 As I tell this story, I sense that you are waiting for something to happen. You're wondering why I'm even talking about it. Quit asking yourself that question. It's not your job to wonder.

7 I watch him prepare lunch. He's wearing an apron and looking confident. He sears chicken in a pan with orange and yellow peppers. It smells fantastic. I thought he was making fajitas, but he just ate everything straight from the pan, standing over the sink. No need for tortillas. "This guy has really got it figured out," I thought.

8 The afternoon is long and hot, just like today. Grueling. But he doesn't use the air conditioner and he doesn't open any windows. He just sweats. He slouches toward the TV and manually turns on a baseball game, but the sound is muted and he barely follows the action. The half-Mexican plays a solitary game I'd seen only in second-rate cowboy movies: He places an upside-down Stetson on his living room floor and tosses a deck of cards into the opening, one by one. It's like he's a monk, but his particular religion venerates an extremely tedious god. I sit across the room and watch him toss cards. Around three o'clock, he looks up—not at me, but toward the ceiling.

"I know you're there," he says.

It was like a punch in the kidney. I'm dumbstruck. Nothing like this had ever happened before.

He tosses two more cards into the hat.

"I know you're there," he says again, this time without looking up. "You can't take all the credit for what happened to me."

This was a new problem.

9 For the next hour, I remain even more motionless than usual. I'm trying to figure out how this half-Mexican had deduced my presence—I had not been careless. Sometimes I make mistakes, but never due to carelessness. I always care. I wait for him to confront me again, or to call the police. I'm sure I can escape if I have to, but I'm hoping that won't be necessary. I want to see what happens. I want to know. Around six o'clock, he begins to make his supper. It's the exact same meal as lunch—chicken and peppers, cooked and consumed in the original pan. No plate required. The only difference was that he had a banana for dessert. As he peeled the banana, he spoke again.

"That wasn't funny," he says. "That's a bunch of lies. That's not the way it is in real life. We don't have dictators in this country."

It was not what I expected to hear.

I mean, I didn't expect to hear anything, but certainly not this.

"No lie," said the half-Mexican to no one.

The phone rings. It's like a woman's scream—the ringer was on the highest possible volume and the phone was right next to my head. He walks over to the phone and picks up the receiver. I become an air statue. It's crazy. He's standing less than three feet from where I'm sitting on the floor. If he knew I was in the room this afternoon, how could he not know I was *right there*? There's a mental disconnect.

"Quit following me," he immediately says into the phone. And then he hangs it up.

Ten seconds later, the phone screams again. He answers mid-ring.

"Listen," he says calmly. "If you don't quit following me, I will kill every man you've got. I'll burn down your house and rearrange your furniture. I will not pray for you and not for your children and not for your children's children. I'll get inside your dreams. I will contact Roberto Duran. We're very close friends. Did you know that? Do you understand me? Good."

Again, he hangs up the receiver. He seemed completely unfazed. This was a man with one omnidirectional emotion. A steadfast state of being we have no English word for: It's some kind of triangulation of boredom, regret, and dignity. Maybe the Germans have a word for it.

The half-Mexican walks up the stairs. I follow. I'm no longer worried about anything.

10 I follow him into this bedroom, which opens up to a balcony veranda. Again, I'm struck by how beautiful this home is—everything is expensive, everything is painted blue or gold. And it's *old*, or at least it looks that way. Disorganized, but classy. I don't know who decorated this place, but I'm pretty sure it wasn't the half-Mexican. A woman must have lived here, once. Maybe recently. There are decorative pillows everywhere.

The half-Mexican sits on his balcony. There are two plastic chairs out there, so I take the other one. We sit and we look. It's pleasant. The insufferable afternoon has broken into a comfortable dusk. His home overlooks a mostly empty, generally dilapidated park. This dilapidated park is built around a dilapidated basketball court—no nets on the rims, weathered wooden backboards, cracked pavement. There are two men playing on the court, and they're the only two men in the park. They're playing one-on-one, full court. The game is ragged and sloppy, but the men are playing hard. One man is black, one man is white. They're sort of reverse stereotypes: The white guy is slick and athletic, but he shoots bricks and seems out of control. The black guy really hustles and knows the fundamentals, but he's slow and predictable and tethered to the earth. Neither man is talented. They're two guys on the cusp of being too old to play basketball against other people, so they play each other instead. For every basket they make, they miss five. They're huffing and puffing too much to talk.

The half-Mexican and I watch the men play. Actually, that's not true—he watches the basketball game and I watch him. His eyes are intense. His mind is alive. I have no idea why this game is so interesting to him. I want to jump into his mind. I want to jump inside his skull and crouch behind his eyes. What is he seeing? I'll never know. It dawns on me that I'll *never* know, no matter how long I watch him. I start second-guessing my entire project. Here I am, sitting with a person who's alone, sitting right next to him, watching him think . . . and yet, nothing. I learn nothing.

"That's not how you do it," he suddenly says.

"He is talking at the basketball players," I think. My dreams have been answered, sort of.

"Don't do it like that," he says. "They tried that once before, in the seventies, with Carter and Echeverría. Nobody cared."

So maybe he's not talking to the basketball players.

Maybe he's not talking to anyone.

"I agree," he says. "I agree, you double-crazy donkey thief. You goddamn double hypocrite."

So now I'm in an awkward position. If the half-Mexican is an insane person—and it seems pretty obvious that he is—there's nothing to be learned from watching him warble. As a society, we expend way too much effort trying to understand the thought processes of crazy people. We're always trying to analyze suicide notes and to interview serial killers. It's a fool's game. Crazy people say things that don't make any rational sense, which is why they're classified as crazy. So why would rational attempts at semantic scrutiny teach us anything of value? It's like trying to use math to figure out history. It's like hypnotism or dream analysis. I certainly had no desire to watch a crazy person speak nonsense for another twenty-four hours. But there was something else at play here, and it was something that seemed worth investigating: Here was a man hearing voices from people who were not there. They were people he couldn't see, because they did not exist. But what if he heard voices from a person he couldn't see who *was* there? Would he be able to differentiate? I mean, this is a guy living in a false reality, right? He's communicating with someone he's constructed. But was the construction itself central to the conversation? Because if it was, that would mean—on some level—he'd be aware that there is a difference between having a voice inside your head and hearing a voice whose presence can't be explained.

I was just curious, I suppose.

I got up from my chair and walked behind where the half-Mexican was sitting. I didn't want the sound of my voice to originate from my chair, for whatever reason . . . it seemed better if I stood directly behind and slightly above him. It seemed fairer, somehow.

I had concerns. I was nervous. What if he jumped off the balcony? I remember thinking that. But he didn't seem the type to panic. There was still a coolness about him, regardless of his age. The man from the bathroom photograph was still the man in the chair. I was confident he'd keep it together.

I swallowed hard, and I spoke. I said: "Who will win this basketball game?"

No response. I said it again: "Who will win this basketball game?"

"The black doesn't have a chance," the half-Mexican said. Beyond that sentence, he offered no reaction whatsoever. It dawned on me that I'd spent too much time thinking about whether I should talk to him and not enough time considering what I'd actually say. I had no material.

"What's your name?" I asked.

"What are you doing in my house?" he said in response.

I tried to seem casual.

"I mean you no harm," I said. I'm not sure why I started talking like a biblical character.

Twenty seconds of silence.

"The black has no chance," he reiterated. "Too fat. Too soft a life for him. Must have a good cook for a wife. The *güero* is a cow, but he can run."

"*Güero*," I say. "You say *güero*. Are you from Mexico?"

"No," he replied. "I'm not Mexican. Only half. My mother was Mexican. My father, he was Irish. Not a drunk, but a fighter."

"You have a nice house," I say. "How did you get such a nice house?"

"I made oil," he said. "Way back when."

"You made oil? You *made* it?"

No response to this.

I knew what he had meant when he spoke. It was stupid of me to correct him.

We watched the basketball game for another five minutes. We didn't talk. We just listened to the faraway basketball sounds—the dribble drives and the missed fallaways. *Tock tock . . . tock TOCK TOCK clang.* It started to get dark. The two sweaty amateurs finally stopped playing and bent at the waist, smiling and panting like cartoon bloodhounds. It was impossible to tell who'd won. I don't think they were even keeping score.

"You can't stay here," said the half-Mexican. "I don't want you sleeping here. Not in my house. I have problems of my own."

"No worries," I said. "I will leave. I want to leave." I did not want to leave.

"Exit through the back door," he said. "And don't call anymore."

"I never called you," I said. "That wasn't me."

"Yes you did," he said. "You called me, and you watched me eat. Twice. You watched me eat twice. You're a pervert."

"Can I use the bathroom before I leave?"

"No," he said. "You can't. Why would I let a pervert in my lavatory? Why do you think you can do whatever you want?"

He made a good point, so I left. And I haven't gone back there, even though I want to. Who knows? Maybe I will tomorrow. There was just something about that guy. I know he's nuts, but there are a lot of people in America who are way, way nuttier. They're just more socialized. North America has more crazy people than every other industrialized continent combined, except for maybe Australia. I'd say 25 percent of our populace has craziness in the blood. It's genetic. It's historical. I mean, what kind of person immigrated to the New World? Not counting slaves, there were only four types, really: people who didn't think Europe was religious enough, people who thought they could make a lot of money, antisocial failures with no other option, and fruitcakes who thought risking their lives on an alien shore might make for an interesting adventure. Those are the four components of the American gene pool, and those are the four explanations behind everything good and everything bad that's ever happened here. Everything. I can't think of a single exception. So this guy, this aging half-Mexican—this guy isn't that outrageous. On balance, he's almost normal. He's probably more like me than you are.

Another Lapse in Judgment

When Y___ finished his story about the elderly biracial gentleman, I asked him a battery of straightforward questions about what he believed the story meant and why it felt significant to him. He didn't respond to either topic. "That should be self-evident" was the closest he came to an explanation. He left my office around eleven a.m. I immediately studied my notes from the session and tried to connect the dots; by this point, I'd followed Y___ to the bottom of the rabbit hole. I still worked under the assumption that every word he said and every thought he expressed had value. Around 11:20, I walked a few blocks to a (now closed) Caribou Coffee, intending to buy a caramel macchiato and return to my work. My next patient wasn't due until one o'clock. When I exited the coffeehouse, I was surprised to see Y___ sitting outside the establishment on a bench, drinking Coca-Cola from a glass bottle. We nodded hello and I began to walk away; like virtually all therapists, I don't fraternize with patients outside the office environment. But because nothing about my experience with Y___ had been normal, I suspended my own rules: I stopped, turned around, and engaged him in casual conversation. I assumed we would talk for ninety seconds.

I'm ashamed to admit that we spoke for almost ninety minutes. The time evaporated. I could have sat there all afternoon.

Obviously, I didn't record this encounter, as it happened by chance. I do not remember most of what we discussed—the conversation was lively, but much of it revolved around mundane subjects like regional housing prices, what neighborhoods in Austin were improving or declining, and various construction problems with local highways and thoroughfares. We talked about the coffeehouse itself, and about coffee in general, and about why Y___ never drank coffee despite his love for how it smelled.

However, three parts of our conversation remain vivid in my mind.

The first stemmed from a question I asked Y___ directly. What I asked him—in an admittedly understated way—was if he honestly believed he needed a therapist to help him. "You essentially talk to yourself for an hour, and you don't seem particularly interested in anything I say in response," I said. I told him that the goal of therapy is to take what we discuss in our session and apply it to the outside world, and that this didn't seem to be happening at all. I conceded that, all things considered, I wasn't completely qualified to work with someone engaged with the life he was living, and that no therapist on earth was trained to help a criminal scientist with the power of invisibility. I told him I loved working with him, but that I wondered if perhaps his state of mind would be better served by writing about his experiences firsthand (if for no other reason than to create a public record of what he was learning through his surveillance).

"If I wrote a book, people would hate it," he replied (*author's note: I'm paraphrasing these sentiments, but my memory is strong*). "There's something wrong with the way I write. It always makes people hate me. And you know, there *will* be a record of all this, eventually. A book will exist, or something akin to a book. But that won't happen for years. Decades, in all likelihood. I can't take notes during my observation periods, so there's no data to report. It's a problem. I mean, imagine if Jane Goodall had no access to pen and paper when she was in Tanzania. Imagine if she had no camera and no colleagues. That's how it is for me. All I can do is remember everything that I see, contextualize those images inside my head, and then recompose my theories several days later, when I return to my apartment. And most of the things I write in my journal aren't specific. Specificity is overrated. It distracts from the theme. The only details I try to record are incidents that suggest something larger and more meaningful than what they'd seem to suggest on the surface. Besides, I wouldn't want to write a book until I've finished with the entire project, and that will take forever. It will take my whole adult life. There can't be a book until there's nothing left for me to see. So until then, I just need someone to remind me that what I'm doing is essential. That's what I pay you for." He laughed at his own joke like a guest on a late-night talk show.

I informed him that was not my job. He said, "Well, of course it isn't. But we can all see the same things differently, can't we? I mean, that's a big part of it."

The second item we discussed was something I'd been thinking about nonstop since May 9: I wanted to know how it felt to be invisible (or at least what I considered "invisible"—I'm sure I used the word *cloaked* when I spoke with Y___ as to not create another argument). I remember thinking how strange it was that we were speaking about this in public; people were walking all around, completely oblivious to the doolally conversation we were having. It was like both of us were invisible already.

"It doesn't feel like anything," he said. "I mean, people can't see me, but I can see myself, even if my eyes tell me otherwise. I know where my arm is. When I wear the suit and I look at my arm, there it is. It looks like a fuzzy, subtle outline of a limb—like a photograph of an arm tacked to the wall of someone's kitchen, but then painted over with four coats of white latex. A visitor would never notice, but the woman who owns the house would always see it immediately. The only time it's strange is if I look at a mirror. If I look directly at myself in a mirror, I see something maddening, because my image just reflects back-and-forth-and-back-and-forth without any concrete substance to recognize. I see a human silhouette of light, and I just have to accept that the light is me. I generally try to avoid mirrors."

That's bizarre, I responded, but it wasn't what I wanted to know. That really wasn't the question I'd asked. I wanted to know how being invisible *felt*. I wanted to know if being invisible was something he liked, or just something he did.

"You're obsessed with feelings," he said. "Which is natural, considering your occupation. You traffic in feelings. And I'm not one of those retrograde automatons who insist they're immune to emotion until they end up having a stroke. I don't have contempt for emotion. But you misread things. People think about themselves constantly, but not in the way you imagine. The only time people are conscious of how they feel is when something hurts them. Most of the time, we train ourselves to ignore the entire sensation. I certainly don't believe it's possible to be successful at anything complicated if you let feelings dictate how you live. It always seems like you're trying to direct me toward some sort of grand realization. I always get the impression that you want me to say something incisive, like, *It makes me feel powerful* or *It makes me feel alone* or *It makes me feel special.* And all of those descriptions are true, some of the time. But none are true all of the time. Everything eventually becomes normal. The first time I realized I could enter someone's home, there was this predictable rush of power. There was an immediate recognition that I could do anything I wanted. I could kill a man and never be captured. I could rape a woman and she'd assume it was just a horrific nightmare. You think about things like this when you're different from the rest of society. You think about them all the time. But the fact of the matter is that *I'm not a rapist,* and the fact that I suddenly had the means to become a world-class rapist wasn't going to change that. We always end up being ourselves, somehow. I was who I was long before I consciously became the person I am. Being unseen makes me feel different than other people, but I've always felt different than other people. Invisibility isn't the issue. The difference is that I've always possessed the single-minded dedication to make an impossible scenario plausible. I have the power to invent my own life. Even if I'd spent the past twenty years sitting on a beach and drinking myself stupid, I would still feel powerful and alone and special. Those are simply the intermittent qualities of who I always am, regardless of how I feel about it."

I was electrified by Y____'s rehearsed bragging; it reminded me of the first time I ever became legitimate friends with one of my college professors outside of class. I wanted him to keep talking, even though the conversation was one-sided and pedantic. I know that must sound masochistic, but there's no influence like the force of personality: It overwhelms everything, even when it defies common sense. Y___ had an effortless, extemporaneous way of explaining complex, personal things. He contradicted me so often (and so deftly) that I started to feel good anytime he agreed with me; I awarded his rare compliments much more weight than they deserved. That imbalance made every conversation charged, which might explain what happened next. This was the third part of our conversation I remember, and it's the part I remember most.

"There's actually something I wanted to talk to you about," Y___ said. "It might seem inappropriate, but I feel like it's necessary."

"Go ahead," I said. "Nothing is inappropriate."

"You say that now," he said. "But here's the thing: I know it's common for therapy patients to misdirect their feelings. I know that therapy patients often develop sexual feelings toward their therapists, simply because they're usually confused people who've never had an experience where they felt open and vulnerable around another person. This is true, no?"

"Yes," I said. "That sometimes happens. Sometimes the misdirection is paternal or maternal, and sometimes it's intimate or romantic."

"Exactly," he said. "Now, the fact that I'm bringing this up probably makes what I'm about to say abundantly obvious."

"Yes," I said. "I think I know what you're getting it."

"What am I getting at?"

"I think you're trying to tell me that you are experiencing misplaced romantic feelings directed toward me."

"Yes," he said. "Obviously. We're all aware of this cliché. But here is my real question—are these misplaced feelings going to create a problem within the context of our work? Are you going to be able to handle my misplaced attraction? Because I'm sure it's misplaced. It has to be."

This confused me. It confused me in two different ways, but I only talked about one.

"Well, you're the one experiencing the attraction," I said. "*You* feel the attraction, and you seem to understand what it means. I don't get the sense that you're confused by what's happening, nor is this the first time I've ever had it happen with a male patient. So I don't see any problem from my end. It's nothing I haven't seen before. The only problem would be if this makes you uncomfortable."

"No, you're not getting it," said Y____. "It's never going to be a problem from my side, because feelings don't dictate my behavior. I'm not like that. What I'm worried about is the possibility of my misdirected feelings becoming uncomfortable for you, and if that discomfort will impact how freely we talk. If it will impact the things I can say to you."

"Like what? I don't follow." Now, certainly, I *did* know what Y____ meant when he said these words. I did follow. I followed completely. But I pretended not to. I suppose I wanted to hear what he was going to say. Sometimes I pretend I don't know certain things about myself in order to force other people to directly voice the compliments I secretly need to hear.

"Okay, here's a hypothetical: Let's say I started thinking about you. Let's say I started to have dreams about you. Sexual dreams. Should this be something I express? Keep in mind I'm not a sexual person."

"Of course," I said.

"You say that now. But what if I told you that I liked to think about you when I masturbated? What if I said that you were what I fantasized about, and that I could orgasm only by thinking about you?"

"We've never talked about your fantasy life," I said. I was a little staggered by the degree to which this dialogue was escalating, mostly because I hadn't expected Y____'s language to be so specific. "I suppose I'd be interested in your willingness to talk about things like that, since, until now, those subjects have always been out of play." I found myself wishing we were having this conversation in my office. Amazingly, I suddenly wondered if Y—— had somehow orchestrated this encounter so that it would happen in public. I felt a sensation of spontaneous paranoia.

"So none of this will be an issue," he asked. "This is all standard?"

"Yes," I said. "I want you to feel safe."

"Even if my thoughts are grotesque? Even if they're dark and detail-oriented? Even if I said something like, 'Well, see you next week, Victoria. I'm just going to go home and masturbate right now. I'm just going to imagine putting my hand up your skirt while I masturbate. I'm going to imagine you're not wearing underwear, and that I can faintly feel your pubic hair with my fingertips. See you next week.' Are you saying that these are things you'd want me to tell you?"

"Not necessarily," I said as impassively as possible. "I don't *want* you to tell me that. Unless you think those details are meaningful, or if you feel a need to say them aloud in order to own them. If those thoughts are important to you, they're important to me. But what *I want* has nothing to do with this. That's not our relationship."

The skin on my face felt warm. Was I blushing? I prayed I was not. This had gone too far.

"That's good to hear, Vicky," said Y——. "Reassuring. Very reassuring. You are a pro. And—like I said—sorry if that seemed inappropriate. Like I said, I'm not a sexual person. I'm not one of those sexual people you read about in magazines. I was just curious, and it seemed relevant."

About five minutes after this exchange, I excused myself and returned to my office to wait for my next patient. Y—— walked in the other direction, leaving his empty Coke bottle on the ground. He waved goodbye with two fingers. I felt good and bad. I knew I'd made another mistake.

June 20:
A memory or a clue?

[This is simply a straightforward excerpt from our June 20 session. I kept waiting for Y___ to revisit the strangeness of our most recent conversation outside the coffeehouse, but he never did. At least not directly.]

Sometimes I'd follow people in hotels. Hotels are much less complicated than residences, because of the access: You just walk around the halls during the afternoon, you locate a maid cleaning the room of a late checkout, and you stroll in while she finishes the bathroom. They always clean the bathroom last. Easy as pie. It was also easier to find decent food, because people leave the remains of their room service outside the door. Sometimes I'd also take snacks from the minibar. Hotels make you lazy.

The problem, of course, is that people aren't natural when they stay in hotels. It's not a realistic depiction of life. The ability to just drop towels on the floor changes the way people view themselves. It causes everyone to act like they're rich. Plus, most people staying in hotels are only in town for business, so they just sit around and look at the Internet all night. They lie on top of the covers and watch HBO. You can usually tell what social class a hotel guest comes from by how long they stay in the shower and how much they appreciate the mattress. If they're staying in a hotel alone, men inevitably masturbate,[10] but women only do so half the time. That might sound reductionist and overstated, but my data is irrefutable.

The other downside to working hotels, of course, is the inescapable likelihood of ending up in a room with two people instead of one. That's when you *really* see people who aren't acting like themselves. When it's a couple on vacation, you can tell a lot about their relationship within the first ten minutes of arrival: If they almost have sex as soon as they enter the room, there's a 95 percent chance they'll have sex later that night; if they just unload their luggage and leave for dinner, they probably won't have sex all weekend. To be honest, I didn't learn much from studying hotel patrons. It was kind of like trying to study the natural behavior of African elephants by visiting a zoo in Portland.

However, I do recall one episode that happened at a Radisson, right here in town. It wasn't an intentional discovery and it didn't fulfill my original goal, but it was a good day. I don't know if you've even been inside the Radisson on Cesar,[11] Vicky, because . . . well, why would you go to a hotel in the city where you already live? But there's a TGI Friday's on the ground floor. I saw this serious forty-something woman eating there, all by herself on a Friday afternoon. She didn't look like she was thanking God for anything. My assumption, of course, was she was staying at the Radisson. And there was something brittle about her I appreciated: It looked like she was unpleasant on purpose. She wore an earth-tone pantsuit and never looked away from the newspaper, even while smearing her chicken fingers with honey mustard. All business, all the time. I decided she'd be my subject for the night; I was drawn to her severity. She seemed like she wouldn't have the patience to become a different person, even when she wasn't at home. I waited for her to pay the bill, and I noticed she didn't charge the food to

10. Was this an aborted segue to our previous conversation? I thought it might be, but it was not. He didn't even look at me when he said this.
11. 111 Cesar Chavez Street.

her room. In fact, she paid cash, which meant she wasn't even on an expense account. That was my first clue that something was afoot.

She leaves the TGI Friday's and walks up to the next level. The mezzanine. The mezzanine? The mezzanine. She enters a conference room. The door is propped open, so I follow. There are maybe ten other people in the room. At first I think, "Goddammit. I've walked into a fucking business conference." But everybody there seems too unalike, and one of these people is clearly a teenager. They all nod hello, but nobody says anyone else's name and nobody shakes hands. About five minutes after five o'clock, they close the door and start talking. For a split second, I'm certain I'm at an AA meeting, which is only slightly better than a business meeting. But nobody talks about being drunk or wanting a drink or regretting things they've lost through drunkenness. These stories are more oblique.

"As you all know, I've been a Little League coach for the past three summers," one man began. He looked like a person from a Nabisco commercial: a good-to-great-looking guy. No facial hair. Nice shirt, no tie. Monotone voice. I don't want to stereotype, but I remember thinking he looked like somebody who used to go to Jimmy Buffett concerts, but only during college. He looked like the kind of guy who traded his SUV for a Saab the same day gas prices went above two dollars a gallon. He looked like the type who hated Obama for completely nonracist reasons.

"My players are all five and six years old," he continued. "It's a 'coach-pitch' league. What this means is that—as their coach—I pitch to my own players. The opposing coach pitches to his own players when they're up to bat. We used to have the little guys hit off a tee, but the league decided that this format was better for their development. Basically, the idea is that—as their coach—I know which kids are good and which kids are bad, and I can challenge or assist them accordingly. We want every kid to know how it feels to get a hit, but we also want them to learn how competition works. That's the concept. It's a good concept, maybe.

"So, we're playing a game this last Wednesday afternoon. It's tight. Our games are five innings long, and we're behind nine to seven in the bottom of the fifth. Two outs, top of the order. This kid named Tommy is our lead-off batter. Tommy is a wonderful kid—quiet, polite. Plays second base. Looks like Justin Bieber, so all the older kids give him shit. I lob him a fat one, and he whacks a single. Nice. Great. I'm happy for Tommy. The next batter is his friend Matt. Matt's a snot, but funny as hell. Reads *Batman* during practice, or whoever the new Batman is supposed to be now. Talks a lot. Talks all the time. Talks about things no one cares about, like some book his grandfather gave him about Vietnam. I love Mattie. Matt already thinks he's interesting. I basically give him the same fat pitch, and *bang*. Another single. So now Tommy's on second and Mattie's on first. It's getting exciting, you know? This is about as tense as a baseball game between kindergarteners can be. The third batter is Cory. Now, the only thing I really know about Cory's life is that his mom is way too attractive to be forty. But Cory's a good player, at least for his age, so I challenge him some. I throw the ball with a little velocity, because I know he can handle it. He pops it straight up, so it looks like the game's over. But the third baseman—remember, these are six-year-olds—totally misplays the ball. It hits him on the top of the head. So now Tommy's at third, Matt's on second, and Cory's on first. Bases loaded. The sacks are juiced. It's a real game. All the parents are suddenly interested. I can tell, because they've stopped checking their cell phones.

"Now, our clean-up hitter is Toby. Toby is almost seven, but he looks like he's ten. He's far and away the best player on our team. We probably should have moved him up to a higher division. I have no doubt he'll be some kind of star by the time he's sixteen. You can already tell he's a jock by the way he walks. But, you know, right now, he's still six. He acts like a six-year-old, even though he's tall and thick and coordinated. And here he is, with the chance to be a six-year-old hero. Here's Toby, in prime position to win the game and be the king of the postgame McDonald's trip. And I want this to happen. In my mind, I want Toby to hit a goddamn grand slam, because he'd remember that forever, or at least until junior high. I'm his coach. My responsibility is his development. But something always stops me from *feeling* this way, even if my mind tells me otherwise. I remembered when I was in high school, when I pitched in the state playoffs. Everyone expected me to close games down, because I was the closer. I was the Mariano Rivera of the Class B San Antonio Catholic League. That's who I was, and that's still how I feel. I know I'm not the same person I was in high school, but sometimes I am. And at that moment—just like always—I quit caring about the economic growth of my insurance dealership or my wonderful wife or my own goddamn kids. I just want to be me. So when I saw Toby digging his stupid little size-five cleats into the dirt, it pissed me off. Fuck that kid. Fuck him. There was no way Toby was going to do this. There's just no way. Time to close the door.

"I lace the first pitch on the inside corner of the plate. Good cheese. I can still bring it. Strike one. Our sixty-pound catcher almost fell backward when it hit his glove. I can tell it kind of scares Toby, which must have been my goal? Next, I throw a breaking ball that runs outside, but he chases it for strike two. I mean, what does Toby know about breaking pitches? I'm sure he can't even spell the word *breaking*. I waste my third pitch high and away, but then I blow off his doors with a split-finger fastball, right down the gullet. The bat never even gets off his shoulder. Strike three. Game over. I get the save against a child on my own team. I'm a monster.

"Later, I tell Toby that he shouldn't have chased strike two, that he needs to be more patient at the plate, but that—next time—I'm sure he'll come through and be the big hero. I let him have extra McNuggets—everyone else got six, but I let Toby have ten. To be honest, he seemed totally okay with what happened. Unchanged. But I felt awful. I felt the way I always do, whenever this happens."

As the Nabisco man finishes his story, I see other people around the table nodding. They all relate to this, somehow. A long-haired man starts yammering; he tells a story about how his wife recently composed a song on the piano, and he goes on and on about how the song was so beautiful. Much better than anything he'd ever written for his own band. Far more sophisticated and nuanced than anything he'd ever created himself. He's clearly proud of his wife. But his wife will never know how proud he was, because he refused to tell her. Instead, he told his wife it is "kind of okay" and that it seemed like something off a late Wings album that Linda McCartney might have co-written. Again, everyone around the table nodded away. The teenage girl spoke third. She said she recently got a 97 on a trigonometry test, but that two other girls in the class got a 100 because they showed their work and she did not. This made her hate the other two students. She could not believe they were being rewarded for doing things on paper that she could do in her head. As a result, she logged onto Facebook under a fake identity and claimed these two girls were lesbians and that she saw them kissing after a National Honor Society meeting. She wanted to ruin their lives and stop them from getting into Rice. She said she felt guilty about this, but not really.

It turns out I had stumbled into a support group for people with "competition disorder," a disorder I had never previously considered. Every person's anecdote expressed an overwhelming sense of helpless entrapment—they all wanted to know how it felt not to obsess over winning. They talked about how they couldn't stop watering and mowing their lawns. They talked about their need to drive faster than the flow of traffic and how they always ruin Christmas by overreacting to minor rules infractions during games of Apples to Apples. The woman I spotted in the TGI Friday's spoke last. She worked for a commodities broker and made $400,000 a year. Her salary meant nothing to her. "I don't like spending money," she said. "I only like watching it accrue." She had no husband and no children. Her social life revolved around her co-workers, all of whom she despised.

"They're so unmotivated," she said. "They smile at me, so I smile back. They ask me to lunch and sometimes I go. I need food like anyone else. They talk about how much things cost and about how their dogs act like cats and about which of our co-workers they suspect are sexist or racist or sympathetic to Elisabeth Hasselbeck, and they all try to convince me to visit their nondenominational churches. It's funny that somebody else mentioned Facebook . . . two years ago, they all told me I needed to join Facebook. They said it was ridiculous that I'd never joined, particularly since my divorce. 'This is just how it is now,' they said. I told them I was too old for that shit. But they kept *insisting* how great it was, how it was no longer just for college kids, how it was this underrated crowd-sourcing resource, how it wasn't what I imagined, how it was this wonderful diversion and this important business tool. So I surrendered. I joined Facebook. And you know what? It turns out the only reason they wanted me to join was so they could show me pictures of their children without having to ask if I was interested in seeing them. This is why Facebook caught on with adults: It's designed for people who want to publicize their children without our consent.

"I suppose I don't mind chatting at the office. It's painless. I just repeat whatever they've already said with different words, and that's usually enough to satisfy their curiosity. They count that as conversation. They're naturally satisfied. I listen to their stories and look for weaknesses. I plot against them. They probably know I'm plotting, but they don't mind. They don't even have the tenacity to think I'm a bitch. They don't care if they lose. Honestly, they don't. They just go home and upload more baby pictures. It's crazy. It's so crazy. This is the life I'm supposed to envy? No way. No fucking way. I want to tell them this. I want to say it to their face. Which, I realize, is unnecessary. It's not their fault, I suppose. They can't help being satisfied with who they are. And it's not like my life is anything to brag about. You know what I do most nights? I watch *There Will Be Blood* in my bedroom. Not the whole movie. Just the middle part. The part where the oilman is talking to his fake brother by the fire and says, '*I have a competition in me. I want no one else to succeed.*' I watch that scene over and over and over again. It's track five on the DVD. It feels so good to watch. I like watching it so much that it scares me. I know this is pathetic, but I wish that oilman was my co-worker. I wish he was in my life. I want to live in a world where *that guy* is normal. I want to sleep with *that guy*. That's who I envy. And that's why I'm such a mess. That's why I'm here. I know it's wrong to feel like this, even though this is how I want to feel."

The meeting ended after an hour. The group left en masse. I stayed behind, unseen, sort of dumbfounded by what I'd heard. Our world is really backward, Victoria. It's backward. Look what society does. It takes the handful of people who know how to succeed and makes them feel terrible for being different. Everyone is supposed to be mediocre, I guess. Everyone is supposed to be dragged into the middle—either down from their success, or up from their self-imposed malfunction. These people didn't need a support group. These people needed someone to tell them they were okay. They needed to be told that the morality they've been forced to accept is manufactured and fake, and that their guilt is just the penalty for not being a failure. Do you know who was the smartest president of the twentieth century, Victoria? Do you know who was the greatest intellectual? Nixon. The bipartisan historians all agree it was Richard Nixon. Bill Clinton is probably second. He was a Rhodes scholar. So this means the two smartest presidents of the twentieth century were the only one we forced to resign and the only one we impeached. That's how it goes. That teenage girl? The one who started the lezbo rumor? She could be president. She's presidential material. She's got brains and she's got guts. But that will never happen. The world will convince her that it's better to lose half the time, because losers are lovable. That's the phrase, right? *Lovable loser*.

I tell you what, Vicky: Sometimes it's terrifying to see how things really are. It makes me want to run away. I mean, I know I'll never get proper credit for the things I've done and the truths I've learned. We both know I won't. People want Santa Claus, and I'm not Santa Claus. I'm more like the guy who invented his magic fucking sleigh. I'm the guy who does the impossible things that need to be done, so that all the normal people can go back to sleep.

[A Personal Aside]

Though I am reticent to discuss my own life (even when it unavoidably intersects with my time with Y——), I need to outline a few pertinent details about what was happening to me during this specific period, purely for the sake of transparency.

I will be brief.

As stated earlier, I had not told anyone—including my husband—about what was happening with Y——. I lied to my own longtime therapist (the aforementioned Dr. Dolanagra) and claimed that Y—— had ended treatment without explanation in May. This required an even denser web of lies: I now had to come up with an ongoing weekly serial for Dr. Dolanagra about what was supposedly happening in my day-to-day life. I initially tried expressing boilerplate complaints about my marriage, but that made me more depressed than I already was. I tried talking about my own childhood, but I couldn't locate any conflict (relative to most, my adolescence was devoid of adversity). I finally made up a crisis about a fictional high school girl I was supposedly mentoring who was considering an abortion (I built a composite "troubled teen" from various ex-patients and tossed in a few plot elements I remembered from *If These Walls Could Talk*—I named the girl "Joan" and focused on the political implications). To my amazement, Dolanagra was totally bamboozled—to this day, she still asks how Joan is coping. I could probably teach an improv class.

My husband, however, was harder to fool. He sensed something strange and hidden; our interactions were now punctuated by long stretches of unnatural silence. Ever since May 9, I'd become a different person—I spent more time alone and went to bed two hours after John was already sleeping. I'd been in a book club, but I quit; I stopped following the news and avoided phone calls. Everything outside of my imagination seemed gray; the world inside my head was more electrifying than the world I had to live in. I started spending days by myself, walking along the lake to the Congress Avenue bridge in order to watch the bats. Every night, thousands of Mexican bats take flight from beneath this bridge, blanketing the sky like an undulating cape. Three thousand bats becoming one massive superbat, a mosquito-eating sky-creature. I did this dusk after dusk after dusk. It was an excuse to be alone and an opportunity to think about Y____. He had become the center of my professional life (and, by extension, my life as a whole).

In the weeks that followed our meeting outside the Caribou Coffee, I started to question my own feelings toward Y____; I started to wonder if I was becoming too entertained by his stories (and if that was damaging my ability to work with other patients and communicate with other people). When we met on June 20, I waited to see if he'd formally revisit the "misplaced" issues we'd casually discussed. I placed the responsibility on Y____ to bring it up. When he ignored me entirely, I decided it was time to tell John what was happening. Hiding this information seemed worse than anything I'd technically done. Moreover, I needed to know if this was really happening. Was I losing my mind? If I was, I knew John would tell me directly. He never has any compunctions about calling me crazy.

When I told John that I needed to talk to him and that he would need to sit down, his initial response was cold and predictable: "Are you having an affair?" he asked without emotion. I said I was not. "Are you sick?" he asked next. "Do you have a disease?" Again, I told him no. "You are not going to be able to guess what I'm going to say," I assured him. "Quit trying. And no matter how you feel, this information must remain only between us."

I told him almost everything.

I told him how my relationship with Y____ had started and what I originally suspected his problem was. I told him about our initial in-person interactions. Obviously, most of what I told him involved the experience of May 9, which felt liberating to say aloud. It was like removing a megalith from the roof. I recounted every detail I could remember about that morning. By the end, I was almost shaking.

I expected John to disbelieve my story, in the same way I never believed Y____ until he proved otherwise. Amazingly, John did not seem skeptical (perhaps he was, but he didn't show it). I also expected him to have a million questions, but he had only a few.

"So, he's not transparent. Am I right? He can be invisible, or mostly invisible. But he's not *transparent*. True? When he eats, you can't see the food going down his invisible throat and lodging in his invisible stomach. You can't see through his invisible skin. Am I right?"

I told him that this was accurate. I reiterated how annoyed Y____ always became anytime I referred to him as an invisible man. Oddly (or maybe predictably), John empathized with that sentiment.

"Is there any chance that this is some kind of hoax?" was his next question. I told him that I couldn't *prove* that it wasn't a hoax, but that I was 99.9 percent certain Y____ was the person he claimed to be. I had not seen him with my own eyes.

It was John's third question that threw me off balance.

"So who is this person?"

I told John I didn't understand the query.

"You can't just become an invisible man these days," he said. "I don't know if you ever could, but you certainly can't now. We live in a bureaucratic nightmare. I mean, does he have a permanent residence? People can't disappear anymore. Does he have a Social Security card? How does he pay taxes? Did he fake his own death? What happens when you plug his name into Google? At the very least, would it be possible to verify his academic records, or his employment in Hawaii? That information must be online. Am I right? I'm right. Who is this person? Who is this person, *really*?"

I told John I did not know the answer to these questions. I told him that our relationship was not focused on those kinds of specifics, and that he hadn't even filled out his insurance form. I told him I wasn't a police officer, and that Y____ came to me for help. I told him that all of those technical details were—on balance—insignificant, particularly when compared with the experience of being inside a room with a person you can't see. Mostly, I was annoyed by John's unsupportive posture. I was annoyed by John himself. Why weren't my personal anxieties worth his concern? I'll never understand why his first reaction is to immediately ask more questions. It's like he can't think about problems in any other way.

"You need to wonder about these things," John said. "If what you're saying is all true—and I have no reason to doubt you, because you're not the kind of person who tells stories—then you need to recognize the import of the situation you're in. True? This is major. This is a totally new landscape. You are the emotional confidante of a *phenomenon*. This needs to be investigated. You have a civic responsibility to investigate this. Am I right? I'm right."

I disagreed with John, at least at first. I told him that my foremost responsibility was to the patient, and that I did not treat interesting clients any differently than uninteresting clients (this was a lie, but it's what I said). John seemed completely oblivious as to why I was telling him about Y——. He never tries to see things from my perspective. He doesn't have that ability.

"That's the wrong way to think," he said. "You're a smart person, but you're not being smart right now. Don't take that the wrong way, but it's true. You're overlooking the obvious. This is not a normal scenario. This is a unique case. Traditional rules don't apply. I would strongly advocate investigating who this person is and what they're really doing. I mean, look: This man does not seem to be seeing you for conventional reasons. True? It doesn't even seem like he's coming to you for the reasons he himself purports. Right? True? Right? You're not handling this case correctly."

I was stunned by this accusation. It was consistent with John's personality, but he'd never before questioned my professional abilities with such directness. It escalated our debate into a far larger argument, much of which gridlocked around issues completely unrelated to Y——: John's unwillingness to take my career seriously, our unresolved decision to remain childless, the way our age difference and racial experience creates an imbalance in our marriage (John is thirteen years my senior and African-American), John's overall condescending tone toward almost everyone we know (particularly my closest friends), and a bunch of complaints and accusations I can't even remember. We fought all night, and—though we both apologized the next morning—it placed a strain on our relationship that had not been there before. It was definitely the most problematic stretch of our problematic marriage.

When John and I got engaged, I knew we were very different people. I told that to everyone at our wedding, and they all made the proper "opposites attract" jokes during their toasts. But it turns out that we were remarkably similar, at least about things that didn't matter. I'd been wrong about all the minor differences I assumed would cause friction: We had different politics, but our fundamental perceptions about fairness were the same; we loved different books and movies, but we had similar ideas about what made a book or movie good; we came from different places, yet we had identical views about how our upbringings shaped us. On a day-to-day level, our marriage has been easier than I would have ever expected. But what I didn't realize on my wedding day—and what John continues to deny, even now, after everything that's happened—is that we're profoundly different in one metronomic respect: There's nothing I care about more than how other people feel, which is the one thing John doesn't care about at all. Or, to put it more on the nose: There's nothing I care about more than how other people (and particularly John) feel about their lives, and there's nothing that interests John less than how anyone (myself included) feels about any issue that doesn't involve him directly. It has nothing to do with my love or his love or loving or levels of love. It's just the way I am and the way he is. All my friends saw this when John and I were dating, but I never did and they never told me.

It took me a while to accept this. Maybe I'm still trying.

I expose these things not to embarrass John or myself, and not because I feel any need to live a public life. I expose them because it had an impact on things that happened later.

Pseudo-Historiography

[What follows is an excerpt from June 27. The session initially dragged, as Y___ seemed less talkative than usual. During a lull in the conversation, I asked Y___ something I'd been wondering: What, exactly, did he feel he was learning from these observations, since he was always so adamant about the pedagogic component of his invisibility. In other words, outside of any espoused scientific revelations, what was he personally learning about himself? He immediately perked up at this query and became the Y___ Character, lecturing in his bombastic, self-aggrandizing style. When I read this transcript now, it strikes me as highly rehearsed. He also didn't answer my question at all. But if this exchange was scripted (and had no relationship to my query), why did he save it until I specifically asked my question?]

Roommate situations were strange. This became a problem whenever I tried to observe someone in their twenties—I'd select a target and I'd follow him into his life, only to realize he wasn't living alone. So then I'd have this claustrophobic situation where two or three or four people were interacting in a small, enclosed area. It was formal and completely fake. Plus, my likelihood of being discovered increased dramatically. If a person is alone, you can get away with a lot. You can get away with more than you should. You can sneeze, and the person will hear you sneeze, and you will see them hearing you sneeze. It will be abundantly clear that they heard an unexplainable noise. They will perk up and look around. They'll give the whole room the once-over. But that's as far as it goes: They notice something, and then they go back to whatever they were doing before. They assume they're hearing things. They return to a state of nonnoticing. But once you have two people in the room, every noise is unforgiving. If you sneeze, the couple will look at each other and wordlessly ask, "Did you hear that?" And then they start wondering. People trust their friends more than they trust themselves. That was something I established straight away. And you'd think that would make them feel more secure, but it doesn't. It has the opposite effect: Unconditional trust destroys relationships. Two people meet as open-minded strangers. They like each other, so they grow closer. It feels good. They become unguarded. Eventually, the two strangers become two friends. But once that boundary of distrust is removed from the equation, they start to learn who the other person really is, and then each starts to resent the other. They end up feeling more distant as friends than they were as strangers. I've seen this happen a million times.

Still, I must be honest: I sometimes enjoyed observing roommates, even when it contradicted my premise. I spent so much time watching lonely people do nothing that group dynamics were a nice change of pace. That said, it's a little shocking how rarely most roommates speak to each other. Especially guys—guys will spend five hours in the same enclosed space and say nothing. Men tend to have zero interest in the lives of others. Women talk about what's on TV, and about boyfriends or potential boyfriends, and about various concerns they have over haircuts. It's disturbing how accurate gender clichés tend to be. They're self-perpetuating. We all direct so much effort toward undermining gender clichés and punching holes through stereotypes, but all that does is remind people how tenacious those sentiments are. Arguing that they're false actually makes people more aware that they're true. I mean, just watch any husband arguing with his wife about something insignificant; listen to what they say and watch how their residual emotions manifest when the fight is over. It's so formulaic and unsurprising that you wouldn't dare re-create it in a movie. All the critics would mock it. They'd all say the screenwriter was a hack who didn't even try. This is why movies have less value than we like to pretend—movies can't show reality, because honest depictions of reality offend intelligent people.

The reality I got to see was not "movie reality." The reality I saw was just reality, without quotes. You want to know what I really learned? I learned that people don't consider time alone as part of their life. Being alone is just a stretch of isolation they want to escape from. I saw a lot of wine-drinking, a lot of compulsive drug use, a lot of sleeping with the television on. It was less festive than I anticipated. My view had always been that I was my most alive when I was totally alone, because that was the only time I could live without fear of how my actions were being scrutinized and interpreted. What I came to realize is that people *need* their actions to be scrutinized and interpreted in order to feel like what they're doing matters. Singular, solitary moments are like television pilots that never get aired. They don't count. This, I think, explains the fundamental urge to get married and have kids, or even just the need to feel popular and respected. We're self-conditioned to require an audience, even if we're not doing anything valuable or interesting. I'm sure this started in the 1970s. I know it did. I think Americans started raising offspring with this implicit notion that they *had* to tell their children, "You're amazing, you can do anything you want, you're a special person." They thought they'd be bad parents if they didn't. They felt a responsibility to give unlimited emotional support. But—when you really think about it—that emotional support only applies to the experience of living in public. We don't have ways to quantify ideas like "amazing" or "successful" or "lovable" without the feedback of an audience. Nobody sits by himself in an empty room and thinks, "I'm amazing." It's impossible to imagine how that would work. But being "amazing" is supposed to be what life is about. As a result, the windows of time people spend by themselves become these meaningless experiences that don't really count. It's filler. They're deleted scenes.

Every once in a while, I'd come across someone who was really happy when they were alone. That was always a little beautiful, but also a little confusing. You know who seemed happiest alone? Consumers. It wasn't the people who read the best books or had the most hobbies. It was the people who bought the most bullshit. I know there's this image in our collective unconscious about the depressed millionaire living alone in an ivory tower, drinking himself drunk on four-thousand-dollar bottles of wine, sadly trying to purchase his childhood sleigh in order to feel something real. But that's a lie. As it turns out, that lonely millionaire is way happier than the lonely pauper. It's not even close, and the explanation is obvious: The rich man can buy things, and those things distract him from loneliness. The rich can take vacations, which isn't nearly as essential to day-to-day happiness as the process of *looking forward* to all the vacations you'll experience later. They have more comfortable furniture and better TVs, and those objects are the single man's sanctuary. They don't need to cook, so cooking becomes this gratuitous, exotic activity. Poor people hate cooking. It's just another chore they need to complete when they get home from the job they hate. But entitled people love to cook. It makes them feel competent and earthy. Of course, rich people don't love cleaning, so they hire maids to do that. That's another thing that really sets the happy apart from the unhappy—how clean the house is, and how much effort it takes to keep the house clean. I've seen a lot of rich people come home to a clean house that they had nothing to do with—the maid service did everything while they were away. You can see the happiness on their face when they open the door and smell the Lemon Pledge. That smell reminds them they're rich. Here again, this all comes back to parenting. That's my theory. The central mistake parents make is telling their kids that making money is not as important as being happy, as if those two things are somehow opposed or disconnected. Movies and TV perpetuate that sentiment, because it makes for counterintuitive plots and happier endings. What parents *should* be telling their kids is that these things *are* connected. They should tell them the single easiest way to be happy is to make a shitload of money. Money doesn't guarantee happiness, but poverty doesn't even come close. I mean, sure, a lot of rich people are unhappy, but sometimes they don't even notice how unhappy they are. They're too busy online shopping. They're too occupied trying to figure out a better recipe for jambalaya. You *can* buy love—not completely, but partially. You can, and never believe otherwise.

Heavy Dudes

[This was the turning point. From the moment Y__ entered the room, our July 11 session was irregular (we had not met on July 4 because of the holiday). Nothing was easy. Y__ sat down, stood up, sat down, stood up, paced around, and told a few nonpersonal anecdotes that seemed irrelevant and disjointed. He was agitated. He kept starting and ending stories, often criticizing himself for wasting my time. This was unusual; he rarely cared about my time. Had Y__ ingested some sort of stimulant that morning? His behavior suggested as much. About twelve minutes into the session, he sat back down, sighed, and dramatically shifted gears. He started telling me a different kind of story—his tone was muted, but the details were rich. It took almost two hours, but I didn't restrict him.

The way Y__ told this story was not remotely chronological; he began in the middle and filled in contextual details intermittently, often repeating the same information multiple times, trampling his own speech patterns. For the purpose of clarity, I have reorganized the story into a straight narrative and removed the gaps and repetitions. The specific time of each statement is in parenthesis, along with its sequence within the original telling.]

1 This is something I've wanted to discuss with you for a while. Of the things that bother me, this is what bothers me most. I mean, I know what happened wasn't my fault, even less so than what happened with Valerie, but it eats at me. Unlike the Val situation, this experience was absolutely a net negative. If I could reverse what happened, I might. In fact, I would. **(12:40 [29])**

2 Flying had become too risky. I had a close call. I'd sneezed on an American Airlines flight to Boston—twice—and everything went pear-shaped. There was a moment when I actually thought there might be a physical altercation on the plane, because a stewardess knew something unusual was happening. I could tell what she was thinking: She was thinking, "There is a terrorist hiding in this fuselage." I could read it on her face. It's exactly what she was trained to think. My only option was to crawl underneath the last row of seats and sweat it out. That was a terrible two hours. After that, I started driving myself everywhere, but that started to have an impact on the process. My agency was unconsciously dictating whom I was observing. I was poisoning the sample by driving to places I'd already been. I decided a better strategy would be to stow away with random people when they passed through Austin. It felt more egalitarian. That was my thinking at the time. (**11:14** [1])

3 Do you care about music? Do you *remotely* care about music? Do you at least read the A & E section of the newspaper? Do you pick up the *Chronicle*? Even if you don't, I'm sure you know about the music festival that happens here every March. It's impossible to live here and not know about it. You can't avoid it, so I'm just going to assume you know what I'm talking about. As a resident, I'm sure it annoys you. It used to annoy me. But it's a great weekend for my objectives, because it makes stowing away supereasy. That weekend, every single year, there are literally hundreds of vans and U-Hauls parked downtown, all filled with equipment—guitars, drum kits, amplifiers, everything. And because these bands tend to play three or four shows over the course of the weekend, the vans get loaded and unloaded constantly. I just amble around Sixth Street on Sunday night and crawl into the back of somebody's shitty van. If the van was a jalopy, I knew the band had no money—and if the band had no money, I knew they'd be leaving that same night, because every hotel in Austin jacks up the price of its rooms during the festival. By Monday, I'd always be somewhere different. (**11:23** [4])

4 There's a club on Red River Street called Red Eyed Fly. Kind of where Red River intersects with Eighth Street? Terrible name for a bar, I don't get the reference, but whatever. There were four bands playing there on Sunday. One was called Suicide by Antelope. One was the Something-Somebody-Somewhere Blues Band, or words to that effect. I can't remember what the third group was called—I didn't *watch* any of these bands, obviously. I'm just trying to remember what was on the marquee. Besides, the only one that really mattered was the fourth band, because they loaded out their equipment last. They were called Jooky MaGoo. That, I can remember, because they had red-and-white JOOKY stickers all over their guitars. **(11:20 [3])**

5 The members of Jooky MaGoo, for whatever reason, did not ride in their own van. The band was three thin bozos and one hot girl, and they traveled separately in an aqua sedan. The Jooky van was driven by two roadies, one guy about twenty and one who might have been forty. That's who I got in with. We drove non-stop, north on I-35, for something like nineteen hours. It was a soul-deadening ride—I don't think the two guys exchanged more than fifteen words on the entire trip, and the van had no radio. That's probably why the band drove separately. I almost skipped out a few times when they were getting gas, but I wanted to stick with my plan. It seemed like such a good plan. We ended up in suburban Minneapolis, late Monday night. After sitting on a speaker for nineteen hours, it felt good to be anywhere. But I wasn't ready for the fucking weather. I did not anticipate being able to see my breath in March, and I wasn't dressed properly. Walking would have been a problem—the suit doesn't break the wind. I elected to stay with the van. The younger roadie dropped the older roadie off at some suburban house and said, "Thanks for the help, man." That was the extent of their relationship—I have no idea how they ended up working together. They didn't seem to know each other at all. The older roadie walked into his house and the young roadie drove the rest of the stuff—and me—to his apartment uptown. By now, it must have been almost midnight. I remember we drove down a road called Hennepin, and maybe past a little frozen lake? It was too dark to tell. No moon. We ended up on Pleasant Avenue, which is an easy avenue to remember. When the kid finally got home, he had to drag all the musical equipment up two flights of stairs, all by himself. I just followed him inside, right through the front door, easy as pie. He was storing all that shit in his living room, which was not an inconvenience, because he really didn't have much furniture. He lived in one of those inexpensive, oversized studio apartments that seem to exist only in self-consciously hip neighborhoods. There was a mattress on the floor and a stereo in the corner. Lots of upright Bose speakers. Nothing on the walls—not even paint. Vinyl records on the floor, in crates. Lots of vinyl. A thick glass coffee table, but no proper chairs and no sofa. He had a crappy set of golf clubs, weirdly. It smelled like an attic and a basement at the same time. He finished hauling the equipment, he took off his shirt and his eyeglasses, and he collapsed on the mattress. Didn't wake up until three in the afternoon. I slept for maybe an hour or two. My mind was fried. (**11:33** [7])

6 Now, this kid: Let me talk about this kid. His name was Dave. He smiled as he slept. That was, and that will always be, the thing I remember most about him. (**11:18** [2])

7 I was pretty sure I was going to hate this kid. He looked like someone I would hate. He looked like someone who put a lot of effort into slacking. The fact that he didn't talk once during a nineteen-hour van ride made me think he was snooty or boring or stoned, or maybe all three. But the second he woke up on Monday, things were different. He seemed so gentle. He carefully folded his dirty T-shirt and placed it inside the cardboard box he was using as a drawer. He put on a different shirt that made him look like a cowboy. He briefly exited the studio and crossed the hallway to knock on his neighbor's door, and the youngish woman who opened it immediately handed him a fat orange cat. She must have been the cat-sitter. He brought the cat back into his apartment and had a little conversation with its furry face. He must have stroked that cat's head for twenty minutes. He played with its ears, asked it if it had had a nice weekend, gave it a bowl of water. He held the cat's face up to the window so it could see outside. They had a real relationship. **(11:32 [6])**

8 Around 5:30, Dave calls his girlfriend on a cell phone. It's clear that this is his girlfriend, because he calls her "Baby" as often as he calls her "Julie" and immediately tells her how much he misses her, and he reiterates that sentiment every time the conversation loses momentum. Obviously, I can hear only one side of this conversation. But most of their dialogue is rote and easy to piece together. *[Y___ holds a hand to his ear with his thumb and pinky extended, mimicking a phone conversation.]* "Don't believe the haters. Austin's still happening." "They played one good show and three bad ones." "It was nice. A lot of people were wearing khaki shorts." "The best deal is Iron Works." "He was supposed to meet us at the Sword show, but he was too drunk." "Tina took care of Murray for me. Tina. From across the hall. The redhead." Just totally normal stuff, the kind of stuff anyone might say to a girlfriend who lives in a different city. They talked for an hour, and she did most of the talking. But there was one thing Dave said near the end of the call that was more opaque. *[Again, Y___ puts his hand to his ear like a phone.]* "They're real heavy dudes. They're the heaviest dudes I know." He elaborated on this, but only slightly. He was extremely enthusiastic. "They're actually coming over here tonight . . . Yeah . . . Julie, I know! But . . . but—exactly. I mean, they're just *so heavy*. I've never hung with dudes like this. They're heavier than everything. They're the heaviest dudes I've ever met." He kept repeating that same phrase: *heavy dudes*. Was some kind of ponderous metal band going to perform in this modest apartment? I was involved with this. I was mentally involved. **(11:35 [8])**

9 Now, I know what you're thinking, Vicky—my whole reason for pursuing this project was to observe people when they were alone. I've stated that thesis time and time again. But—remember—all the rules I've outlined are my own rules, created by me, for my own motives. I can break them whenever I want. Any self-imposed rule can be suspended without explanation. People forget that they have that ability. You forget that, too, Victoria. **(11:27 [5])**

10 Dave cleans his apartment, or at least he cleans everything that might get touched. The bathroom is too gross to salvage, but he makes the kitchenette livable and files half of the loose records. He listens to piano jazz as he cleans—that Charlie Brown music that makes everyone happy. He leaves for twenty minutes and brings back a case of Guinness and a case of Bass. He washes his biggest, coolest beer glasses and dries them with a towel. He talks to his cat. "Don't let these heavy dudes scare you, Murray. They're just heavy." The cat stares at him for a long time. He's like a cat from a cat food commercial. He's an actor cat. I think to myself, "This cat should be on TV." **(11:37 [10])**

11 Around nine o'clock, men start arriving at the apartment, sometimes solo and sometimes in pairs. And these are *men*. Like, they're all six feet four or six feet five. Most of them weigh in the neighborhood of three hundred pounds. Everyone has a beard. A few have ponytails. Three of them are wearing bib overalls and work boots. Dave's empty apartment is instantly devoid of emptiness: It's now a room of ten massive mountain men, sitting comfortably on unplugged Marshall amplifiers, drinking twenty-four-ounce black-and-tan schooners of beer that Dave mixed over the kitchen sink. It was two tons of flesh and bone and hair. *So this is all that Dave meant,* I thought. *They're literally heavyset people.* But then they start playing the stereo, and I notice they like only certain types of music. One type, really. They play Black Sabbath's *Master of Reality*. They play Neil Young's

Live Rust. They listen to a bunch of bands no civilian would ever enjoy—bands with monosyllabic names like Sleep and Tool and Karp. They listen to the Beatles' "I Want You (She's So Heavy)" twice in a row. They listen to Electric Wizard, and they define all other bands influenced by Blue Cheer as "compromised." So now I'm thinking, "*This* is what he meant. *This* is why they're heavy." But that's only part of it. Around 9:45, these acid-rock gorillas start eating mushrooms. Like, whole handfuls of dried, shit-colored, hallucinogenic mushrooms. They offer some to Dave, but he says, "I'll stick with beer." It was crazy. But what made it even crazier is that these mushrooms didn't seem to affect them at all. They didn't trip, or at least they didn't act trippy. Maybe the mushrooms didn't work. That seems to happen more often than not. But regardless, their personalities remained static—if I hadn't watched them eat the mushrooms, I'd have never known it happened at all. The only thing that changed was what they started talking about. That's when I finally deduced what Dave had meant. (**11:42 [11]**)

12 I don't know if this was an organization or a club or just an ad hoc collective of friends. That was ambiguous. That was never defined. They clearly knew one another, although they must not have been overly familiar, because they all shook hands when they arrived and again when they left. But whatever excuse brought these guys together was exactly that—an excuse. These dudes wanted only one thing: They wanted to sit around and get heavy. It was the heaviest possible conversation, conducted by the heaviest possible humans, held under the heaviest of circumstances. All they did was argue about morose, heavy shit: The possibility of a world without morality. Ethical justifications for revenge. The concept of genocide as a necessary extension of Darwinism. Someone would ask a question, somebody else would answer it with a different question, and that would turn into a third question. It was like taking a philosophy class with a herd of minotaurs. They debated politely, rarely cutting anyone off and always conceding minor points. But they'd also insult each other, flatly and without tact. "That's naïve," they'd tell each other. "Your words are entertaining, but you think like a child." **(11:40 [9])**

13 Part of me wants to call these heavy dudes "brilliant," but I don't know if that's true. They'd all read a lot, certainly, and they all had a lot of opinions. But that's not really the same as being *smart*, you know? It's related, but it's not the same. Like, they were all prone to conspiracy theories. Every time someone really started to impress me, the conversation would unravel into something stupid. Like, a certain song came on the stereo, and they started talking about the way music was recorded during the 1950s. This one dude starts talking about Pro Tools and studio technology, and he's fixated on how music producers can now do most of their editing by watching sound waves on a computer. He wasn't for this or against this—he just thought it was meaningful and super-duper deep. "We now measure the quality of sound through visual means," he said. "This means a product designed for one specific sense is built through criteria that are measured by a totally unrelated sense. This means something for our *ears* is created by someone's *eyes*. That's a huge leap. This would be like if it suddenly turned out that the most accurate way to judge the quality of wine was by how it felt when you rubbed it between your fingers, so all the world's sommeliers started using their hands instead of their mouths and noses. Judging wine would become a tactile occupation, just as judging sound has become an optical occupation." When he first described this, I was impressed; it was, I suppose, a new way to think about sound. But he just kept going, and his logic went congo-bongo. He kept talking and talking and talking, until he ended up insisting that there's some massive underground vault in rural New Mexico that's owned by the Church of Scientology, and that this vault houses a solar-powered turntable with pictogram illustrations explaining how it operates. They devised pictograms, apparently, in case written language disappears over time. This dude insists that the vault was built in preparation for a nuclear holocaust, because no one really knows what will happen to the U.S. power grid if a bunch of nuclear weapons are detonated at sea level. The best assumption, or at least *his* best assumption, is that all our hard drives will be spontaneously fried and the Internet will collapse and every digital file in existence will either be deleted or spontaneously corrupted. So when human society eventually tries to rebuild itself in some distant future, this underground bomb shelter will be the only source for recorded sound. Scientologists will own the only working record player on earth. Hence, Scientologists will control all the music in the world. He was pretty concerned about this. (**11:48 [12]**)

14 The question I had while watching all this, of course—and probably the question you have right now—is, "Why were these people in Dave's apartment?" Dave was thin, didn't seem like a philosopher, didn't talk much, didn't act or posture or trip, and seemed to be into Vince Guaraldi. But it was obvious he *wanted* these guys in his apartment, and he listened to their conversation with a real intensity. He was a listener. He did a lot of affirmative nodding. And he obviously had some kind of preexisting outside relationship with Zug. That was obvious from the get-go. Zug was the difference maker. (**12:44 [30]**)

15 Zug was kind of their leader. I say "kind of" because I suspect he might not have said that about himself, and I *know* none of the other heavy dudes would have said that about him. But—in reality—he was. Zug spoke the most and was more willing to abruptly change the trajectory of the conversation. He'd read more than the others, or at least he was the most willing to casually cite the books he'd read. He was the largest person from a physical standpoint, and he had the most body hair. He ingested the most mushrooms. He laughed the least and was the most nihilistic. Zug was the heaviest of the heavy dudes. (**11:50 [14]**)

16 I didn't like the way Zug spoke to Dave. He would kick back his head and snort whenever Dave tried to enter the conversation. Sometimes he'd kind of loom over him and glare. They must have liked each other on some level, but Zug was dismissive. He was cruel, and for no apparent reason. Have you ever seen *Goodfellas*? Do you remember the scene where Joe Pesci shoots the teenager in the foot? It was too much like that. (**12:46 [31]**)

17 There was a dispute. What can I say? It was a minor dispute, but it seemed not-so-minor at the time. It certainly doesn't seem minor now, in light of what happened. (**12:20 [22]**)

18 It was late. It was well past one in the morning. They were talking about "honor cultures"—societies where everything is based around status and there's just a collective, accepted notion that any kind of threat or negative action will be met with immediate violence. This is how it is in prison, for example, and—apparently—how it was in Iceland during the tenth century. I don't know where they were getting their information, but they all seemed to know a shitload about tenth-century Iceland. The larger point, according to Zug, is that honor cultures have more nobility than nonhonor cultures, because they're more egalitarian and more functional and ultimately more polite. If everyone has the potential to become a vigilante, everyone becomes equal. I could tell Dave was getting annoyed by this, just by the way he kept wrinkling his nose and shaking his head. After five minutes of this crap, he finally interrupted Zug's lecture. He said the concept sounded childish and anti-intellectual, and that it seemed like Zug was glamorizing a primitive world he'd never want to honestly experience, and that the whole theory was basically just a complicated way of saying, "An eye for an eye and a tooth for a tooth." Now, if anybody else had made this argument, I think Zug would have been civil. But because it came from Dave, Zug started raising his voice. "Don't you

realize that the phrase 'an eye for an eye' is actually an argument
for restraint?" Dave said he didn't want to waste time on semantics. He seemed nervous, or maybe even scared. So then Zug says,
"Well, you've certainly read William Henry Miller's [sic][12] books
on this subject, right?" Fully aware that Dave had no reason to be
familiar with some random academic nobody's ever heard of. So, of
course, Dave told him he didn't know who that person was, which
immediately made Zug roll his eyes. To which Dave quietly replied,
"Now you're just showing off." And that's when Zug started yelling.
He totally lost whatever cool he might have had. "You're an idiot,
go fuck yourself, let the grown-ups talk," on and on like that. Loud.
Embarrassingly loud. Embarrassing in general. (**12:23 [24]**)

19 Dave just sat there and took it. It went on forever.
(**12:24 [25]**)

20 There was a knock on the door, right after the yelling. It was the red-haired woman from across the hall.
Dave answered the door. Everybody in the room got
quiet—that unnatural variety of quiet that happens when the cops
try to break up a party. She was obviously asking about the yelling,
although we couldn't really hear what was being said. Dave finally
came back inside and said, "You guys should probably leave. It's
later than I thought." Nobody argued. The heavy dudes got off the
amps and started filing out, shaking hands with Dave as they said
goodbye, mentioning how they'd had a great time. They all left at
the same time. But Zug didn't leave. Zug stayed. He went to the
fridge, opened a Guinness and a Bass, and poured himself another
black-and-tan. Nobody seemed to think this was unusual. I suppose
I did, but I was the only one. (**12:27 [23]**)

---

12. It's my belief that "Zug" was attempting to reference William Ian Miller
of the University of Michigan. This is assuming Y____ was telling the truth about
what he remembered.

21 Dave started cleaning up the apartment, placing empty schooners in the sink. Zug was leaning against the kitchen counter with beer foam in his mustache. He says, "I'm sorry I yelled at you, D." Dave says something along the lines of, "I just don't understand why you do that." Again, Zug says he's sorry. But then he just starts lecturing Dave all over again. "You need to have more sophisticated ideas," he insists. He tells Dave that he doesn't read enough, and that the books he does read are facile, and that he's sometimes embarrassed by the things Dave says. He's not yelling when he says this, but he's talking like a bad father. He says, "All your opinions are received wisdom." He says, "If you don't have an original idea, it's better to just listen to the people who do." This was real perverse, real condescending shit. It was appalling. I was appalled. Dave just sort of shrugged it off and didn't say anything. He acted like he was concentrating on half-ass organizing his totally unclean apartment. Finally, Zug stops talking. He downs half his beer in one gulp. Then something peculiar happened: Dave turned to him and casually said, "Are you staying over here tonight?" Zug took another drink of beer and said, "We'll see." **(12:31 [26])**

22 What was going on there? I don't know. I have an idea, obviously, but I don't think it matters. **(12:30 [27])**

23 I was upset. I don't like to admit when I get upset, but I was. He was an awful person. I regret what happened, but only the last part. I don't regret the first part very much. I suppose I regret it a little, but just barely. I can see the absurdity in what transpired. I can recognize the irony. It's probably not the worst thing I've ever done. **(11:53 [13])**

24 Zug is walking around the apartment, looking at the guitars and finishing his drink. And I'm looking at this huge, hairy, heavy dude, and I just hate him. I'm a pretty good judge of character. Everybody thinks that about them-selves, but I'm right. I'm different. Zug was a bully. It wasn't like he was doing anything for the world, or producing anything the world needed. He was just an educated cretin who took advantage of people like Dave, probably in lots of bizarre psychological ways. I was thinking about how Zug had talked all that bullshit about the nobility of honor cultures, and how transparent that was. Sometimes it's wrong to let people get away with their behavior. **(11:56 [16])**

25 I was only going to freak him out. That was the totality of my intention. I thought I would just scare him, fuck with his mind, fuck with his reality, put him in a sub-ordinate position. Was it out of character for me to do this? Yes. But I did it for Dave. Dave deserved my help. **(11:55 [15])**

26 I didn't overthink it. It was just an honest reaction to what was happening at the time. Dave goes into the bathroom and closes the door. I see the light come on under the crack of the door, and I hear the fan running. By now, I have a strategy: I'm going to walk up to Zug, poke him in the chest, and tell him he's a coward. I'm going to tell him that he's fake and that everyone knows he's fake, and that everything he believes about the world is wrong. If nothing else, I want him to think he's having an extremely bad trip. Then I'll just run out the door and spend the night in the hallway. He'll flip. That was my thinking. **(12:50 [32])**

27 Okay, I get it. I get it. You're still not getting it. Let me try to simplify the situation: Dave's still in the bath-room. I can hear him working in there. It's gross. Zug is standing in the middle of the living room, looking back toward the kitchen. The positioning seems perfect. I walk straight toward Zug's face. I can tell he can't see me at all—and, even if he could, this is a person who'd probably had ten or twelve beers and a bushel of psychedelics. I have all these brilliant things in my head that I want to say, but I don't say them. I choke. I just say, "Fuck you, man," real fast, almost like it's one three-syllable word. And I poke him in the chest with my finger. Hard. I poke him hard in the chest. But, you know, it was only a poke, and this was a huge man. Normally, I don't think I could have knocked him down if I'd punched him in the face. But this poke *really* surprised him. Really, totally surprised the shit out of him. He got this hilarious look on his face, like he'd just remembered something awful. His arms shot out. His eyes were like bicycle tires. He tried to back up, and he fell. And he fell straight back, real fast. And his fucking head went right through the fucking table. His skull went through that glass coffee table like a cannonball. It shattered into a million fucking pieces. My first thought was "This is bad." But then I saw the blood. It was pouring out of the back of his head. It seemed like it was being forced out by a pneumatic pump. Blood was pooling up under his neck, crawling across the floor in every direction, seeping into his beard. His hair was like a wet red sponge. So my second thought was "This is as bad as it gets." **(12:39 [28])**

28 His head struck one of the metal legs of the table, and it punctured the bone. Put a hole in his head the diameter of a golf ball. That's exactly how it was explained in the *Pioneer Press*—the reporter was weirdly graphic about the trauma, almost like he was getting off on describing it. You can read it for yourself. The details are all online, if you're curious. Their archives are free. It turns out Zug's real name was Marion. Just like John Wayne! **(11:59 [17])**

29 These are vivid memories. Vivid, vivid, vivid. I close my eyes and everything happens again. The toilet flushes and Dave flies out of the bathroom, his belt still unbuckled. He doesn't scream. He just says, "Jesus." He tries to help Zug, but what can he do? He gets blood on his hands, blood on his shirt, blood on his pants. It's now a room of blood and amplifiers. It looks like a photo shoot for *Vice* magazine. Dave starts frantically searching for his cell phone. He calls 9-1-1, explaining the situation as best he can. He explains everything too calmly, actually. His voice was perfectly composed. This would come back to haunt him. I know they played that 9-1-1 call for the grand jury in an attempt to portray him as unfeeling. **(12:10 [19])**

30 Waiting for the cops to show up was a strange fifteen minutes. Dave just stood over Zug's corpse, kind of hugging his own body with both arms. The dude was so clearly dead. He turned white when he bled out. The cat started licking some of the blood, so Dave picked it up and patted its little orange head, real gentle. The cat didn't care about Zug. He understood. Animals are like that. **(12:12 [20])**

31 As soon as the police arrived, I left. A room full of police is not a good place to hide, even if you're the best hider on the planet. People were constantly coming in and out of the door, so it wasn't hard to exit. I read that they interviewed redheaded Tina the very next morning, and she told them about the loud argument. All the other heavy dudes gave depositions, too. The newspaper wouldn't directly say what the relationship between Zug and Dave was, but several of the heavy dudes implied it was complicated. That was the word they all used: *complicated.* It was too frigid for me to go out into the night, so I spent the rest of it on the second-floor landing. They took Dave to the station around 3:30 a.m. He wasn't in handcuffs, but they charged him with murder when he got downtown. I saw him walk out with two cops. He looked guilty. He did. Just before they went down the stairs, he asked one of the cops if he could run back and give his cat to the woman across the hall, but they said they'd take care of it for him. He said, "Thank you. I'd appreciate that." **(12:15 [21])**

32 I can tell you have questions, Victoria. I can see them on your face. But just let me finish. I don't care if our session goes long. You can charge me extra. We'll address your concerns next week. Next week, you can ask me anything you want. But I just need to power through. (**12:04 [18]**)

33 As you might expect, I've been following this case pretty closely over the Internet. The daily papers don't write about it much, but some of the weeklies report almost everything. Personally, I don't think he'll go to prison. Maybe he'll take a hit for manslaughter, but certainly not for second-degree homicide. That's what the prosecution wants, but I see a lot of holes in their case. Why would you murder a man by pushing him through a coffee table? Is that even something you can do on purpose? Plus, Zug's blood alcohol level was jacked through the roof, and he still had some uneaten mushrooms *in his pocket*. The fact that they had an argument hurts, of course. Tina's testimony was a problem. And—of course—Dave's lawyer won't allow Dave to testify on his own behalf, which makes it seem less like an accident and more like an *incident,* especially with all this "complicated relationship" crap that the heavy dudes keep repeating. You know, if I didn't know better, I'd be a little suspicious myself. I saw an AP photo of Dave in the courtroom, wearing an ill-fitting suit, looking like he hadn't slept in weeks. His hand was over his mouth. He looked worse than Zug's corpse. I hope this hasn't ruined his life. I mean, I'm sure it hasn't made his life better, but I like to imagine he's got some grit. (**12:58 [34]**)

34 Part of me wanted to get inside Tina's apartment to check on the cat, just because I feel like I owe it to Dave. I owe him that much. But now there's too much risk, and I'm never going to Minneapolis again. Too many nutcases in that town. Too many weirdos. I'll stay here. (**12:51 [33]**)

Heavy Dudes
Part II (The Interrogation)

[I've generally avoided using two-sided transcripts in this manuscript, partially to keep the focus on Y___'s words but primarily because I'm uncomfortable with my own elocution. However, I'm suspending that rule temporarily in order to illustrate why certain things were said in our July 18 session. My queries have been streamlined for clarity. This is not the full conversation; I am including only the opening thirteen minutes. I'm mildly embarrassed by some of the things I said in this exchange, but it was a confusing time.]

> **VV: Last week, you said you'd be open to questions about what happened in Minneapolis. Are you still open to that?**
>
> Y___: I am. Did you read about the case online? I'm curious as to whether you were curious.
>
> **VV: I did not. Is that important to you? Is this something you want me to be interested in? Is it something you need me to know about?**
>
> Y___: I don't need you to know anything. I was just curious. I'm curious about what interests you.
>
> **VV: A great deal of what you said was interesting. And . . .**
>
> Y___: And?

VV: Troubling.

Y——: I accept that. What troubles you? I'm open to all of this. I want you to understand this, Victoria. I don't *need* you to, but I want you to. And I must admit—I'm a little surprised you didn't look this up on the Internet. Why didn't you do that? I'm just curious. I would have done that immediately, had I been in your pumps.

VV: I wanted to talk about this first, before I did anything. I wanted to talk about if this really happened.

(Long pause.)

Y——: I don't follow you.

VV: Did this really happen?

Y——: What do you mean? Is that a nonliteral question? Or is this some René Descartes horseshit?

VV: My question is self-explanatory.

Y——: I just told you to check the Internet in order to read about it. Wouldn't that be a pretty stupid thing for me to say if I'd made the whole thing up? I don't understand where this is going.

VV: Oh, I'm confident that the event you described happened. I do not doubt—if I rummaged around the Internet—that I'd find a story very similar to what you described. But I want to know if you were actually there. I want to know if you actually played a role in what happened, or if you merely saw it happen, or if maybe you just read about it and decided it would make a good story. I'm not trying to catch you in some sort of a lie. I just want to establish the real reason you told me that story.

Y___: So . . . even though you've seen me cloaked, and even though you believe that I can become what you classify as "invisible," and even though I stood in front of you and you could not see me—you're still skeptical of what I tell you. You're skeptical of my story.

VV: Don't misinterpret what I'm saying. I'm not making accusations. I've seen you when you can't be seen. I know that's real. I know you have the ability to be unseen. But that doesn't mean *everything* you tell me is real. Sometimes people tell stories about themselves that aren't impossible, but still untrue. Do you know what I mean? I'm not saying I think you're a liar, or that there's no way this could have happened. I'm just asking if everything you told me is how it really was. All you have to do is answer yes, and I'll move on.

(Pause.)

Y___: I see what you're doing, Victoria. *(Another pause.)* This is actually a little sophisticated. I can't deny that you've thought about this. I appreciate that. It's sort of like television, I suppose. Right? From your perspective, my stories are like reality television: You start with the idea that what you're seeing is real, even though everyone watching at home knows it's constructed entertainment. But then there's another level, where an actual reality emerges from the simulated reality. All the fake relationships become real relationships. And then there's a third level after that, the level of *received* realness, where all that universal fakeness ends up being closer to formal reality than the show's original intention. That's impressive, Victoria. You should get a job at MTV.

VV: Does this mean you're not answering my question?

Y___: You already know the answer to your question. You're taping these conversations, right? Go back and tell me what parts you think are unreal. I would be fascinated to hear which parts you think are fabricated. It would be truly fascinating.

VV: Please don't be offended. That's not why I'm asking you these questions. You said you would be open to whatever I wanted to ask about . . . You know, I'm curious about something else: Have you ever heard of something called the Theory of Mind?

Y___: Of course I have.

VV: Of course you have.

Y___: And? So?

VV: Tell me what it means.

Y___: Are you serious? Don't *you* know what it means? This is idiotic.

VV: Humor me.

Y___: Okay, fine, whatever. *(Exhales deeply.)* The Theory of Mind. The Theory of Mind[13] describes, basically, the ability to understand what people are really thinking. It's what autistic people don't have.

VV: Keep going.

Y___: Um, well . . . Christ, I didn't expect the GRE today . . . one way of looking at it is . . . Okay, let me start again: It's the ability to know what other people mean when they say

---

13. Technically speaking, this is the ability to conceive of mental activity in others, particularly how children conceptualize mental activity in other children, how they attribute intentions, and how they predict the behavior of others.

things. The ability to understand how your own words are received by others. The ability to understand how words and actions are understood differently by different people. Is that what you're looking for? I don't know—I mean, I know what the Theory of Mind is, okay? But I probably can't explain it in the way you want me to. I'm not some fucking Wikipedia writer.

VV: Oh, you understand it. You do. You understand it completely. But sometimes I think you understand it so intuitively that you use it to manipulate others. To manipulate me.

Y___: Really.

VV: Your stories, in many ways, are all the same. They're so similar, in fact, that I suspect you're pre-anticipating my reactions in order to make me conclude certain things about who you are and what these stories represent. The Beatles, for example. Whenever you talk about observing people, you inevitably make some reference to music, and that music is inevitably the Beatles. There's no possible way that this is a coincidence. It makes me think that you assume the Beatles are so well known that everyone—including someone like me—will take that repetition in some explicitly metaphoric way. It makes me think you're *trying* to make me conclude something, even though I don't know what that something is.

Y___: The Beatles are popular.

VV: Pardon?

Y___: The Beatles are fucking popular. People listen to their music all the time. Different kinds of people. All generations, all subcultures. They're ubiquitous. I mean, seri-

ously, what the fuck are we debating here? I like music.
I took ten years of piano and four years of classical guitar. All mathematicians love music. I can't relate to people
who don't. Also, and not to be a jerk about this, but do you
remember when I told you that story about watching the
kid through his bedroom window? Who did I say that kid
was listening to? Rush. He was listening to Rush. So why
didn't I lie about *that*? Why didn't I claim he was listening
to "Strawberry Fields"?

**VV: But that's exactly what I mean. That story, the one
about the boy and the window and Rush—I'm certain that story is authentic. I have no doubt whatsoever. I think that story would be almost impossible
to make up. But that story is different from some
of the others you've told me. That story is a pure
memory. It doesn't have an intention.**

Y——: I must admit, Vicky, this is *not* what I thought you'd want
to ask me about when I came in here today. I accidentally
kill a guy, and you want to talk about the Beatles.

**VV: But did you *really* kill anyone? This is important.
We have to face this. Did you really kill him?**

Y——: Well . . . I didn't *murder* him, if that's what you mean. I
didn't *intend* to kill him. That wasn't my intention. It just
worked out that way.

**VV: I just can't believe you killed someone, Y——. Or,
more accurately, I can't believe you could kill someone and simply move on. I don't think you could kill
someone without feeling anything, and I don't think
you'd joke about someone you killed accidentally. I
don't think you're that kind of person.**

Y——: What kind of person is that? I already told you that I
didn't murder him. I'm not a murderer. I'm not *that kind*

of person, if that's what you're implying. It's much worse to want to kill someone and fail than it is to successfully kill someone by accident. And I do feel guilt. I never said I didn't feel guilty. What I said is . . . I just don't think I *should* feel guilt, which is why I came to you in the first place. Because I haven't done anything wrong.

VV: I don't think you've done anything wrong, either. I don't think you could do the things you've said you've done. I think you possess the ability to do bad things, and you've overstepped some significant social boundaries. I think you fantasize about doing terrible things, just as we all do. But I don't think you have the capacity to end a stranger's life—and to wreck a second stranger's life—without feeling profound grief. You don't think I know you, but in some ways I do. I know you're not the person you want me to think you are.

Y___: I suppose I do want you to like me, Victoria.

VV: I know that.

Y___: But not so much that I'd lie to you.

VV: Try to see this from my perspective, just for a moment. You end up in a room with a bunch of large, hairy men. I think you referred to them as "gorillas." And from your description, they all seem roughly identical. But you have no idea why they're meeting at this apartment, who these people are, or why this is happening. Don't you see how this might seem implausible? It seems more symbolic than realistic.

Y___: I'm sure it does. But this isn't a play. Isn't that obvious? If that had never happened—if this was just something I concocted in my head—I would have made up a reason for those guys to be in the apartment. I could have said it was a birthday party, or a meeting of anarchists or One Percenters,[14] or some kind of orgy. I could have said a hundred different things. If I was lying, I would have the answer to every question you ask. But I can't control the parts of the story I don't know, Victoria. Sometimes things happen and we never know why. That's the difference between fiction and nonfiction. Only fictional stories require an explanation. Only fictional stories can't have accidents.

VV: You're an amazing storyteller. You really are. We can build on that.

Y___: I don't need compliments, Victoria.

VV: I disagree. I think you need compliments as much as anyone else, and maybe more.

Y___: That's ridiculous. Come on. Get serious. You can't just take everything I say and pretend that the "real truth" is actually the opposite. That's not analysis. You're acting like a TV psychiatrist again.

VV: That's not true. You're wrong. This is something you're consistently wrong about, Y___. You need compliments. You're desperate for them. But you can't *accept* my compliments, because you're afraid doing so would make me stop giving them. And maybe that fear is justified.

Y___: We are so off topic, Victoria. This is not why I came here. I'm not interested in having a debate over what's real and

14. "One Percenters" refers to a sect of outlaw motorcycle gangs who regularly engage in criminal activity. The term comes from the (likely apocryphal) belief that the American Motorcycle Association once argued that 99 percent of bikers were not criminals; members of the One Percenter society embrace the concept of being the "1 percent" who do live a life of crime.

what's not real and how everything straightforward is actually its reverse.

VV: **We're not debating anything. I just want you to know that you're a good storyteller, and that I appreciate that. It's part of who you are.**

Y___: Well, wonderful. I got blisters on my fingers.

VV: **What?**

Y___: Exactly.

An Incident?

On the Sunday following our July 18 session, I traveled to Missouri to briefly visit my mother (who was ill with shingles). Around eleven p.m., my husband called me on my cell phone; this was surprising, as John rarely calls me (or anyone) on the telephone, even if I'm away for weeks at a time. We don't have the kind of relationship where talking on the phone is necessary. But he called on this night, agitated and terse.

"Someone was in the house," he said. "Your patient was in my house. I know it." John is immune to panic, but I could detect traces of alarm.

I asked why he believed this.

"Because an invisible man was in this house, and you have a relationship with an invisible man. It's not like this is a mystery. I don't need Basil Rathbone to explain what just happened."

John says he was working in our upstairs office when he "felt" (*his word*) someone else in the room. He insists he could "feel" (*his word*) someone's "presence" (*his word*). These were strange words for John to select—he regularly criticizes the use of such words in other people's arguments, particularly in historical and persuasive writing. He said he turned on every light on the second level of our home and loudly asked, "Who's there?" He claims he asked this question ten or fifteen times. After several minutes without response, he considered calling the police. "I am going to call the police," he said aloud, although I doubt he seriously considered doing so. He returned to work. It was at this point that he heard someone (or something) tumble down the stairs. He rushed out to

184

the second-floor landing and looked toward the base of the staircase (these stairs descend into our living room and have about twenty carpeted steps). He saw nothing. He walked down the stairs, picked up a poker from the fireplace, and jabbed around the floor of the living room. He says he stabbed every square foot of the living room floor. It was at this point he heard (or claims to have heard) someone exiting our residence through the kitchen door (which leads into the backyard). However, that door was locked from the inside when he later checked it.

John was outraged by what he believed had transpired. He was demanding and performative. At the time, I remember thinking his anger seemed funny.

"You will end your professional relationship with this person," he said. "You will end it this week."

I told him I could not and would not. I told him that I did not believe Y___ had been inside our house.

"Then explain what happened tonight," John said.

"Nothing happened tonight," I responded. "Had I not told you about Y___, this entire hallucination would have never even occurred to you."

"You're overlooking the obvious," John said. "You're refusing to see what's obviously happening here. There was a deranged person in our home, and it's your fault. If something happens, it will be your fault." He hung up the phone. I called him back immediately, but he declined to pick up.

I didn't sleep much that night. I was annoyed at John and skeptical of his motives (and I was tired of feeling those things on such a consistent basis). I didn't believe Y___ had entered our home. I wasn't 100 percent certain, because anything is possible. I didn't discount the prospect entirely. But it seemed unlikely. I refused to believe he was there.

Here, of course, is where I see the irony and absorb the shame: I can't make a good argument as to *why* I felt that way, particularly since breaking into strangers' homes was the main thing I knew about this person. He'd told me dozens of stories that were either bald-faced lies or disturbing truths, yet I still found myself trusting him more than my husband. I'm tempted to say it was because we were (finally) making real progress with our therapy and because Y___ was (finally) seeing me as something approaching his equal. But as I look back now with clearer vision, I realize those arguments contradict the veracity of my denial; the fact that our relationship was improving probably amplified the likelihood of Y___'s home invasion. Sad as this sounds, I probably thought Y___ was innocent simply because John believed the opposite. John is the type of person who's always certain about his perceptions; the fact that he *suspected* Y___ was there was all he needed for that to become true. John never doubts himself. Granted, his arrogance is not without merit—he's a brilliant man, and he doesn't make accusations without cause. Even his most vitriolic academic critics concede this. But brilliance can make the unreal seem reasonable. I believed John was just smart enough to be totally wrong.

Tuesday afternoon, I returned from Missouri. John apologized for the way he'd spoken to me over the phone, although he still wanted me to end my work with Y___. I told him I'd consider doing so, but not before directly asking Y___ about the alleged incident. It was my intention to do exactly that when I met with Y___ on Friday. However, the moment I saw him on July 25, I could tell he'd done nothing wrong. If he'd been in our house that Sunday, his behavior would have been different—he would have immediately told me he was there, or he would have acted nervous and evasive, or he would have come across as too casual and nonchalant. He would have volunteered an alibi without any prompting. He definitely would have done *something*. I would have noticed *something*. But he seemed exactly the same. If anything, he seemed extra chipper and unusually polite. I never even brought it up.

When I returned from work that evening, John asked what Y___ had said when I asked if he'd been in our home. I told him that Y___ had traveled to Corpus Christi that weekend to observe a collection of born-again Christian oil drillers he'd read about in the newspaper. Y___ had returned with a brutal second-degree sunburn, I insisted, and he spent most of our session peeling the dead skin off his arms and shoulders. "It was a little disgusting," I noted. "It was unseemly. There was dead skin all over my office carpet. I had to use the vacuum after he left."

At the time, John believed me completely, or at least he said he did.

August

It was a nuclear detonation, and it was my fault. A superstructure of shallow feelings collapsed into one bottomless feeling, and we both lost control of who we were and what we were doing. I don't like to think about it, but now I have to.

"Television is a form of one-way entertainment," Y___ said in the middle of our August 15 session. What made August so convoluted was that we quit talking about problems and more often just *talked*, about nothing and everything, exactly like we had on the afternoon outside the coffeehouse. It wasn't anything close to therapy. I didn't even realize how much things had changed until I went back and listened to the tapes. "Television is a form of one-way entertainment, but that's not how people want to think about it. They want to believe they're somehow involved. This is why they talk back to the TV. This is why they get upset if certain characters don't behave in a likable fashion. This is why they complain when the story moves further from their own personal definition of interesting. This is why they criticize boring episodes on the Internet and expect the show's writers to study their thoughts and care what they think. This is why they love shows that involve voting. They believe their personal experience with television effects what television is. But television is the only place where this belief exists. Within their actual life, they feel powerless. They believe voting is frivolous. They think caring is a risk. They assume they have no control over anything, so they don't even try. They perceive reality backward."

I don't watch much television, but I knew what Y___ was talking about. It was what I was doing with him (and I'm sure that's why he brought it up). Y____ was a television show. He would come in each week and talk about his life, and he'd treat me in whatever manner he chose (with no regard for how I felt). I would accept that treatment, because I was somehow convinced my reactions had an impact on future episodes. Over time, I treated him like a poorly written television show I wanted to adore—I changed the meanings of things I could not control and ignored the things I could.

During our five sessions that August, Y____ continued to tell anecdotes about the strangers he watched and the data he gathered. But he no longer lectured me; now he dropped these snippets into conversation like insouciant scraps of meat, and I chewed them like a puppy who'd earned a reward. There was the story of a man named Byron who lost his job because he couldn't resist pulling practical jokes around the office; he was fired when he filled a co-worker's desk with tampons (the co-worker had been on leave for sexual reassignment surgery). He mentioned a woman who threw a cat out of her third-story window every night, apparently because the cat enjoyed it (Y____ saw this as some kind of allegory for the economy). He detailed human sleeping patterns and graphically described the sound of grinding teeth; he told countless stories about acts people had committed on Ambien, most notably a woman who'd pour herself full glasses of vodka and tell her boyfriend it was "dream water." He mercilessly mocked any homeowner who adopted feng shui design principles. He exhausted twenty minutes of one session outlining the strengths and weaknesses of various U.S. airports (Pittsburgh and Portland were his favorites). My favorite story was about an obese woman who mentally masturbated while watching horse racing on television. "She didn't even touch herself. She didn't need to," said Y____. "What I could never figure out was the catalyst for her pleasure. Was it the horses? Was it the jockeys? It might have been the race itself, because she always seemed to orgasm at the precise moment the lead horse approached the finish line. 'And down the stretch they come,' or whatever. I think she was from Saratoga. Some sick childhood thing, I suppose."

All of these vignettes, told in their conversational totality, can be accessed in the U of T archives. Some of them are funnier than others, and I'm tempted to detail the best stories here. But that would be a ruse. That would be nothing more than a way to avoid writing about what was really happening between Y___ and myself, which is probably what I've been trying to avoid since I started this project.

We were not in love.

I did not fall in love with Y___. People will accuse me of this, just as John has, and sometimes I wonder if I protest too much. But what happened between us certainly did not feel like love. It was a different type of problem, accompanied by a different type of buzz. I want to be clear about this. I don't want people saying I fell in love with this patient, because I did not. I don't know why that's so important to me, but it is. My new therapist has asked me questions like, "What did you possibly appreciate about this evil person? Was it pure apophenia[15]?" But those seem like such unreal, unfair questions. I mean, honestly: How many rational people end up in irrational relationships? How many marital affairs are the manifestation of deep consideration? Think about your own circle of friends—how many of them have been intertwined in romantic liaisons that contradict logic? The mistake I made was not seeing goodness where it didn't exist, because that's what all romantic people do. My mistake was allowing something professional to become something personal, solely because my client refused to differentiate between those two idioms.

He spoke to me differently than other people did. That was the crux of it. Y___ talked the same way John does, but with a deeper kind of authority; it was spongier. More elastic. John is the kind of person who can instantly recall every single passage from every book he's ever read, and that instantaneous recall is the foundation of who he is. He's a perpetual remembering machine. But Y___ wasn't like that. He was the kind of person who would say, "I'm

15. The experience of making deep connections and/or seeing meaningful patterns within random data.

familiar with that book, and it's a good book, and you can certainly read that book if you want—*but here's the truth.*" He didn't need to know something in order to be confident. Now, obviously, that's a dangerous way to live. That brand of thinking is what starts world wars. But it was this autodidactic self-assurance that made conversation such a blast. Whenever John tells me that something I say is *interesting,* it's almost like he's saying, "That's something I could have thought of myself." When Y___ told me I was *interesting,* he was authentically engaged. He treated my words like a new thought. Sometimes he was cruel, but that's because he respected me. And I know that sentence reads like the words of a battered wife, but it wasn't like that. Y___ wasn't an arrogant intellectual, even though he was both arrogant and intellectual. I'd be lying if I said that made me enjoy him less.

He gave me such specific compliments.

They were all so excruciatingly detailed. "I like when you wear two-inch chunk heels," Y___ might say. "They make you look more relaxed than when you wear pumps. When you wear pumps, I always feel like you're too conscious of your own feet. They make you anxious when you stand up to shake my hand." Now, I'm not even sure if this was true. But who cares if it wasn't? It was a delightful thing to hear. If you asked John a hundred questions about my shoes, he wouldn't be able to answer one of them. He might know when clogs were first popularized in America, but he'd have no idea if I actually owned a pair.

But still: Let's not pretend that this is an objective reading of what went down. I'm culpable. I only believed what Y___ said when his words humanized him, or when I could make them human through my own devices. This was most evident during our conversation about the "heavy dudes," but it was happening all the time. In those early days following May 9, I didn't know how to feel about Y___. It was impossible for me to know what he was capable of. He seemed capable of anything. But something changed as we exposed ourselves, just as it does in any relationship built on words instead of deeds. His sociopathic parables became neutral.

It was almost like he wanted me to think he was dangerous in order to compensate for the fact that he wasn't. That was how I chose to view him. I processed every story as metaphorical autobiography. He could never admit he was wrong. He couldn't admit that he was pretending to observe strangers for all these high-minded, altruistic reasons, even though he wasn't learning anything of value. His project, or at least the project he claimed to be pursuing, was a total failure. None of his alleged discoveries improved my understanding of the human condition. As far as I was concerned, he was telling me other people's stories so that I'd understand secrets about him. I elected not to believe the things about Y___ that were troubling; I saw those details as part of his fantasy life and (sadly) as a pathetic way to impress me. For a time, I even toyed with the notion that Y___ had never entered *any* of these residences and was just projecting what he imagined his power of invisibility might allow him to do. Why did I think this? I don't know. Why do people get mad at the TV?

When I reread the conversations I've typed into this manuscript, I see Y___ the way others will see him. I suspect every third-party reader will see him more transparently than I did. But he wasn't a one-dimensional fiend. He wasn't. Sometimes I'd see glimpses of a vulnerable person, and that would make me rethink all my previous thoughts. I remember him once saying, half-jokingly, as he got up to leave my office: "You know, I've been everywhere in the world. I've been all over America, all over Europe. I spent a few weeks in Australia. I traveled through Asia in high school, I traveled through Africa in college. I've been everywhere there is to go. But you know what? I don't think I've ever met anyone I wanted to see again."

Even the invisible are insecure. It's the most universal problem we have. It's so universal, it might not even count as a problem.

During our last session in August, I asked Y___ something I had been wondering since spring: Why me?

"You weren't the first therapist I called," he said. "You were the fifth. But the first four were unsatisfactory. Actually, that's giving them too much credit—they were wretched. We never finished the initial phone call. They were inflexible. Control freaks. They were dictatorial. Therapists forget that they have issues, too."

So how was I different, I asked. Certainly, I had no fewer issues than anyone else. In fact, I might have had more.

"You didn't immediately assume things. You asked questions, but you didn't pretend like you already knew the answers," he said. "Nobody else was comfortable with the information I refused to provide. They always assumed my unwillingness to tell them information was an unconscious attempt to tell them something deeper."

"Give me an example," I said.

"Oh, you know what I mean," Y___ replied. "Look: You have a black husband. Right? And I'm sure the fact that you married a black man made certain people in your life skeptical of your motives. I'm sure close-minded people assumed that his blackness was part of the reason you were attracted to him, or that this had something to do with your father or your upbringing or your education or your liberal guilt, or that this relationship was somehow *political*. But would any of those assumptions be remotely true? Should you be required to deny those accusations, lest they become the conventional wisdom? I can't accept someone who *forces* me to explain how I feel, simply to contradict a preexisting opinion they incorrectly applied in the first place."

"I know what you mean," I said. "I know that feeling. But when did I ever talk to you about my husband?"

"When we were sitting on the bench that day," Y___ said. "Outside the coffee shop. You talked about your husband. He's an academic, right? A historian? A big nineteenth-century guy, no?"

I didn't remember that part of our conversation, but maybe it happened. It probably did. My memory is good, but Y___'s was always better. It probably happened. I'm going to believe it happened.

Sometimes he was just a weirdo.

"You never talk about your romantic relationships," I said one morning. "Most of my patients talk about those things constantly. But you never do. Have you ever had a serious relationship?"

"Oh, not really," he said. "There was a woman I dated in college—Alejandra Llewellyn. She was half Argentinean and half British. She had beautiful, condescending eyes. She listened to techno and cooked a lot of steaks. We were only together for seventy-four days. It was like having sex with the Falkland Island war."

"Come on," I said. "Be real with me."

"Men who talk about the details of their sex life are not real people," he said. "I'm not a rapper. I'm not a Jewish novelist."

It seems obvious to me now—and, in fact, it *felt* obvious to me, even then—that Y___ has never had a girlfriend and is probably a virgin. That he had been skipped two grades during his adolescence surely contributed to this; it's not unusual for academically accelerated males to enter college with the stigma of asexuality. Very often, they embrace that discomfort as a personality trope. Y___'s unconventional physical appearance and his inability to understand human behavior (much less the needs of an adversarial gender) compounded that problem exponentially. I felt for him. It was ironic: It seemed so many of my insecure patients reveled in their over-the-top sexual histories; somehow, finding partners for empty intercourse was the one thing they could always succeed at. Over time, these oversexed patients would inevitably come to accept that unfeeling physicality complicated their mind and eroded their self-worth. It was an impulse they needed to overcome. Yet here sat the most self-assured, knottiest patient I'd ever encountered . . . and in his world, the act of physical intimacy was so terrifying he refused to engage with the concept on any level. He couldn't even talk about it. Instead, he pretended not to care. He made jokes about it and tried to position me as prurient and intrusive. It was a hard thing to watch. I wanted to help him. It made me think his problems were profound, but still solvable. Maybe he was only missing that one chip?

When our final August session ended, Y___ started to collect his things and leave (sometimes he brought a tote bag with him, usually filled with notebooks and half-empty water bottles). We were both smiling; our conversation had been lively. Our meetings were no longer work, and I felt guilty for charging him. I wasn't thinking like a therapist anymore. I wanted Y___ to think I was spontaneous and laid-back. I wanted him to enjoy talking to me, so I asked a stupid question.

"When won't I see you again?" I asked.

"What?"

"When won't I see you again?" I asked again. I thought this was so droll.

"You'll see me next week," said Y___. "I look forward to it." He wasn't getting it. He didn't get me.

"Of course," I said. "But I want to know when I *won't* see you again. Will I ever get to see you cloaked? That first time I saw you, it was too intense. I couldn't keep it together. I couldn't appreciate it. But I think I could, now. I'd love to not see you again. Or is it too much hassle? I can understand why you wouldn't want to come here in the suit. I was just curious."

(I have no idea what I thought I was doing here. Any criticism of my decision-making is justified. I was lost in my own head.)

Y___ looked at me for a long time. The smile left his lips, but he was still smiling with his eyes. He was a supermodel.

"What are you doing tomorrow afternoon?" he eventually asked.

"Tomorrow? What am I doing tomorrow? Nothing."

"Meet me at noon," he said.

"Where? Here?"

"No, not here," he said. "Somewhere else."

"Like where?"

"I'm not sure. How about the Capitol Building? Meet me outside the Capitol Building, where the tourists take pictures," Y___ said.

"Why the Capitol Building?"

"Because it's a place," he said. "Just be there, unless this is some sort of mean joke. I'll find you. Try to stand apart from other people. Don't stand in a crowd. And come by yourself, obviously."

"Obviously," I repeated.

"Are you sure about this?" Y___ asked. His smile returned. "If I show up and you're not there, I'll be devastated. It will ruin my weekend."

"Don't worry," I said. "I'm not the kind of person who doesn't show up."

Today, as I type the words from that exchange and consider the choices I was making, I want to vomit. It's like remembering I'd forgotten a baby in the backseat of a car. But on that summer Friday, I was excited. I was as excited as I get about anything. It was all I thought about for the next twenty-four hours. It was what I wanted, and I almost knew why I wanted it.

The Thirtieth of August

It was twenty minutes to 12:00 when I arrived on the grounds of the Capitol. John didn't ask where I was going when I left the house. He always assumes there's a predictable reason for everything I do. Y___ had said I should avoid crowds. This was not a problem; almost no one else was there. I sat on a metal bench and looked at the white dome in the distance. I remember thinking, "Why do so many capitol buildings look exactly the same? Who made that decision?" I also remember thinking, "This is such a picturesque place. It's so lush. Why have I never visited before?" I also remember thinking, "The sky looks a little gray. Maybe it will rain. Will today not happen if it rains?" And then, suddenly, I was no longer alone with my thoughts.

He was on the bench.

"Good afternoon," said Y___, his words slightly muffled by the fabric covering his lips. I looked directly at the sound of his voice. I saw no one, but I saw *something*. Imagine watching an IMAX movie with the dead center of the screen softly out of focus; that's what it was like. I tried to locate his eyes, but that proved impossible. I brushed the back of my hand against his leg to get a fix on his location. He was exactly where I anticipated. I looked into the area where I should have seen his lap; I saw nothing but the coils of the bench and the grass underneath (its greenness looked muted, but the difference was only perceptible when I forced myself to search for it). It was shocking, but not like before.

"Hello," I said, turning to face the body that wasn't there. "We're both early." It occurred to me that—as far as the rest of the world was concerned—I was talking to my imagination. I was a schizophrenic. I pulled out my cell phone and held it to my ear. I was smiling. I assume Y___ was smiling, too. "This is incredible," I said into my phone. I felt like a spy. "No matter how many times I remind myself that you can do this, I never really believe it."

"Believe," he said. "Believe." He didn't speak in a stage whisper, but in a low register that sounded like talk radio played through paper-thin hotel walls.

I imagined strangers looking at us from across the lawn, completely bored by their own colorless reality, reasonably assuming I was merely having a phone conversation in public. I pretended that I could see Y___, even though I could not; I constructed his facial expression and the intensity of his stare. Somehow, my projection was more attractive than who he actually was. In my mind, he was no longer Ichabod Crane. Now he was Conan O'Brien, or maybe Adrien Brody.

We talked for ten or fifteen minutes about nothing worth mentioning—recycled conversations from the past four months. I wanted to say clever things, but my words were like bricks. He made a complimentary joke about my age, which should have been a signal. Because he was speaking so quietly (and because there were no physical cues to respond to), I can't say for sure that Y___ wasn't nervous, but I took my own insecurity as proof that he was at ease. He complimented me on my prescription sunglasses, which prompted me to instantly remove them. I was a teenager.

"What should we do," he asked. "What should we do today?"

I had no idea. I asked if he planned on observing someone. He said, "Not today. Today is recreational. Today is for you."

We bantered over possibilities. He suggested we walk up to BookPeople and Waterloo Records, a pair of stores on North Lamar Boulevard about fifteen minutes away. It was something to do. We started walking; I turned off the ringer but kept my phone to my ear. As he moved, Y___ totally disappeared into the ether—no matter how closely I looked or how hard I squinted, the combination of movement and refraction dissolved him into nothingness. We passed dozens of people on the sidewalk; no one noticed anything. A bulldog looked at him quizzically but did not bark. It was godlike. I was godlike, or maybe just on a date with somebody who acted the way an obnoxious god might behave.

We talked as we walked, but only sporadically. He was cautious, sheepishly admitting that he'd never been cloaked around a person who truly understood what was happening. I mentioned how difficult it was to talk with a person I could not see, because I didn't know how my words were being taken. It was harder than the telephone, somehow. "In twenty-five years, that's how it will be for everyone," he said. "Kids live through computers now. They make all their friends over the Internet, so they don't understand how non-verbal communication works. They don't understand body language or casual sarcasm. They love irony, but they never understand any joke they don't make themselves. In a hundred years, no one will be able to talk in public. Talking will be like blacksmithing."

He was in control. I was just a prop.

We reached the record store and walked inside (I could feel him behind me as I pushed open the door, even though we never made physical contact). It had been years since I'd entered an actual record store, but the smell of patchouli was immediate, familiar, and transportive. The shop was full of customers who didn't seem to be buying anything. The music was dissonant and deafening. It was too loud for talking and I had nothing to shop for. I flipped through posters of women posing with beer logos and tried to act like I was supposed to be there. My eyes kept darting around the space, constantly trying to figure out where Y____ was located—I often thought I knew, but perhaps I was wrong every time. After maybe five minutes, I felt a tug on my shirtsleeve. "Outside" was all he said.

As we crossed the street to BookPeople, Y____ put his mouth next to my ear and asked, "Are you having fun? Or is this boring?" I said it was beyond fun. We walked inside the bookstore and wandered the aisles, avoiding congested sections and potential bottlenecks, pretending to look at books about philosophy and sex and advertising. Every so often, Y____ would knock a random hardcover off the shelf to watch me jump in surprise. It amused us both.

We walked down to the store's lower level. It was desolate. We were essentially alone, except for one female clerk behind a register. Suddenly, Y___ tapped me on the shoulder twice. "Listen," he said. I listened. There was music playing over the sound system. At first I thought it was Muzak, but then I heard a pair of dulcet voices; there was a female voice and a male voice, but I recognized only the former (and just vaguely). The song seemed familiar, but I could not place it. "What song is this?" I finally whispered. "Go ask," Y___ replied.

The ectomorphic girl behind the counter had a nose ring loosely attached to her earlobe on a chain. The highlights in her bangs were the color of Mountain Dew. She was reading a magazine called *Decibel.* "Who is this?" I asked her. "The music. Who is this?"

"It's a music service," said the ectomorph. "It's, like, I don't know, satellite radio or something. Whatever replaced satellite radio. Pandora? Not sure." We listened together for another ten seconds. Suddenly, I saw recognition in her face. "Actually, this is so random, but I think I used to have this in junior high. I think it's the *I Am Sam* soundtrack." She looked at the ceiling and listened for three seconds more. "Yeah, I remember buying this. I sucked."

"What song is this?" I asked. "Do you remember?"

"It's Aimee Mann and her husband, or maybe her ex-husband, or whoever he is," she said. "It's called . . . oh, man . . . it's called 'Two of Us.' The whole soundtrack was bad Beatles covers. Actually, that's not true. There was an okay Grandaddy song near the end. And I guess this song is okay. I mean, it's okay for you to like it." The clerk returned to her magazine, uninterested by my interest.

"Thanks," I said. I walked away from the counter, back toward where I thought Y___ might be standing. I guessed right. He was waiting for me.

"See," he said. He said it so quietly the ecto-clerk never lifted her head. "See. What did I tell you? The Beatles are popular. Not everything is symbolic of something else. Not everything is a trope. Sometimes music is music."

"Are you sure?" I asked. The clerk looked up when I spoke. I had spoken louder than I needed to. She glared at me like I was naked.

We left the store soon after. It was just past one o'clock. I asked what was next. Y___ said, "Let's find a bar." I found this suggestion surprising, and I told him so. "Just for ten minutes," he said. "Let's check on the Horns. Just wanna see the score."

It had never occurred to me that Y___ would care about the local college football team, but he was a man living in Texas.

We walked to a bar where the game was playing on six televisions. It was too crowded. There was another bar up the block with only one TV, but the room was only a quarter full. It was ideal. "Follow me," he said. "How?" I asked. He grabbed my left hand. I could feel the creamy grit from his glove. It reminded me that this situation was more precarious than I was allowing myself to recognize.

Y___ led me to a booth and sat down, facing the TV behind the bar. I sat across from him. "No," he rasped. "Sit on this side, next to me." I followed his order immediately. "What if someone you know inexplicably walks into this bar," he said. "Or what if some random bachelor decides he wants to chat up a lonely Longhorns fan drinking in the middle of the afternoon? He'd come over and sit down, and he'd sit right on top of me. This is safer. The closer you stay to me, the safer we are."

We sat together on the same side of the vinyl booth—two of us, riding nowhere. Texas was playing Rice. It was the first game of the year, and there were two minutes until halftime. The Longhorns were already ahead by thirty points. "Let's just watch until the end of the half," Y___ said. "Let's see if the Owls get something going." I wondered if John was watching the same game at home. He probably wasn't. He probably didn't even know it was happening, and if he did, he was probably mad about it.

A waitress came over to our table. Would she notice anything? Would she *sense* that there were two people in this booth? Would she sense that the hazy, unpredictable shadow against the wall was not an accident, and that this was a moment unlike any she would ever again experience, and that I was in a bar with an invisible man who was not my husband?

Of course she didn't.

"What can I get for you?" she asked. I ordered a Diet Coke. "Do you need a food menu?" I did not. She walked away. I was alone in this.

I felt myself blushing. Something was wrong with me. Part of me felt exhilarated and part of me felt humiliated. My Diet Coke arrived. It tasted awful: flat, warm, and mostly syrup. Every component had something missing or something unnecessary.

Again, I placed the cell phone to my left ear. "Do you like football?" I asked Y____. "I didn't think you'd like football."

"I don't know if I necessarily *like* it, but I follow it," he said. "I follow the Longhorns, I follow the Aggies, I follow Texas Tech. I watch the Cowboys on Sunday, and sometimes I'll try to get down to Lake Travis on a Friday night. It's a diversion. It's in the newspaper, and I read the newspaper. You?"

"Oh, I never watch football," I said. "But I don't have any, you know, *ethical* problem with the concept. I'm not one of those. My father loved it. I just never have the time. The rules seem more complicated than necessary."

"What about your husband?" asked Y____. "Does he like to watch?"

"Oh, no," I said. "I don't think he likes football. I mean, maybe he does, but I don't think so." It occurred to me that I didn't know the answer to this question.

"What does he like?" asked Y____. "What are his interests?"

"He's interested in working," I said. "He's very, very interested in history. Very interested. If he could read all day, every week, for every minute of every month, he'd be ecstatic. Reading is his favorite thing, followed by writing about whatever he just finished reading. He likes to watch documentaries about the Reconstruction. He likes to look at those maps on the Internet that predict how all the different states will vote in the electoral college. He likes to fact-check Wikipedia articles. He listens to jazz, but only the ear-liest known recordings. He's just an intense man. His interests are intense."

"It must be fascinating to live with such a recondite person," said Y___.

"Not really," I said. "I don't even know what *recondite* means, exactly, but I know it's not something that makes for a fascinat-ing husband. He was different when I met him. I mean, he was the exact same person, but still different, somehow. It's hard to explain. We talked about the same things we talk about now, but the conver-sations were more like regular talking."

The first half was over. Rice had still not scored.

I looked at Y___. He still wasn't there.

I looked down at my right hand, which was resting on the surface of the table. I could see it, but it was fuzzy. It felt trapped. There was a hand on top of it.

"I don't think your husband is a good person," said Y___. His voice was borderline inaudible. I had to lean closer. "And I don't think he's as smart as you think he is."

"No, you're wrong. You don't know what you're talking about," I protested into my phone, still staring at the TV, which now showed a commercial for dog food. "If you read his books, you wouldn't say that. He invented a new way to write about the Civil War. He *invented* it. Do you know how rare that is? To invent a new way of writing?"

"That's not what I mean," said Y___.

I knew what he meant.

I pulled my palm away from the table; I could see sparkles on the back of my hand, the glove's residue. I wiped it on my pant leg. "I need to go home," I said. "It's time for me to go home."

"Why?" he asked. "What else do you have to do today? Why don't you come over to my apartment? It's not far. It's a short walk. I won't try anything untoward. I'm not a sexual person."

"I need to go home," I said. "Maybe I can visit some other time."

"Why?"

"I just need to go home," I repeated.

"Why? Give me the real answer."

"My answer is my answer."

"That's not an answer. Quit talking like an infant."

"That's insulting. That's inappropriate," I said. "I don't need to give you an answer. I don't understand why you're suddenly acting like this. You were so nice before."

"I wasn't any different than I always am," he said. "All I want is to know why you're leaving. Do you even have a reason? Is it so your husband can explain why you're always wrong about everything? So that you can keep living a life you find unsatisfying?"

"You don't know anything about my life," I said.

"I know everything about your life, Victoria."

That sentence was all it took to remind me how disturbed this man was, and how stupid I had been for far too long.

I left three dollars on the table and walked out the door. It was a ten-minute walk to my car, but I can walk fast. Did Y___ follow me? It felt like he did. In my imagination, he was never more than ten steps behind. But how could I know? When I got into my car and locked the doors, I punched around the backseat and the shotgun side of the vehicle with my fists, just to make sure I was alone. My hands were shaking when I gripped the steering wheel. It made the entire steering column shake.

When I got home, John was in his office, working on an essay about Jefferson Davis. He didn't ask where I'd been until we were eating take-out Chinese food at dinner; he barely listened to the fake answer I provided. I asked if he had seen any of the football game. He said, "There was a football game?"

Sabbatical

Lying in bed that Saturday night, it became clear I needed to make some decisions about how to move forward.

If I didn't feel safe around Y——, I couldn't treat him. That was obvious. But did I really feel "unsafe"? Perhaps I'd overreacted that afternoon. Y—— had never gotten physical, and—as he himself noted—his language and posture hadn't been any more or less abrasive than it had been on the first day I met him.

Was I partially at fault for what had transpired? Absolutely. It was certainly not unusual for patients to become attracted to their therapists, but I had accentuated that risk by asking for a meeting outside of our established safe zone. I had allowed our conversation to become too intimate and I'd allowed myself to view Y—— differently than my other patients. I was responsible for my actions.

But this situation *was* different. It was.

Y—— had subterranean problems that made his problematic behavior a virtual afterthought. We weren't even confronting his central issues. I mean, here was a patient I'd spoken with every week for half a year, and we'd barely even touched on the fact that he was a habitual drug user. His other problems were so profound that the denial of his stimulant addiction didn't even seem worth mentioning! There was growing evidence that I was not helping Y—— in any way. He had ostensibly come to me to talk about his sense of guilt, but now I was just a sounding board. I was validating his solipsism. The sociocultural conditions he pretended to obsess over didn't matter a fraction as much as his own desire to be seen as intelligent. He was not interested in changing. If anything, he wanted to be more like himself.

Still, there were other issues to consider, many of which were tied to my own personal ambition as a psychological practitioner. Would I ever have a patient this interesting again? Never. This was like being Hitler's therapist, or Springsteen's, or Superman's. This was an opportunity to work with that rare variety of person who lives other people's dreams. Moreover, my time with Y___ had changed how I viewed my own self-worth; I still knew that helping bulimic college girls and unsatisfied commodities brokers was important, but now it seemed unremarkable. Their dilemmas seemed so obvious . . . so self-indulgent . . . so traditional. Working with Y___ was *real work*. If I could solve this riddle, who knew what the result might be? What if Y___ evolved from the selfish person he was into a man who wanted to make the world better? Is there anything more valuable I could do for any one person? Is there anything more valuable I could ever do for society as a whole?

I either had to walk away from Y___ or I had to embrace his treacherous imperfections. There were only two options, and I had to pick one.

So, of course, I tried to choose both.

Here was my plan: I would call Y___ on the telephone and cancel our next session (I would not even go to the office that day, just in case he refused to accept my cancellation). I would tell him that it was currently impossible for us to continue our relationship. If he had romantic feelings for me (which now seemed undeniable), we needed some tangible distance to reestablish those boundaries; I was confident that any misplaced attraction would dissipate if we removed the structured intensity of our dialogue. Then—if we both understood what our relationship was and Y___ was willing to accept conventional two-way communication and traditional therapeutic methods—we could renew our sessions in six weeks. That seemed like the proper time frame: It was long enough to prompt change, but not so long that we'd lose whatever progress we'd already made. On Sunday morning, I explained all of this to John during brunch, as casually and stoically as possible. He agreed that it was the proper decision. "This is the intelligent move," he said over the top of the newspaper. "You're being the intelligent person here."

On Monday morning, I called Y____ to talk this over. He did not pick up. I called again Monday evening; again he didn't pick up, so I left a message urging him to return my call. I called again on Tuesday and did not get a response. On Wednesday, I called a fourth time and finally outlined all my intentions in a voice mail message. There is nothing in the previous paragraph that I did not directly say to Y____. I told him he could call me if he wanted to talk this through, and that I would contact him in five weeks time to see if he was still interested in my offer to reconvene. I called again on Friday morning to make sure he'd gotten the message, but his cell phone no longer rang. The number had been discontinued.

At 4:04 a.m. on Friday, I received this voice mail message from a blocked number:

"Victoria. This is Y____ speaking. I received your call and message . . . I'm disappointed. I'm very disappointed . . . if I'd known that our afternoon together was going to end so negatively, I would have never agreed to the meeting. I'm sorry about what happened, whatever it is you think that it was . . . I'm still not certain how you feel about what's happening here. I get the impression you're having a difficult time differentiating between our personal relationship and our professional relationship . . . I want you to know that my feelings for you are very real and important, but also ideological. That should mean something to you. We share ideologies and [*inaudible*], and that matters. Like I've said, I'm not a sexual person . . . I'm sorry I said those things about your husband, even though those things are true, and you know this . . . Perhaps we will continue my therapy again in two or three weeks, depending on how we feel. But I'll gladly skip our next session. We both need some time to regroup and decide what we want,

and I'm extremely busy right now. But I'll see you again.
You'll see me again. Thanks for watching the game with
me. I had a nice time. Don't lose those sunglasses. This was
Y___."

It has been my experience that patients who elect to temporarily
suspend treatment rarely return to the same therapist (often, they
give up therapy entirely). This being the case, I wondered if that
message would be the last interaction with Y___ I'd ever have. As
I replayed his message, it seemed like things were over; he spoke
with the skittish, sheepish syntax of a man who knows he's going
to be late for dinner but can't admit it up front. I was relieved, but
also a little sad. I'm embarrassed to concede that Y___ was right,
at least on one point: Once he disappeared from my life, I was just
a person again.

Something That
May Have Happened
(September 11)

It was ten o'clock at night. I was watching television in my bathrobe (the E! network was broadcasting a retrospective on theorists who believe 9/11 was planned by the U.S. government). John was in his office, talking over Skype; an Australian writer was remotely interviewing him about the long-term consequences of the Monroe Doctrine. His office door was closed, but I could faintly hear John's steady delivery and the stilted, digitized voice of the Aussie. The information on the TV was repetitive. I began to fall asleep. Nothing seemed unusual, until the couch changed.

It changed.

I was sitting on one end of the couch. It's an expensive, high-end couch—plush microfiber, three cushions, not a sectional, good for napping. You sink into the softness, just like they say on the commercial. But—suddenly, and *almost* imperceptibly—the gravity of the couch shifted. It seemed like my seat raised up half an inch, the way it does when something heavy comes to rest on the other side. I swiveled my head. I looked at the far cushion of the couch. Was it slightly depressed? Was a person I could not see sitting three feet away? I had no idea, but that was my first thought. I'd never sat on a couch with an invisible person, so I didn't know how it was supposed to feel. I tried to remember how it had felt to sit on the vinyl booth in the bar, but I couldn't conjure a memory. I picked up a pillow and tossed it toward the other end of the couch. It landed on the arm, softly, in a manner that suggested no one was in the way.

Is this how insanity begins?

It wasn't that I'd forgotten how it feels to be alone. It was more like I had never even thought about how being alone was supposed to feel, until that very moment.

I was scared (not horrified, but nervous enough to remember the feeling). I wanted to yell up to John, but I could still hear his voice through the door ("A hands-off policy on the Western Hemisphere seems reactionary today . . ."). He'd be annoyed if I interrupted his interview, especially if this was only my imagination. Instead, I paced around the living room, trying to remember what the empty atmosphere of life is supposed to feel like. I checked the door locks and the windows. At one point, I said "Hello" aloud, but not loud enough for John to hear. Around eleven p.m., I made a cup of coffee and watched two consecutive episodes of *Project Runway,* followed by two black-and-white episodes of *The Twilight Zone.* Nothing else happened. I still have no evidence that anyone besides me was ever in the room.

Normally, I'd view this as nerves. That's what I would tell anyone else. It's easy to believe there's a monster under the bed if you've spent the last six months arguing with a monster. Maybe I was ridiculous. But I probably wasn't as ridiculous as I wanted to be. I probably wasn't ridiculous at all.

Something That

Probably Happened

(September 15)

"He was here again."

This was what John said when I returned from work. My instinctive reaction was to ask, "Who was here?" But even as those words escaped my mouth, I knew whom John was talking about.

"The invisible man," he said. "Your invisible boyfriend."

"He's not an invisible man," I responded. "It's impossible for a person to be invisible."

"Enough semantics," he said. "I can't see him. True? You can't see him. True? So he's invisible, and he keeps coming into our house. We need to do something about this. This is a crime. He's a criminal."

I had not told John about what (I suspected) had happened a few nights before, and this didn't seem like an especially good time to bring it up. But I was worried now. I didn't know if this was really happening, but I knew it couldn't continue if it was. It was time to think like a victim. I asked John to explain what happened.

"I bumped into him," he said. "I literally ran into his body. I was in the living room, and I started to walk toward the stairs. But I remembered that I'd left my glasses on the coffee table, so I turned around and walked the other way. I suppose it was a sudden movement on my part. I ran right into him. I'm sure of it. I know how it feels to run into a person, and that's what it felt like. He must have been directly behind me. He was trailing me. That's the only explanation."

I asked what happened next.

"I confronted him."

"How did you confront him?"

"I made it clear that I knew who he was, that I knew everything about him, and that he was doing something illegal. I told him that breaking into someone's house nullified his constitutional protection. And I made it clear that I was *extremely* unhappy about this."

That seemed like a lot of information to deliver on the spot. I asked John how he worded those sentiments.

"It doesn't matter how I worded it," he said. "I'm sure your boyfriend inferred the proper meaning." Had Y___ responded? "No. There was no response. I even took a swing at where I expected him to be. All I hit was air. But he was in this room. I know it. He was here. He might *still* be here, for all I know. This is a problem. Are you finally going to accept that this is a problem?"

John and I discussed our options. Going to the police was the logical move, but that felt hopeless (and borderline comical). There was just no way to explain our situation to a law enforcement official; I wouldn't even know where to begin, and there was no way to come across as normal. Who would I claim was doing this? I wasn't even certain I knew Y___'s real name. I didn't know where he lived or how to find him. His cell phone was no longer active. We would essentially be filing a report that read, "A man we can't see and that you can't find may (or may not) be breaking into our home in order to steal nothing and hurt no one." It's hard to place a restraining order against a person who doesn't exist.

We agreed to pay extra attention to our doors and windows, but that was a limited solution; if a mostly invisible man wants to break into your house, there's no way to stop him. We considered an alarm system with a motion detector, but we didn't know if Y___'s "motion" was even "detectable." We tried to outline just how serious this menace was, and we tentatively wondered if Y___ was nothing more than a terrifying nuisance. We also wondered if any of this was happening at all—what if our collective anxiety was causing both of us to turn every unclear moment into a brush with Y___? I was still rational enough to consider the possibility of being wrong, regardless of how true our feelings might have felt. But John was cracking.

"I'm taking this situation over," said John. "I won't let this person infiltrate our lives. I won't. You say he's harmless, but I disagree. If he comes back here again, I'm going to deal with him. I'll hammer him."

"How?" I asked.

"With this," said John. He held up a hammer.

I didn't even know we owned a hammer. I knew we had paintings on the walls, but I had never considered how they got there.

"You can't be serious," I said.

"I'm as serious as Truman," said John. "I've had enough. I almost hope he comes back tonight. Violence doesn't scare me. I've seen violence. I've experienced violence. I know my rights." He slid the handle of the hammer into his belt loop and looked straight at me, defiant. He had made his decision. "I'll knock his goddamn block off."

So this is what my life had become: I was married to an aging historian who carried a hammer everywhere he went, with the sole intent of bludgeoning an invisible man as punishment for falling in love with me.

Unlike the rest of my life, it was too crazy to regret. I just had to swallow it.

A Point of No Return

The next two days passed without irregularity. I was still upset and out of sorts, but each day got easier; I started to wonder if we'd all overreacted. John had phoned a security company the day after his alleged collision, but now we weren't sure it was necessary to schedule an appointment. The more I thought about it, the less hazardous Y___ seemed. Perhaps he was just lonely and I'd become his only friend. Maybe I misled him. Maybe I gave him the wrong impression about my intentions. Maybe I was scared of him only because he was smart enough to do the impossible, and maybe I was punishing him for being different than other people.

These are the kind of thoughts I entertained, because I was just smart enough to be totally stupid.

It was a Thursday. I was with a patient. I can't write too much about this individual, as she has her right to privacy and I have an obligation to protect that right. However, this patient's problems were so common they'd be impossible to tag on any specific person: She was an attractive young woman with irrational body issues, she wasn't sure what she wanted as a career, and she was often devastated by anonymous comments posted on her blog. At the time, I probably had five other patients exactly like her. She talked about her life for forty minutes, I responded with five minutes of commonsense advisement, and she left to go home. The door to my office slammed shut and I began typing a few details from our session into an e-mail addressed to myself. And then, from across the room, I heard the voice.

"She's pretty awful," it said.

I was startled, but I was getting used to being startled. I was sick

of being startled. I was more angry than surprised. I took a deep
breath and tried to be the adult.

"I can't believe it," I said slowly. "I can't believe you'd do this.
I can't believe you'd interfere with my work. I can't believe you'd
completely disregard what I do for a living. And I can't believe
you'd judge a perfectly nice woman who has legitimate problems,
but I suppose that's just the person you are. I can't believe you'd
come here. Get out. Now. I never want to be around you again. Get
out of my office or I'll call the police."

"Oh, quit pretending you care," said Y____. "You can't fool me.
I know you. You're concerned about this woman? *This* woman? Do
you honestly believe either of us learned anything meaningful about
her fake life? At least you got paid. I could solve her in two minutes.
She has body issues because she has a body. Tell her to cancel her
magazine subscriptions. She doesn't have a career because she isn't
interested in working. People write cruel things on her blog because
she's a lazy thinker who actively courts the attention of self-loathing
strangers. These are all things she intuitively understands. Haven't
you noticed how she always answers her own questions? All she
wants is a temporary friend who'll tell her that she's no different
than anyone else, and she knows you have to be that person as long
as her father writes you checks."

"I'm calling the police," I said, and I picked up the phone.

"Turn on the tape recorder," Y____ said.

"What?"

"Turn on the tape recorder. Let's get this on the record."

It was so like Y____ to make that request. It was so like him to
demand indulgence. My microcassette recorder was on the desk. I
picked it up and pointed it at him like a handgun. I hit RECORD with
my thumb. I don't know why I made such a dramatic gesture, but
I did. I'm sure it looked ridiculous, but I couldn't help it. I wanted
to shoot him.

I recorded only the next minute and fourteen seconds. This is
the only segment of the interaction that isn't a reconstruction from
memory.

Y___: Is the red light on? It is. Excellent. You know, not that it's any of my business, but you should really buy a digital recorder, Victoria. It's going to be impossible to find micro-cassettes in a few years. But I digress. Victoria, please tell the jury why you met me on a Saturday afternoon, recreationally, without informing your husband of who you were seeing. Or who you were *not* seeing, since that's probably something you'd like to say in order to seem clever.

VV: Come on. Really? This is what you want to do?

Y___: Are you denying that we were together?

VV: What does that have to do with anything?

Y___: I'm just curious over whether you view our time together as social or professional. Because, you know, you didn't charge me anything. We didn't talk about my life or my problems. We went to a record store, a bookstore, and a bar. We went to a bar. Is that the accepted standard of care for licensed therapists in the state of Texas?

VV: You know, you're pathetic. This is sad.

Y___: No. No, not really. Not sad. Curious. I'm curious about your side of the story. Obviously, our relationship is broken. I'm just trying to understand who's at fault here. I want to hear both sides. I'm that kind of open-minded dude. You act as if this situation was entirely predictable. It strikes me that—

[I turned off the recorder. I had to stop giving him what he wanted.]

"Stay out of our house," I said in the most threatening way I could muster. "Don't come into our house, ever again. I'm not playing around. Stay out of our house."

"I've never been in your house," said Y___ (or words to that effect). "Why do you think I was inside your house? I don't even know where you live. What's your address?"

"Stay the fuck away from our house! Jesus Christ. Are you deaf? Stay away from this office, and stay away from me." I was losing my handle, so I took a few breaths and tried to become the person I was supposed to be. "You can't come into our house anymore. You just can't. My husband will hurt you. He's more upset than you realize. This is not a funny situation or an interesting situation or whatever type of situation you want to pretend that it is. This is serious."

"Your husband will hurt me? *Your* husband," said Y____. "Does he intend to shoot me with a musket?"

"Don't come into our house. I'm begging you. What do I need to do to convince you to stay away? Do you need me to start seeing you again professionally? If I *have* to keep seeing you, *here*, in my office, I will. But stay away from the house."

"So you *do* want to spend time with me. That contradicts what you just said, Victoria. Are you sure your thoughts and feelings are the same? Because you never think mine are."

It was no use. There was no way I was going to convince Y____ of anything, and all he was going to do was contradict everything I said in a desperate attempt to keep us talking. In his mind, that was the only way to keep our relationship from ending. As I listened to his regressive arguments, I had a flashback to my freshman year at Davidson: I remembered how impossible it was to break up with my boyfriend from high school, and how he seemed to believe that starting a nightly fight over the telephone was not terribly different than being together as a couple. I realized this had already gone way too far, and the only remedy was to detonate every bridge we'd ever crossed. I chose the nuclear option. I told Y____ that I loved my husband, even though our marriage was not perfect. I told Y____ my interest in his life was solely a product of what he'd done scientifically (and not remotely related to his qualities as a man). I flatly told him, "You're not a good person." I explained how I was not physically attracted to him, and that it was no coincidence he had to be invisible in order for me to spend time with him in public. I said I sometimes enjoyed talking with him, but not enough to put up with his thoughts and actions. I said that I didn't want to know who he really was, because that person was probably worse than the person he was pretending to be.

I could not see how these words affected him. I could not see his face. But I knew. I could see him, in my mind.

After I finished my speech, there was a wordless gap that felt louder than the conversation. Eventually, I heard a few scrapes from across the room (he must have been sitting on the floor against the wall and was finally standing up). For a moment, I thought he might just walk out without saying a peep. But that, of course, is not his way. He had to say something. He couldn't stop himself.

"I was too kind to you," he finally said. "You liked me when I insulted you, because you like men who treat you like shit. That's your problem. As soon as I started treating you like a real person, you lost interest. I know I have problems, but your problems are worse."

With that, the door to my office unmagically opened and unmagically closed. "Are you still there?" I asked aloud. I had to make sure he was gone, even though I'd never truly know. But I received no response, and I took that at face value. It was an agonizing brand of relief; I felt sick, but I also felt better. It was over. I really believed that. I don't know why, but I did. I guess I'll always be an optimist, even if that makes me a fool.

The Worst-Case Scenario

What happened on the night of September 18 is, for understandable reasons, painful to re-create. Though the event lasted only minutes, it's become the central fracture of my existence; I now see my life as having two distinct halves. It will probably seem that way forever. I hope I'm wrong about this, but I doubt it.

Whenever I've anecdotally described what happened that evening to other people, they inevitably ask the same question: "Did it seem like a movie?" I know exactly what they mean by this, and I understand why it's something they'd ask. Our exposure to media makes everyone believe they can conceptualize certain popular impossibilities; by now, we've all seen so many "invisible man" movies that we assume we can imagine the unimaginable. But that's not how it was. It wasn't like a movie, except at the very end. So my stock answer to the question is this: "Not at all, except when it was." This allows people to laugh at something that isn't funny.

After my disturbing office conversation with Y___, I counseled two more patients and returned home. I immediately told John what had transpired. He was not surprised. When I told him that things were really over and that I might have (finally) hurt Y___ in an irreconcilable way, he scoffed. "We're installing a motion detector next week," he said. "The security people are coming Monday morning. I've already scheduled an appointment." John knew less about Y___ than I did, but—in many important ways—he understood him better.

The early part of our evening was fine—uncharacteristically idyllic, to be totally honest. I made chicken stir-fry. John and I did the dishes together. I asked John if he had any work to do, but he said, "Not tonight." We took a walk around the neighborhood as the sun went down. After we returned, we watched a documentary titled *Visions of Light* on IFC. I think we went to bed around eleven p.m. We both read for an hour and fell asleep. As I drifted away, I remember being pleasantly surprised by how little I'd thought about Y___ that entire night. It really seemed finished. My mind was clear. Sleeping was easy.

But something woke me up.

I don't know what that something was—it could have been a sound, it might have been the sense of being watched, or perhaps both. But something woke me up and I immediately felt sick. I felt like I was about to have a car accident. I sat up in bed. I looked toward our open bedroom door. The doorway was empty, but it didn't look the way an empty doorway should: Within an utterly dark room, the doorway looked *darker*. The blackness had a shimmer. I reached for my glasses and put them on my face. The shimmer disappeared, but the darkness did not. My scalp felt hot. My palms were damp.

"John," I said. "John."

John woke up like a patient after surgery.

"There's someone here, John."

In an instant, John was vigilant. He grabbed his glasses and reached for the hammer below the bed. He jumped up from under the covers and said, "Where? Where?"

Now, this is mildly embarrassing, but it needs to be said for transparency: John doesn't wear clothes when he sleeps. I typically wear sweatpants, but I always sleep topless. When I looked at John, it did seem a bit tragically comedic—there he was, an old, nude man with eyeglasses on his face and a hammer in his hand, crouched at the knees like a high school shortstop. "This is going to end badly," I thought to myself. "We are not ready for this." But we had no choice. This was happening. I got out of bed and pointed at the doorway. "There," I said. "He's there. Or he's out there. He's either there or out there."

John rushed the door and swung his hammer through the open space. It struck nothing. He swung again, wildly. Again, nothing. He walked through the doorway onto the second-floor landing. He swung in every direction. Nothing. I turned on the reading lamp next to the bed and followed my husband through our bedroom door.

Why did I turn on the reading lamp? No idea. Habit, I suppose. But it made a huge difference. The dim light emanating from our bedroom cast huge shadows across the rest of the house. My five-foot-five body generated a thirty-foot shadow on the living room floor. John's shadow was just as large. And now we could see a third massive shadow, longer than either of ours. I grabbed John by the arm and said, "Look at the walls!" For a moment, I thought I was a genius. I'd cracked the code. But then Y____ simply said, "I'm right here."

The voice was calm and the voice was close. He could not have been more than ten feet away, standing on the same second-floor landing, looking at two naked people who had run out of ideas.

"Call the police," said John. I'd left my cell phone in the kitchen, so down the stairs I ran. Despite everything that was happening, I still felt self-conscious about Y____ seeing me topless. Certain insecurities never disappear. Upstairs, I could hear my husband yelling at Y____, unleashing a concentration of profanity I'd never heard him utter. I could also hear Y____ laughing and asking sarcastic questions about the hammer. I dialed 9-1-1 and pleaded for assistance. When the operator asked what my emergency was, I only said, "There's a man in our house. Please get here soon." There was no sense in trying to explain.

Before leaving the kitchen, I should have grabbed a carving knife or a rolling pin. But I didn't. The thought never even occurred to me. I rushed back into the living room and looked toward the banister on the second level. It was like John had taken LSD: He was naked, standing on the landing, raving like a lunatic, yelling at nothing. "I'm gonna fucking kill you, you fucking cunt," he said. "I'm going to rip off your fucking head and jam it down your faggot throat." But Y____'s voice never changed. He never seemed nervous. He didn't seem menacing. He just seemed like a jerk.

"I've grown fond of your wife," said Y____. Even now, he talked like an asshole. "And she's falling in love with me. Now put down that hammer and get some clothes on. Let's talk about this like men."

"I'm not gonna fucking talk to you," yelled John. "Get out of my house!"

"No," said Y____. He sounded bored.

"I'll kill you," said John.

"You won't," said Y____. "Don't try." And with that, John rushed forward, straight toward Y____'s voice, swinging the hammer in a huge diagonal stroke across the front of his body. Once again, he hit nothing. He was thrown off balance, like a boxer who'd overpunched his target. And then it happened: I saw John's lithe body lift off the floor, float over the banister, and fall twenty-five feet, straight down to the wood below. He tumbled end over end, like a bowling pin knocked into the air. His body rotated 270 degrees as it fell.

It was absolutely the worst thing I've ever seen. The fall seemed to last longer than our marriage.

For one terrible instant, it looked like he would hit the hardwood headfirst. That would have killed him instantly. But his body kept rotating, and he landed on his tailbone. He screamed. I screamed. I rushed over to him. He said, "Get away!" I didn't know what to do. I looked up at the second-floor landing, and (of course) saw nothing. What did I expect to see? Human nature is impossible to overcome.

I could hear Y____ walking down the stairs. He was taking his time. I looked around for the hammer, which John had released as he fell. I was going to kill Y____, or at least I was going to try. That was my final decision. A lot of problems I'd been grappling with suddenly seemed simple.

"We can go now," said Y____.

"Are you out of your goddamn mind?" I screamed. "You just killed my husband." This wasn't exactly true (and probably didn't give John a lot of confidence about his condition), but my mind wasn't right. John was still on the floor, moaning.

"Come with me," said Y___. I'll never get over how calm he sounded. "They won't be able to find us. I can promise you that. They'll never find us."

"You're so sick," I said.

"We're running out of time," said Y___. "We can't have one of those conversations where we go back and forth about why I'm right and why you're nervous. We need to leave *now*. Everything will be okay." It was as if he did not even hear John's groans. He was blocking them out entirely. To Y___, John was already a carcass.

"You're fucking crazy," I said.

"Don't do this, Victoria," Y___ said. "We need each other. You know that I'm right."

"Kill yourself," I said. "You're a liar."

As I knelt beside John, I looked at Y___. He wasn't there, but I could see him as clearly as I could see the body of my broken husband. I'd never seen him so easily. And Y___ could tell. He knew I could see him now. That's why he was in my house.

It was at this point that my existence became a movie, if only for five seconds. John's hammer was laying in the middle of the rug. In a flash, it levitated off the ground. The hammer hung in the air like a cheap special effect from the unpopular eighties, bobbing and weaving, cocked and loaded. It was an amazing moment. What can I say? It was an amazing thing to see. But it was also terrible, because I thought it was going to crush me. "This is it," I thought. "This is where Y___ beats me to death." Maybe he'd torture me. Maybe he'd rape me first, or maybe he'd do it after I was dead. I had been wrong about Y___ so many times that nothing seemed off the table. I waited for his attack and wondered if I could fight him off long enough for the cops to arrive; I wondered what the cops would do when they saw a topless woman wrestling with herself on the floor.

But he didn't attack.

He didn't even talk.

He dropped the hammer, and the hammer went thud. I heard him casually walk toward the door, and I watched our deadbolt unlock itself. The door swung open and swung itself shut. I started crying uncontrollably. I tried to help John stand, but he couldn't move. I ran into the kitchen (still crying) to fetch him a glass of water; when I returned, I could see rolling blue and red lights through our picture windows. I sprinted to the front door, opened it wide, and yelled, "Get an ambulance," at the first cop I saw.

I went back inside, covered John's midsection with a towel, and tried to figure out how I was going to explain my life to other people.

Epilogue

It would be wrong to classify John as "paralyzed." He still has some feeling in his feet and lower extremities, and he can pivot his right ankle forty-five degrees. If he were truly paralyzed, he'd have no pain around his coccyx, and the pain is definitely there, every minute of every day. But he can't stand and he can't walk, and he'll spend the rest of his days in a wheelchair. We both accepted that certainty very early on, immediately following his surgery. However, he can still read and he can still write, and—if the pain subsides by next fall—he'll resume teaching full-time. He's excited about that. John's become a totally different person. Amazingly, there's been an upside to this incident, something I could never have imagined. But before I get to that, I need to explain what happened in the wake of Y___'s final, destructive cameo.

Try to put yourself in the position of the first police officer on the scene: You've been summoned to investigate a home invasion, but when you arrive no one is there except the two residents. One resident is injured, seemingly from a fall. He's in no position to explain anything. The other is topless and hysterical. You're informed that a man was in the house, that this man was familiar with the homeowners, and that he'd escaped (on foot) just minutes ago. But you're also told that any attempt to search for this man in the immediate area will be completely useless. You ask, "In what direction did he flee?" You are told, "That doesn't matter." You start to wonder what's really going on here; you start to wonder if this is some kind of domestic dispute, or maybe that drugs are involved. You start to wonder if you need to take the hysterical woman into custody, so that's what you do.

After John was rushed to the hospital, I spent six hours in Austin City Jail. They never charged me with anything, probably because they didn't know what to charge me with. I never got the sense they saw me as a perpetrator, but they were certainly confused. The next morning, I began a series of interviews with Detective Paul LaBour. To his credit, Paul never seemed to doubt any detail of the story (even when he admitted there wasn't much he could do about it).

Knowing what was at stake, I explained the situation like this: I told Detective LaBour that the intruder had been my patient. This, right away, seemed to remove any suspicion about my motives. I was conscious not to use the word *invisible*—it dawned on me why Y___ had always been so careful about using that word flippantly. It hijacks every conversation. Instead, I said that this patient had detailed a long history of entering people's homes, and that he was exceedingly adroit at urban camouflage. I mentioned the "heavy dudes" case in Minneapolis that Y___ had described in June, and the authorities were immediately able to confirm that such a crime had occurred.[16] I described the events of the previous evening as accurately as possible, once again avoiding the word *invisible* (instead, I would use phrases like "we could not really see him"). I also made an off-the-cuff decision that proved invaluable: I told Paul that he could interview John immediately after he recovered from his emergency spinal surgery, even before I had a chance to see him myself. This was an extremely difficult decision, and perhaps a bit cruel. Considering his condition, I'm sure John wanted to see me even more than I wanted to see him. But it was the rational move. Paul needed just five minutes with John to conclude that the details of our stories matched.[17] Had we not done this, I wonder if

16. Unfortunately, my subsequent deposition regarding this case was deemed inadmissible by the Minnesota court. As of this writing, the defendant remains in custody and is awaiting appeal.

17. Interestingly, John claims he directly referred to Y___ as "invisible" as soon as he met with the police. To the best of his memory, they never really questioned that detail—but John was also under fairly heavy sedation at the time of

they'd ever have believed a word of what we said. Beyond the broken latch on our back door, there was no evidence of anything. The finger smudges on the hammer were useless—they matched nothing in the FBI database.

The hunt for Y____ continues to this day. But it's a feeble hunt, devoid of doggedness. In my opinion, the authorities have lost interest.

It is, I suppose, a paradox: Despite listening to Y____ talk about himself for nearly one hundred hours, I'd learned almost nothing useful about him. I knew his name, but it's a common name and probably fake. I had his previous cell phone number, but the number was registered to a person who'd been dead for years. I didn't know Y____'s specific address or where he was born. He paid for everything in cash. I turned over all the audiotapes in my possession, and investigators have scoured the transcripts for any clue that might illustrate who this person was. Yet every time they find a useful detail, it's inevitably contradicted by something different Y____ would say later. His deception, it seems, was conscious.

Our strongest lead, certainly, were the dialogue passages about his time at Chaminade as a researcher. That period was key to every crime he would later commit. But this presented its own kind of problem: Whatever happened in that Hawaii laboratory has been artlessly stricken from the public record. The school has no information about the program, and the building where such research would have been conducted has been converted into married student housing. On his own, John has tried to ascertain details about the espoused military program through the Freedom of Information Act, but the FOIA documents we received were useless: All the names of the researchers have been blackened out, and the explanation for what was being studied is so simultaneously vague and technical that it's virtually unreadable. We didn't learn anything, beyond proving that some kind of military program did, in fact, exist in Hawaii.

---

the conversation. Perhaps they took him for a superstoned drama queen? More likely, they just accepted his story because he had no reason to lie.

Did we ever encounter Y__ again? No. For weeks after the attack, I was certain we would. I feared he would show up at the hospital, so I spent almost every night in John's room. But he never appeared. If he did, I was not aware of it (and as one might expect, I've grown hyperconscious of every sound and movement that would indicate the presence of a man who isn't there). The nights are still the worst. I wake up a lot. I probably wake up five times a night. But that used to happen twice as often, so I suppose that's progress.

I still think about Y__ all the time. I know I should hate him, but I don't. Whenever I try to hate him, it doesn't work. All his worst qualities were totally transparent, but so were the things that made him different than other people. What can I say? I can't deny that he was interesting, even if he was interesting in a negative way.

Almost six months after John's fall, Y__ contacted me one final time. He sent me a postcard, addressed to my office. The postmark was from Golden, Colorado, but he claimed to be writing from Canada. Did he think I'd fail to notice the discrepancy? I've given up trying to understand his lies. The image on the front of the card was of all four members of the Beatles in lab coats, curiously adorned with decapitated baby dolls and hunks of raw meat. I have no idea if this is supposed to indicate an unhinged state of mind, a sick inside joke, or nothing at all. Y__'s message was handwritten in blue ink; his printing was minuscule and exacting. The message was as follows:

Victoria:

I'm sorry about what happened. I did not enter your
home with the intention of hurting your husband. He should
not have attacked me with a hammer, but I forgive him. It
sounds like he got the worst of it. Obviously, I'm sad about
how we left things. It's hard to be a private person, I suppose.
I miss you, and I hope you miss me as well. I am as much
to blame for all this as you are, so don't beat yourself up. I

would like to think we'll meet again, but I know that can't happen. We were no good together, but try to remember me as best you can. I am doing well here in Montreal. The subway system is very efficient.

Votre ami,
Y___

To the very end, he stayed in his lane.

John was (predictably) angry when I showed him Y___'s post-card. I believe his initial comment was, "So he thinks he's Hanni-bal Lecter now?" But—to John's credit—he eventually conceded that these were not words written by a reasonable person, so there's really no point in despising him from afar. Maybe John has forgiven him, too. Since his accident, he's become a different man. Gone is the condescending person devoid of empathy; in his place, I have a husband who needs me, and who admits that he needs me, and who realizes that I am the only person who can help him when he wants help. I am the only person who can pull up his pants or get his books out of the attic or help him go to the toilet in a restaurant lavatory. It was jarring to see him realize these things. He speaks differently. He listens more. We share our lives equally, but I make the real decisions. John's perspicacity will always be present, but he comprehends his own weakness (and, by extension, the weak-nesses of others). I am by no means *happy* that he cannot walk, and his condition makes our life difficult. But not every tragic situation is tragic in totality.

I must be frank: There are many reasons why I'm writing this book, but the main one is money. John and I both have large life insurance policies, but neither of us ever thought to purchase disability insurance—it didn't seem applicable to our nonphysi-cal careers. Since his fall, we've had to remodel most of our home (including all the bathrooms) and install ramps and chairlifts. Many types of physical therapy are prohibitively expensive. My only option was to sell this story. It's the only thing I have that's worth anything. Much of the advance money is already gone, but at least we are comfortable and John is recovering. We needed the money. We did. Y___ wasn't wrong about everything.

Still, if I'm going to be straight, I need to go all the way: Beyond the money, I'm pleased with the work. I'm happy this record of Y___'s life exists, and I'm proud to be the person who heard it firsthand.

Is the publication of this book precisely what Y___ wanted all along? Probably. It probably is. I can imagine him reading it wherever he's hiding, scribbling in the margins, consumed by its minor inaccuracies. He will probably send me a letter outlining the revisions he wants to see in the paperback. Y___ could never see the things about himself that were obvious, but that's not atypical. It might have been the only thing about him that was normal. The only thing I hope is that—wherever he is—he's reading this book alone. He needs to be alone, and he needs to stay alone. He's not ready to be the person he is.

DA NOV 09 2011